A master at depicting both the legends and the lore of Ireland and the tender, enchanting passions of its people, Nora Roberts "just keeps getting better and better" *(Milwaukee Journal Sentinel)*. Now, together in one volume, these delightful stories of magic and romance capture the everlasting beauty of this charming land—and prove that this #1 *New York Times* bestselling author is truly "at the top of her game" *(People)* . . .

In "Spellbound," a beautiful lady casts a thousand-year spell on the man of her dreams—and unleashes a nightmare only love can conquer . . . "Ever After" follows an enchanting woman as she journeys to an otherworldly land—and introduces a handsome artist to the transforming power of love . . . "In Dreams" links a young woman to a stranger's past—and to the curse that has trapped him forever in the eternity of his own dreams . . .

"Roberts weaves a story like no one else."

—*Rocky Mountain News*

"A consistently entertaining writer."

—*USA Today*

"Roberts is indeed a word artist, painting her story and her characters with vitality and verve."

—*Los Angeles Daily News*

Turn the page for a complete list of titles by
Nora Roberts and J. D. Robb from The Berkley Publishing Group . . .

A LITTLE MAGIC

NORA ROBERTS

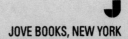
JOVE BOOKS, NEW YORK

THE BERKLEY PUBLISHING GROUP
Published by the Penguin Group
Penguin Group (USA) Inc.
375 Hudson Street, New York, New York 10014, USA
Penguin Group (Canada), 90 Eglinton Avenue East, Suite 700, Toronto, Ontario M4P 2Y3, Canada
(a division of Pearson Penguin Canada Inc.)
Penguin Books Ltd., 80 Strand, London WC2R 0RL, England
Penguin Group Ireland, 25 St. Stephen's Green, Dublin 2, Ireland (a division of Penguin Books Ltd.)
Penguin Group (Australia), 250 Camberwell Road, Camberwell, Victoria 3124, Australia
(a division of Pearson Australia Group Pty. Ltd.)
Penguin Books India Pvt. Ltd., 11 Community Centre, Panchsheel Park, New Delhi—110 017, India
Penguin Group (NZ), Cnr. Airborne and Rosedale Roads, Albany, Auckland 1310, New Zealand
(a division of Pearson New Zealand Ltd.)
Penguin Books (South Africa) (Pty.) Ltd., 24 Sturdee Avenue, Rosebank, Johannesburg 2196,
South Africa

Penguin Books Ltd., Registered Offices: 80 Strand, London WC2R 0RL, England

This is a work of fiction. Names, characters, places, and incidents either are the product of the author's imagination or are used fictitiously, and any resemblance to actual persons, living or dead, business establishments, events, or locales is entirely coincidental. The publisher does not have any control over and does not assume any responsibility for author or third-party websites or their content.

A LITTLE MAGIC

A Jove Book / published by arrangement with the author

PRINTING HISTORY
Berkley trade paperback edition / January 2002
Jove mass-market edition / August 2004
Special $4.99 edition / September 2006

ISBN: 0-515-14287-5

JOVE®
Jove Books are published by The Berkley Publishing Group,
a division of Penguin Group (USA) Inc.,
375 Hudson Street, New York, New York 10014.
JOVE is a registered trademark of Penguin Group (USA) Inc.
The "J" design is a trademark belonging to Penguin Group (USA) Inc.

PRINTED IN THE UNITED STATES OF AMERICA

15 14 13 12 11 10 9 8 7 6 5

CONTENTS

SPELLBOUND

*To all my wonderful friends
in this life and all the others*

PROLOGUE

LOVE. *My love. Let me into your dreams. Open your heart again and hear me. Calin, I need you so. Don't turn from me now, or all is lost. I am lost. Love. My love.*

Calin shifted restlessly in sleep, turned his face into the pillow. Felt her there, somehow. Skin, soft and dewy. Hands, gentle and soothing. Then drifted into dreams of cool and quiet mists, hills of deep, damp green that rolled to forever. And the witchy scent of woman.

The castle rose atop a cliff, silver stone spearing into stormy skies, its base buried in filmy layers of fog that ran like a river. The sound of his mount's bridle jingled battle-bright on the air as he rode, leaving the green hills behind and climbing high on rock. Thunder sounded in the west, over the sea. And echoed in his warrior's heart.

Had she waited for him?

His eyes, gray as the stone of the castle, shifted, scanned, searching rock and mist for any hole where a foe could hide. Even as he urged his mount up the rugged path cleaved into the cliff he knew he carried the stench of war and death, that it had seeped into his pores just as the memories of it had seeped into his brain.

Neither body nor mind would ever be fully clean of it.

His sword hand lay light and ready on the hilt of his weapon. In such places a man did not lower his guard. Here magic stung the air and could embrace or threaten. Here faeries plotted or danced, and witches cast their spells for good or ill.

Atop the lonely cliff, towering above the raging sea, the castle stood, holding its secrets. And no man rode this path without hearing the whispers of old ghosts and new spirits.

Had she waited for him?

The horse's hooves rang musically over the rock until at last they traveled to level ground. He dismounted at the foot of the keep just as lightning cracked the black sky with a blaze of blinding white light.

And she was there, just there, conjured up out of storm-whipped air. Her hair was a firefall over a dove-gray cloak, alabaster skin with the faint bloom of rose, a generous mouth just curved in knowledge. And eyes as blue as a living star and just as filled with power.

His heart leaped, and his blood churned with love, lust, longing.

She came to him, wading through the knee-high mists, her beauty staggering. With his eyes on hers, he swung off his horse, eager for the woman who was witch, and lover.

"Caelan of Farrell, 'tis far you've traveled in the dark of the night. What do you wish of me?"

"Bryna the Wise." His hard, ridged lips bowed in a smile that answered hers. "I wish for everything."

"Only everything?" Her laugh was low and intimate. "Well, that's enough, then. I waited for you."

Then her arms were around him, her mouth lifting to his. He pulled her closer, desperate for the shape of her, wild to have whatever she would offer him, and more.

"I waited for you," she repeated with a catch in her voice as she pressed her face to his shoulder. " 'Twas almost too long this time. His power grows while mine weakens. I can't fight him alone. Alasdair is too strong, his dark forces too greedy. Oh, love. My love, why did you shut me out of your mind, out of your heart?"

He drew her away. The castle was gone—only ruins remained, empty, battle-scarred. They stood in the shadow of what had been, before a small house alive with flowers. The scent of them was everywhere, heady, intoxicating. The woman was still in his arms. And the storm waited to explode.

"The time is short now," she told him. "You must come. Calin, you must come to me. Destiny can't be denied, a spell won't be broken. Without you with me, he'll win."

He shook his head, started to speak, but she lifted a hand to his face. It passed through him as if he were a ghost. Or she was. "I have loved you throughout time." As she spoke, she moved back, the mists flowing around her legs. "I am bound to you, throughout time."

Then lifting her arms, raising palms to the heavens, she closed her eyes. The wind roared in like a lion loosed from a cage, lifted her flaming hair, whipped the cloak around her.

"I have little left," she called over the violence of the storm. "But I can still call up the wind. I can still call to your heart. Don't keep it from me, Calin. Come to me soon. Find me. Or I'm lost."

Then she was gone. Vanished. The earth trembled beneath his feet, the sky howled. And all went silent and still.

He awoke gasping for breath. And reaching out.

1

"CALIN Farrell, you need a vacation."

Cal lifted a shoulder, sipped his coffee, and continued to brood while staring out the kitchen window. He wasn't sure why he'd come here to listen to his mother nag and worry about him, to hear his father whistle as he meticulously tied his fishing flies at the table. But he'd had a deep, driving urge to be in the home of his childhood, to grab an hour or two in the tidy house in Brooklyn Heights. To see his parents.

"Maybe. I'm thinking about it."

"Work too hard," his father said, eyeing his own work critically. "Could come to Montana for a couple of weeks with us. Best fly-fishing in the world. Bring your camera." John Farrell glanced up and smiled. "Call it a sabbatical."

It was tempting. He'd never been the fishing enthusiast his father was, but Montana was beautiful. And big. Cal thought he could lose himself there. And shake off the restlessness. The dreams.

"A couple of weeks in the clean air will do you good." Sylvia Farrell narrowed her eyes as she turned to her son. "You're looking pale and tired, Calin. You need to get out of that city for a while."

Though she'd lived in Brooklyn all of her life, Sylvia still referred to Manhattan as "that city" with light disdain and annoyance.

"I've been thinking about a trip."

"Good." His mother scrubbed at her countertop. They were leaving the next morning, and Sylvia Farrell wouldn't leave a crumb or a mote of dust behind. "You've been working too hard, Calin. Not that we aren't proud of you. After your exhibit last month your father bragged so much that the neighbors started to hide when they saw him coming."

"Not every day a man gets to see his son's photographs in the museum. I liked the nudes especially," he added with a wink.

"You old fool," Sylvia muttered, but her lips twitched. "Well, who'd have thought when we bought you that little camera for Christmas when you were eight that twenty-two years later you'd be rich and famous? But wealth and fame carry a price."

She took her son's face in her hands and studied it with a mother's keen eye. His eyes were shadowed, she noted, his face too thin. She worried for the man she'd raised, and the boy he had been who had always seemed to have . . . something more than the ordinary.

"You're paying it."

"I'm fine." Reading the worry in her eyes, recognizing it, he smiled. "Just not sleeping very well."

There had been other times, Sylvia remembered, that her son had grown pale and hollow-eyed from lack of sleep. She exchanged a quick glance with her husband over Cal's shoulder.

"Have you, ah, seen the doctor?"

"Mom, I'm fine." He knew his voice was too sharp, too defensive. Struggled to lighten it. "I'm perfectly fine."

"Don't nag the boy, Syl." But John studied his son closely also, remembering, as his wife did, the young boy who had talked to shadows, had walked in his sleep, and had dreamed of witches and blood and battle.

"I'm not nagging. I'm mothering." She made herself smile.

"I don't want you to worry. I'm a little stressed-out, that's all." That was all, he thought, determined to make it so. He wasn't different, he wasn't odd. Hadn't the battalion of doctors his parents had taken him to throughout his childhood diagnosed an over-developed imagination? And hadn't he finally channeled that into his photography?

He didn't see things that weren't there anymore.

Sylvia nodded, told herself to accept that. "Small wonder. You've been working yourself day and night for the last five years. You need some rest, you need some quiet. And some pampering."

"Montana," John said again. "Couple of weeks of fishing, clean air, and no worries."

"I'm going to Ireland." It came out of Cal's mouth before he'd realized the idea was in his head.

"Ireland?" Sylvia pursed her lips. "Not to work, Calin."

"No, to . . . to see," he said at length. "Just to see."

She nodded, satisfied. A vacation, after all, was a vacation. "That'll be nice. It's supposed to be a restful country. We always meant to go, didn't we, John?"

Her husband grunted his assent. "Going to look up your ancestors, Cal?"

"I might." Since the decision seemed to be made, Cal sipped his coffee again. He was going to look up something, he realized. Or someone.

IT was raining when he landed at Shannon Airport. The chilly late-spring rain seemed to suit his mood. He'd slept nearly all the way across the Atlantic. And the dreams had chased him. He went through customs, arranged to rent a car, changed money. All of this was done with the mechanical efficiency of the seasoned traveler. And as he completed the tasks, he tried not to worry, tried not to dwell on the idea that he was having a breakdown of some kind.

He climbed into the rented car, then simply sat in the murky light wondering what to do, where to go. He was thirty, a successful photographer who could name his own price, call his own shots. He still considered it a wild twist of fate that he'd been able to make a living doing something he loved. Using what he saw in a landscape, in a face, in light and shadow and texture, and translating that into a photograph.

It was true that the last few years had been hectic and he'd worked almost nonstop. Even now the trunk of the Volvo he'd rented was loaded with equipment, and his favored Nikon rested in its case on the seat beside him. He couldn't get away from it—didn't want to run away from what he loved.

Suddenly an odd chill raced through him, and he thought, for just a moment, that he heard a woman weeping.

Just the rain, he told himself and scrubbed his hands over his handsome face. It was long, narrow, with the high, strong cheekbones of his Celtic forefathers. His nose was straight, his mouth firm and well formed. It smiled often—or it had until recently.

His eyes were gray—a deep, pure gray without a hint of green or blue. The brows over them were strongly arched and tended to draw together in concentration. His hair was black and thick and flowed over his collar. An artistic touch that a number of women had enjoyed.

Again, until recently.

He brooded over the fact that it had been months since he'd been with a woman—since he'd wanted to. Overwork again? he wondered. A byproduct of stress? Why would he be stressed when his career was advancing by leaps and bounds? He was healthy. He'd had a complete physical only weeks before.

But you didn't tell the doctor about the dreams, did you? he reminded himself. The dreams you can't quite remember when you wake up. The dreams, he admitted, that had pulled him three thousand miles over the ocean.

No, damn it, he hadn't told the doctor. He wasn't going that route again. There had been enough psychiatrists in his youth, poking and prodding into his mind, making him feel foolish, exposed, helpless. He was a grown man now and could handle his own dreams.

If he was having a breakdown, it was a perfectly normal one and could be cured by rest, relaxation, and a change of scene.

That's what he'd come to Ireland for. Only that.

He started the car and began to drive aimlessly.

He'd had dreams before, when he was a boy. Very clear, too realistic dreams. Castles and witches and a woman with tumbling red hair. She'd spoken to him with that lilt of Ireland in her voice. And sometimes she'd spoken in a language he didn't know—but had understood nonetheless.

There'd been a young girl—that same waterfall of hair, the same blue eyes. They'd laughed together in his dreams. Played together—innocent childhood games. He remembered that his parents had been amused when he'd spoken of his friend. They had passed it off, he thought, as the natural imagination of a sociable only child.

But they'd been concerned when he seemed to know things, to see things, to speak of places and people he couldn't have had knowledge of. They'd worried over him when his sleep was disturbed night after night—when he began to walk and talk while glazed in dreams.

So, after the doctors, the therapists, the endless sessions, and those quick, searching looks that adults thought children couldn't interpret, he'd stopped speaking of them.

And as he'd grown older, the young girl had grown as well. Tall and slim and lovely—young breasts, narrow waist, long legs. Feelings and needs for her that weren't so innocent had begun to stir.

It had frightened him, and it had angered him. Until he'd blocked out that soft voice that came in the night. Until he'd turned away from the image that haunted his dreams. Finally, it had stopped. The dreams stopped. The little flickers in his mind that told him where to find lost keys or had him reaching for the phone an instant before it rang ceased.

He was comfortable with reality, Cal told himself. Had chosen it. And would choose it again. He was here only to prove to himself that he was an ordinary man suffering from overwork. He would soak up the atmosphere of Ireland, take the pictures that pleased him. And, if necessary, take the pills his doctor had prescribed to help him sleep undisturbed.

He drove along the storm-battered coast, where wind roared in over the sea and held encroaching summer at bay with chilly breath.

Rain pattered the windshield, and fog slithered over the ground. It was hardly a warm welcome, yet he felt at home. As if something, or someone, was waiting to take him in from the storm. He made himself laugh at that. It was just the pleasure of being in a new place, he decided. It was the anticipation of finding new images to capture on film.

He felt a low-grade urge for coffee, for food, but easily blocked it as he absorbed the scenery. Later, he told himself. He would stop later at some pub or inn, but just now he had to see more of this haunting landscape. So savagely beautiful, so timeless.

And if it was somehow familiar, he could put that down to place memory. After all, his ancestors had roamed these spearing cliffs, these rolling green hills. They had been warriors, he thought. Had once painted themselves blue and screamed out of the forests to terrorize the enemy. Had strapped on armor and hefted sword and pike to defend their land and protect their freedom.

The scene that burst into his mind was viciously clear. The flash of sword crashing, the screams of battle in full power. Wheeling horses, wild-eyed, spurting blood from a severed arm and the agonizing cry of pain as a man crumpled. The burn as steel pierced flesh.

Looking down as the pain bloomed, he saw blood welling on his thigh.

Carrion crows circling in silent patience. The stench of roasting flesh as bodies burned on a pyre, and the hideous and thin cries of dying men waiting for release.

Cal found himself stopped on the side of the road, out of the car, dragging air into his lungs as the rain battered him. Had he blacked out? Was he losing his mind? Trembling he reached down and ran his hand over his jeans. There was no wound, and yet he felt the echoing ache of an old scar he knew wasn't there.

It was happening again. The river of fear that flowed through him froze over and turned his blood to ice. He forced himself to calm down, to think rationally. Jet lag, he decided. Jet lag and stress, that was all. How long since he'd driven out of Shannon? Two hours? Three? He needed to find a place to stay. He needed to eat. He would find some quiet, out-of-the-way bed-and-breakfast, he thought. Somewhere he could rest and ease his mind. And when the storm had passed, he would get his camera and go for a long walk. He could stay for weeks or leave in the morning. He was free, he reminded himself. And that was sane, that was normal.

He climbed back into the car, steadied himself, and drove along the winding coast road.

THE ruined castle came into view as he rounded the curve. The keep, he supposed it was, was nearly intact, but walls had been sheared off, making him think of an ancient warrior with scars from many battles. Perched on a stony crag, it shouted with power and defiance despite its tumbled rocks.

Out of the boiling sky, one lance of lightning speared, exploded with light, and stung the air with the smell of ozone.

His blood beat thick, and an ache, purely sexual, began to spread through his belly. On the steering wheel his fingers tightened. He swung onto the narrow, rutted dirt road that led up. He needed a picture of the castle, he told himself. Several studies from different angles. A quick detour—fifteen or twenty minutes—then he would be on his way to that B and B.

It didn't matter that Ireland was dotted with ruins and old castles—he needed this one.

Mists spread at its base like a river. So intent was he on the light and shadows that played on stone, on the texture of the weeds and wildflowers that forced their way through crevices, that he didn't see the cottage until he was nearly upon it.

It made him smile, though he didn't realize it. It was so charming, so unexpected there beside the ancient stones. Inviting, welcoming, it seemed to bloom like the flowers that surrounded it, out of the cliffside as if planted by a loving hand.

It was painted white with bright blue shutters. Smoke trailed up out of the stone chimney, and a sleek black cat napped beside a wooden rocker on the little covered porch.

Someone made a home here, he thought, and tended it.

The light was wrong, he told himself. But he knew he needed to capture this place, this feeling. He would ask whoever lived here if he could come back, do his work.

As he stood in the rain, the cat uncurled lazily, then sat. It watched him out of startlingly blue eyes.

Then she was there—standing in the lashing rain, the mists swirling around her. Though he hadn't heard her approach, she was halfway between the tidy cottage and the tumbling stones of the old castle. One hand was lifted to her heart, and her breath was coming fast as if she'd been running.

Her hair was wet, hanging in deep-red ropes over her shoulders, framing a face that might have been carved out of ivory by a master. Her mouth was soft and full and seemed to tremble as it curved into a smile of welcome. Her eyes were star blue and swimming with emotions as powerful as the storm.

"I knew you would come." The cloak she wore flew back as she raced to him. "I waited for you," she said with the musical lilt of Ireland before her mouth crushed his.

2

THERE was a moment of blinding, searing joy. Another of dark, primal lust.

Her taste, sharp, potent, soaked into his system as the rain soaked his skin. He was helpless to do anything but absorb it. Her arms were chained around his neck, her slim, curvy body pressed intimately to his, the heat from it seeping through his sodden shirt and into his bones.

And her mouth was as wild and edgy as the sky thundering above them.

It was all terrifyingly familiar.

He brought his hands to her shoulders, torn for a staggering instant as to whether to pull her closer or push her away. In the end he eased back, held her at arm's length.

She was beautiful. She was aroused. And she was, he assured himself, a stranger. He angled his head, determined to handle the situation.

"Well, it's certainly a friendly country."

He saw the flicker in her eyes, the dimming of disappointment, a flash of frustration. But he couldn't know just how deeply that disappointment, that frustration cut into her heart.

He's here, she told herself. He's come. That's what matters most now. "It is, yes." She gave him a smile, let her fingers linger in his hair just another second, then dropped them to her sides. "Welcome to Ireland and the Castle of Secrets."

His gaze shifted toward the ruins. "Is that what it's called?"

"That's the name it carries now." She had to struggle to keep her eyes from devouring him, every inch, every expression. Instead she offered a hand, as she would have to any wayward traveler. "You've had a long journey. Come, sit by my fire." Her lips curved. "Have some whiskey in your tea."

"You don't know me." He made it a statement rather than a question. Had to.

In answer, she looked up at the sky. "You're wet," she said, "and the wind's cold today. It's enough to have me offer a seat by the hearth." She turned away from him, stepped up onto the porch where the cat stirred itself to wind through her legs. "You've come this far." Her eyes met his again, held. "Will you come into my home, Calin Farrell, and warm yourself?"

He scooped dripping hair out of his face, felt his bones tremble. "How do you know my name?"

"The same way you knew to come here." She picked up the cat, stroked its silky head. Both of them watched him with patient, unblinking blue eyes. "I baked scones fresh this morning. You'll be hungry." With this, she turned and walked inside, leaving him to come or go as he willed.

Part of him wanted to get back in the car, drive away, pretend he'd never seen her or this place. But he climbed onto the porch, pushed the front door open. He needed answers, and it seemed she had at least some of them.

The warmth struck him instantly. Welcoming warmth redolent with the fragrances of bread recently baked, of peat simmering in the hearth, of flowers just picked.

"Make yourself at home." She set the cat on the floor. "I'll see to the tea."

Cal stepped into the tiny parlor and near to the red eye of the fire. There were flowers, he noted, their petals still damp, filling vases on the stone mantel, pots on the table by the window.

A sugan chair sat by the hearth, but he didn't sit. Instead he studied the room with the sharp eye of an artist.

Quiet colors, he thought. Not pale, but soothing in the choice of deep rose and mossy greens. Woven rugs on the polished floors, mirror-bright woods lovingly cared for and smelling lightly of beeswax. Candles everywhere, in varying lengths, standing in holders of glass and silver and stone.

There, by the hearth, a spinning wheel. Surely an

antique, he mused as he stepped closer to examine it. Its dark wood gleamed, and beside it sat a straw basket heaped with beautifully dyed wools.

But for the electric lamps and their jewellike shades, the small stereo tucked into a stack of books on a shelf, he might have convinced himself he'd stepped into another century.

Absently he crouched to pet the cat, which was rubbing seductively against his legs. The fur was warm and damp. Real. He hadn't walked into another century, Cal assured himself. Or into a dream. He was going to ask his hostess some very pointed questions, he decided. And he wasn't going anywhere until he was satisfied with the answers.

As she carried the tray back down the short hallway, she berated herself for losing her sense in the storm of emotion, for moving too quickly, saying too much. Expecting too much.

He didn't know her. Oh, that cut through the heart into the soul. But it had been foolish of her to expect him to, when he had blocked out her thoughts, her need for him for more than fifteen years.

She had continued to steal into his dreams when he was unaware, to watch him grow from boy to man as she herself blossomed into womanhood. But pride, and hurt, and love had stopped her from calling to him.

Until there had been no choice.

She'd known it the moment he stepped onto the ground of her own country. And her heart had leaped. Had it been so wrong, and so foolish, to prepare for him? To fill the house with flowers, the kitchen with baking? To bathe herself in oils of her own making, anointing her skin as a bride would on her wedding night?

No. She took a deep breath at the doorway. She had needed to prepare herself for him. Now she must find the right way to prepare him for her—and what they must soon face together.

He was so beautiful, she thought as she watched him stroke the cat into ecstasy. How many nights had she tossed restlessly in sleep, longing for those long, narrow hands on her?

Oh, just once to feel him touch her.

How many nights had she burned to see his eyes, gray as storm clouds, focused on her as he buried himself deep inside her and gave her his seed?

Oh, just once to join with him, to make those soft, secret sounds in the night.

They were meant to be lovers. This much she believed he would accept. For a man had needs, she knew, and this one was already linked with her physically—no matter that he refused to remember.

But without the love in the act of mating, there would be no joy. And no hope.

She braced herself and stepped into the room. "You've made friends with Hecate, I see." His gaze whipped up to hers, and her hands trembled lightly. Whatever power she still held was nothing compared with one long look from him. "She's shameless around attractive men." She set the tray down.

"Won't you sit, Calin, and have some tea?"

"How do you know who I am?"

"I'll explain what I can." Her eyes went dark and turbulent with emotions as they scanned his face. "Do you have no memory of me then? None at all?"

A tumble of red hair that shined like wet fire, a body that moved in perfect harmony with his, a laugh like fog. "I don't know you." He said it sharply, defensively. "I don't know your name."

Her eyes remained dark, but her chin lifted. Here was pride, and power still. "I am Bryna Torrence, descendant of Bryna the Wise and guardian of this place. You're welcome in my home, Calin Farrell, as long as you choose to stay."

She bent to the tray, her movements graceful. She wore a long dress, the color of the mists curling outside the window. It draped her body, flirted with her ankles. Columns of carved silver danced from her ears.

"Why?" He laid a hand on her arm as she lifted the first cup. "Why am I welcome in your home?"

"Perhaps I'm lonely." Her lips curved again, wistfully. "I am lonely, and it's glad I am for your company." She sat, gestured for him to do the same. "You need a bit of food, Calin, a bit of rest. I can offer you that."

"What I want is an explanation." But he did sit, and because the hot liquid in his cup smelled glorious, he drank. "You said you knew I would come, you knew my name. I want to know how either of those things is possible."

It wasn't permitted to lie to him. Honesty was part of the pledge. But she could evade. "I might have recognized your face. You're a successful and famous man, Calin. Your art has found its way even into my corner of the world. You have such talent," she murmured. "Such vision." She arranged scones on a small plate, offered it. "Such power inside you."

He lifted a brow. There were women who were willing, eager to rock onto their backs for a man who had a hold on fame. He shook his head. "You're no groupie, Bryna. You didn't open the door to me so that you could have a quick bout of sex with a name."

"But others have."

There was a sting of jealousy in her voice. He couldn't have said why, but under the circumstances it amused him. "Which is how I know that's not what this is, not what you are. In any case, you didn't have the time to recognize my face from some magazine or talk show. The light was bad, the rain pouring down."

His brows drew together. He couldn't be dreaming again, hallucinating. The teacup was warm in his hand, the taste of the sweet, whiskey-laced brew in his mouth. "Damn it, you were waiting for me, and I don't understand how."

"I've waited for you all my life." She said it quietly, setting her cup down untouched. "And a millennium before it began." Raising her hands, she laid them on his face. "Your face is the first I remember, before even my own mother's. The ghost of your touch has haunted me every night of my life."

"That's nonsense." He brought a hand up, curled his fingers around her wrist.

"I can't lie to you. It's not in my power. Whatever I say to you will be truth, whatever you see in me will be real." She tried to touch that part of his mind, or his heart, that might still be open to her. But it was locked away, fiercely guarded. She took one long breath and accepted. For now. "You're not ready to know, to hear, to believe." Her eyes softened a little, her fingertips stroking his temples. "Ah, Calin, you're tired, and confused. It's rest you're needing now and ease for your mind. I can help you."

His vision grayed, and the room swam. He could see nothing but her eyes, dark blue, utterly focused. Her scent swam into his senses like a drug. "Stop it."

"Rest now, love. My love."

He felt her lips brush his before he slid blissfully into the dark.

CAL awoke to silence. His mind circled for a moment, like a bird looking for a place to perch. Something in the tea, he thought. God, the woman had drugged him. He felt a quick panic as the theme from Stephen King's *Misery* played in his head.

Obsessed fan. Kidnapping.

With a jolt, he sat straight up, terrified, reaching

for his foot. Still attached. The black cat, which had been curled on the edge of the bed, stretched lazily and seemed to snicker.

"Yeah, funny," Cal muttered. He let out a long breath that trailed into a weak laugh. Letting your imagination turn cartwheels again, Calin, he told himself. Always been a bad habit of yours.

He ordered himself to calm down, take stock of the situation. And realized he was buck naked.

Surprise ran a swift race with embarrassment as he imagined Bryna undressing him with those lovely tea-serving hands. And getting him into bed. How in the hell had the woman carted him into a bedroom?

For that was where he was. It was a small and charming room with a tiny stone hearth, a glossy bureau. Flowers and candles again, books tucked into a recessed nook. A doll-size chair sat near a window that was framed in white lace curtains. Sunlight slipped through them and made lovely and intricate patterns on the dark wood floor.

At the foot of the bed was an old chest with brass fittings. His clothes, clean and dry, were folded neatly on it. At least she didn't expect him to run around in his skin, he decided, and with some relief reached quickly for his jeans.

He felt immediately better once they were zipped, then realized that he felt not just better. He felt wonderful.

Alert, rested, energized. Whatever she'd given him, he concluded, had rocked him into the solid, restful sleep he hadn't experienced in weeks. But he wasn't going to thank her for it, Cal thought grimly as he tugged on his shirt. The woman went way past eccentric—he didn't mind a little eccentricity. But this lady was deluded, and possibly dangerous.

He was going to see to it that she gave him some satisfactory answers, then he was going to leave her to her fairy-tale cottage and ruined castle and put some miles between them.

He looked in the mirror over the bureau, half expecting to see a beard trailing down to his chest like Rip Van Winkle. But the man who stared back at him hadn't aged. He looked perplexed, annoyed, and, again, rested. The damnedest thing, Cal mused, scooping his hair back.

He found his shoes neatly tucked beside the chest. Putting them on, he found himself studying the patterns the sunlight traced on the floor.

Light. It struck him all at once, had him jumping to his feet again. The rain had stopped. For Christ's sake, how long had he been sleeping?

In two strides he was at the window, yanking back those delicate curtains. Then he stood, spellbound.

The view was stunning. He could see the rugged ground where the ruined castle climbed, make out the glints of mica in the stone where the sun struck. The ground tumbled away toward the road, then the road gave way to wave after rolling wave of green fields, bisected with stone walls, dotted with lolling cattle. Houses were tucked into valleys and on rises, clothes flapped cheerfully on lines. Trees twisted up, bent by the years of resisting the relentless wind off the sea and glossy green with spring.

He saw quite clearly a young boy pedaling his blue bike along one of the narrow trenches of road, a spotted black-and-white dog racing beside him through thick hedgerows.

Home, Cal thought. Home for supper. Ma doesn't like you to be late.

He found himself smiling, and reached down without thinking to raise the window and let in the cool, moist air.

The light. It swelled his artist's heart. No one could have described the light of Ireland to him. It had to be seen, experienced. Like the sheen of a fine pearl, he thought, that makes the air glimmer, go luminous and silky. The sun filtering through layers of clouds had a softness, a majesty he'd never seen anywhere else.

He had to capture it. Now. Immediately. Surely such magic couldn't last. He bolted out of the room, clattered down the short flight of steps, and burst out into the gentle sun with the cat scampering at his heels.

He grabbed the Nikon off the front seat of his car. His hands were quick and competent as he changed lenses. Then swinging his case over his shoulder, he picked his position.

The fairy-tale cottage, he thought, the abundance of flowers. The light. Oh, that light. He framed, calculated and framed again.

3

BRYNA stepped through the arched doorway of the ruin and watched him. Such energy, such concentration. Her lips bowed up. He was happy in his work, in his art. He needed this time, she thought, just as he'd needed those hours of deep, dreamless sleep.

Soon he would have questions again, and she would have to answer. She stepped back inside, wanting to give him his privacy. Alone with her thoughts, she walked to the center of the castle, where flowers grew out of the dirt in a circle thick with blooms. Lifting her face to the light, raising her arms to the sky, she began her chant.

Power tingled in her fingertips, but it was weak. So weak that she wanted to weep in frustration. Once she had known its full strength; now she knew the pain of its decline.

It was ordained, this I know. But here on ground where flowers grow, I call the wind, I call the sun. What was done can be undone. No harm to him shall come through me. As I will, so mote it be.

The wind came, fluttering her hair like gentle fingers. The sun beat warm on her upturned face.

I call the faeries, I call the wise. Use what power you can devise. Hear me speak, though my charms are weak. Cast the circle for my own true love, guard him fast from below, from above. Harm to none, my vow is free. As I will, so mote it be.

The power shimmered, brighter, warmer. She fought to hold it, to absorb what gift was given. She thrust up a hand, the silver of the ring she wore exploding with light as a single narrow beam shot through the layering clouds and struck. The heat of it flowed up her arm, made her want to weep again. This time in gratitude.

She was not yet defenseless.

Cal clicked the shutter again and again. He took nearly a dozen pictures of her. She stood, still as a statue in a perfect circle of flowers. Some odd trick of the wind made it blow her hair away from her glowing face. Some odd trick of the light made it beam down on her in a single perfect diagonal shaft.

She was beautiful, unearthly. Though his heart stumbled when her fingers appeared to explode with light, he continued to circle her and capture her on film.

Then she began to move. Just a sway of her body, rhythmic, sensual. The wind whipped the thin fabric of her dress, then had it clinging to those slim curves. The language she spoke now was familiar from his dreams. With unsteady hands, Cal lowered the camera. It was unsettling enough that he somehow understood the ancient tongue. But he would see beyond the words and into her thoughts as clearly as if they were written on a page.

Protect. Defend. The battle is nearly upon us. Help me. Help him.

There was desperation in her thoughts. And fear. The fear made him want to reach out, soothe her, shield her. He stepped forward and into the circle.

The moment he did, her body jerked. Her eyes opened, fixed on his. She held up a hand quickly before he could touch her. "Not here." Her voice was raw and thick. "Not now. It waits for the moon to fill."

Flowers brushed her knees as she walked out of the circle. The wind that had poured through her hair gentled, died.

"You rested well?" she asked him.

"What the hell is going on here?" His eyes narrowed. "What the hell did you put in my tea?"

"A dollop of Irish. Nothing more." She smiled at his camera. "You've been working. I wondered what you would see here, and need to show."

"Why did you strip me?"

"Your clothes were damp." She blinked once, as she saw his thoughts in his eyes. Then she laughed, low and long with a female richness that stirred his blood. "Oh, Cal, you have a most attractive body.

I'll not deny I looked. But in truth, I'm after preferring a man awake and participating when it comes to the matters you're thinking of."

Though furious, he only angled his head. "And would you find it so funny if you'd awakened naked in a strange bed after taking tea with a strange man?"

Her lips pursed, then she let out a breath. "Your point's taken, well taken. I'm sorry for it. I promise you I was thinking only of giving you your ease." Then the humor twinkled again. "Or mostly only of that." She spread her arms. "Would you like to strip me, pay me back in kind?"

He could imagine it, very well. Peeling that long, thin dress away from her, finding her beneath. "I want answers." His voice was sharp, abrupt. "I want them now."

"You do, I know. But are you ready, I wonder?" She turned a slow circle. "Here, I suppose, is the place for it. I'll tell you a story, Calin Farrell. A story of great love, great betrayal. One of passion and greed, of power and lust. One of magic, gained and lost."

"I don't want a story. I want answers."

"It's the same they are. One and the other." She turned back to him, and her voice flowed musically. "Once, long ago, this castle guarded the coast, and its secrets. It rose silver and shining above the sea. Its walls were thick, its fires burned bright. Servants raced up and down the stairways, into chambers.

The rushes were clean and sweet on the floor. Magic sang in the air."

She walked toward curving steps, lifted her hem and began to climb. Too curious to argue, Cal followed her.

He could see where the floors had been, the lintels and stone bracings. Carved into the walls were small openings. Too shallow for chambers, he imagined. Storage, perhaps. He saw, too, that some of the stones were blackened, as if from a great fire. Laying a hand on one, he swore he could still feel heat.

"Those who lived here," she continued, "practiced their art and harmed none. When someone from the village came here with ails or worries, help was offered. Babies were born here," she said as she stepped through a doorway and into the sun again. "The old died."

She walked across a wide parapet to a stone rail that stood over the lashing sea.

"Years passed in just this way, season to season, birth to death. It came to be that some who lived here went out into the land. To make new places. Over the hills, into the forests, up into the mountains, where the faeries have always lived."

The view left him thunderstruck, awed, thrilled. But he turned to her, cocked a brow. "Faeries."

She smiled, turned and leaned back against the rail.

"One remained. A woman who knew her fate was here, in this place. She gathered her herbs, cast her spells, spun her wool. And waited. One day he came, riding over the hills on a fine black horse. The man she'd waited for. He was a warrior, brave and strong and true of heart. Standing here, just here, she saw the sun glint off his armor. She prepared for him, lighting the candles and torches to show him the way until the castle burned bright as a flame. He was wounded."

Gently she traced a fingertip on Cal's thigh. He forced himself not to step back, not to think about the hallucination he'd had while driving through the hills toward this place.

"The battle he had fought was fierce. He was weary in body and heart and in mind. She gave him food and ease and the warmth of her fire. And her love. He took the love she gave, offered back his own. They were all to each other from that moment. His name was Caelan, Caelan of Farrell, and hers Bryna. Their hearts were linked."

He stepped back now, dipping his hands into his pockets. "You expect me to buy that?"

"What I offer is free. And there's more of the story yet." The frustration at having him pull back flickered over her face. "Will you hear it, or not?"

"Fine." He moved a shoulder. "Go ahead."

She turned, clamped her hands on the stone balustrade, let the thunder of the sea pound in her head. She stared down at that endless war of water and rock that fought at the base of the cliff.

"They loved each other, and pledged one to the other. But he was a warrior, and there were more battles to fight. Whenever he would leave her, she watched in the fire she made, saw him wheel his horse through smoke and death, lift his sword for freedom. And always he came back to her, riding over the hills on a fine black horse. She wove him a cloak out of dark gray wool, to match his eyes. And a charm she put on it, for protection in battle."

"So you're saying she was a witch?"

"A witch she was, yes, with the power and art that came down through the blood. And the vow she'd taken to her heart, as close as she'd taken the man she loved, to harm none. Her powers she used only to help and to heal. But not all with power are true. There was one who had chosen a different path. One who used his power for gain and found joy in wielding it like a bloody sword."

She shuddered once, violently, then continued. "This man, Alasdair, lusted for her—for her body, her heart, her soul. For her power as well—for she was strong, was Bryna the Wise. He came into her dreams, creeping like a thief, trying to steal from her what belonged to another. Trying to take what she refused to give. He came into her home, but she would not have him. He was fair of face, his hair gold and his eyes black as the path he'd chosen. He thought to seduce her, but she spurned him."

Her fingers tightened on the stone, and her heart began to trip. "His anger was huge, his vanity deep. He set to kill the man she loved, casting spells, weaving charms of the dark. But the cloak she had woven and the love she had given protected him from harm. But there are more devious ways to destroy. Alasdair used them. Again in dreams he planted seeds of doubt, hints of betrayal in Caelan's sleeping mind. Alasdair gave him visions of Bryna with another, painted pictures of her wrapped in another man's arms, filled with another man's seed. And with these images tormenting his mind, Caelan rode his fine black horse over the hills to this place. And finding her he accused her.

"She was proud," Bryna said after a moment. "She would not deny such lies. They argued bitterly, tempers ruling over hearts. It was then that he struck—Alasdair. He'd waited only for the moment, laughing in the shadows while the lovers hurled pain at each other. When Caelan tore off his cloak, hurled it to the ground at her feet, Alasdair struck him down so that his blood ran through the stones and into the ground."

Tears glinted into her eyes, but went unshed as she faced Calin. "Her grief blinded her, but she cast the circle quickly, fighting to save the man she loved. His wound was mortal and there was no answer for him but death. She knew but refused to accept, and turned to meet Alasdair."

She lifted her voice over the roar of the sea. It came stronger now, this story through her. "Then the walls of this place rang with fury, with magic loosed. She shielded her love and fought like a warrior gone wild. And the sky thundered, clouds dark and thick covered the full white moon and blotted out the stars. The sea thrashed like men pitched in battle and the ground trembled and heaved.

"In the circle, weak and dying, Caelan reached for his sword. But such weapons are useless against witchcraft, light and dark, unless wielded with strength. In his heart he called for her, understanding now his betrayal and his own foolish pride. Her name was on his lips as he died. And when he died, her heart split in two halves and left her defenseless."

She sighed, closed her eyes briefly. "She was lost without him, you see. Alasdair's power spread like vultures' wings. He would have her then, willing or not. But with the last of her strength, she stumbled into the circle where her lover's blood stained the ground. There a vow she made, and a spell she cast. There, while the walls rang and the torches burned, she swore her abiding love for Caelan. For a thousand years she would wait, she would bide. She sent the fire roaring through her home, for she would not let Alasdair have it. And the spell she cast was this."

She drew a deep breath now, kept her eyes on his. "A thousand years to the night, they would come back and face Alasdair as one. If their hearts were strong, they would defeat him in this place. But such spells have a price, and hers was to vow that if Caelan did not believe, did not stand with her that night as one, her power would wink out. And she would belong to Alasdair. Pledging this, she knelt beside her love, embraced him. And vanished them both."

He waited a moment, surprised that he'd found her story and the telling of it hypnotic. Studying her, he rocked back on his heels. "A pretty tale, Bryna."

"Do you still see it as such?" She shook her head, her eyes pleading. "Can you look at me, hear me, and remember nothing?"

"You want me to believe I'm some sort of reincarnation of a Celtic warrior and you're the reincarnation of a witch." He let out a short laugh. "We've waited a millennium and now we're going to do battle with the bad witch of the west? Come on, honey, do I look that gullible?"

She closed her eyes. The telling of the tale, the reliving of it had tired her. She needed all her resources now. "He has to believe," she murmured, pacing away from the wall. "There's no time for subtle persuading." She whirled back to face him. "You had a vivid imagination as a child," she said angrily. "It's a pity you tossed it aside. Tossed me aside—"

"Listen, sweetheart—"

"Oh, don't use those terms with me. Haven't I heard you croon them to other women as you guided them into bed? I didn't expect you to be a monk waiting for this day, but did you have to enjoy it so damn much?"

"Excuse me?"

"Oh, never mind. Just never mind." She gestured impatiently as she paced. " 'A pretty tale,' he says. Did it take a millennium to make him so stubborn, so blind? Well, we'll see, Calin Farrell, what we'll see."

She stopped directly in front of him, her eyes

burning with temper, her face flushed with it. "A reincarnation of a witch? Perhaps that's true. But you'll see for yourself one simple fact. I am a witch, and not without power yet."

"Crazy is what you are." He started to turn.

"Hold!" She drew in a breath, and the wind whipped again, wild and wailing. His feet were cemented to the spot. "See," she ordered and flung a hand down toward the ground between them.

It was the first charm learned, the last lost. Though her hand trembled with the effort, the fire erupted, burning cold and bright.

He swore and would have leaped back if he'd been able. There was no wood, there was no match, just that golden ball of flame shimmering at his feet. "What the hell is this?"

"Proof, if you'll take it." Over the flames, she reached out a hand. "I've called to you in the night, Calin, but you wouldn't hear me. But you know me—you know my face, my mind, my heart. Can you look at me and deny it?"

"No." His throat was dust-dry, his temples throbbing. "No, I can't. But I don't want this."

Her hand fell to her side. The fire vanished. "I can't make you want. I can only make you see." She swayed suddenly, surprising them both.

"Hey!" He caught her as her legs buckled.

"I'm just tired." She struggled to find her pride at least, to pull back from him. "Just tired, that's all."

She'd gone deathly pale, he noted, and she felt

as limp as if every bone in her body had melted. "This is crazy. This whole thing is insane. I'm probably just having another hallucination."

But he swept her up into his arms and carried her down the circle of stone steps and away from the Castle of Secrets.

4

"BRANDY," he muttered, shouldering open the door to the cottage. The cat slipped in like smoke and led the way down the short hall. "Whiskey. Something."

"No." Though the weakness still fluttered through her, she shook her head. "I'm better now, truly."

"The hell you are." She felt fragile enough to dissolve in his arms. "Have you got a doctor around here?"

"I don't need a doctor." The idea of it made her chuckle a little. "I have what I need in the kitchen."

He turned his head, met her eyes. "Potions? Witch's brews?"

"If you like." Unable to resist, she wound her arms around his neck. "Will you carry me in, Calin? Though I'd prefer it if you carried me upstairs, took me to bed."

Her mouth was close to his, already softly parted in invitation. He felt his muscles quiver. If he was caught in a dream, he mused, it involved all of the senses and was more vivid than any he'd had in childhood.

"I didn't know Irish women were so aggressive. I might have visited here sooner."

"I've waited a long time. I have needs, as anyone."

Deliberately he turned away from the steps and started down the hall. "So, witches like sex."

That chuckle came again, throaty and rich. "Oh, aye, we're fond of it. I could give you more than an ordinary woman. More than you could dream."

He remembered the jolt of that staggering kiss of welcome. And didn't doubt her word. He made a point of dropping her, abruptly, on one of the two ladder-back chairs at a scrubbed wooden table in the tiny kitchen.

"I dream real good," he said, and she smiled silkily.

"That I know." The air hummed between them before she eased back, tidily folded her hands on the table. "There's a blue bottle in the cupboard there, over the stove. Would you mind fetching it for me, and a glass as well?"

He opened the door she indicated, found the cupboard neatly lined with bottles of all colors and shapes. All were filled with liquids and powders, and none were labeled. "Which one of these did you put in my tea?"

Now she sighed, heavily. "Cal, I put nothing in your tea but the whiskey. I gave you sleep—a small spell, and a harmless one—because you needed it. Two hours only, and did you not wake feeling well and rested?"

He scowled at the bottles, refusing to argue the point. "Which blue one?"

"The cobalt bottle with the long neck."

He set the bottle and a short glass on the table. "Drugs are dangerous."

She poured a careful two fingers of liquid as blue as the bottle that held it. "'Tis herbs." Her eyes flickered up to his, laughed. "And a touch or two of magic. This is for energy and strength." She sipped with apparent enjoyment. "Will you be sitting down, Calin? You could use a meal, and it should be ready by now."

He'd already felt his stomach yearn at the scents filling the room, puffing out of the steam from a pot on the stove.

"What is it?"

"Craibechan." She smiled as his brows drew together. "A kind of soup," she explained. "It's hearty, and your appetite's been off. You've lost more than a pound or two in recent weeks, and I feel the blame for that."

Wanting to see just what craibechan consisted of—and to make sure there was no eye of newt or tongue of frog in the mix, he had started to reach for the lid on the pot. Now he drew back, faced her. He was going to make one vital point perfectly clear.

"I don't believe in witches."

A glint of amusement was in her eyes as she pushed back from the table. "We'll set to working on that soon enough."

"But I'm willing to consider some sort of . . . I don't know . . . psychic connection."

"That's a beginning, then." She took out a loaf of brown bread, set it in the oven to warm. "Would you have wine with your meal? There's a bottle you could open. I've chilled it a bit." She opened the refrigerator, took out a bottle.

He accepted it, studied the label. It was his favorite Bourdeax—a wine that he preferred chilled just a bit. Considering, he took the corkscrew she offered.

The obsessed-fan theory just didn't hold, he decided, as he set the open bottle on the slate-gray counter to breathe. No matter how much information she might have dug up about him, she couldn't have predicted he would come to Ireland—and certainly not to this place.

He would accept the oddity of a connection. What else could he call it? It had been her voice echoing through his dreams, her face floating through the mists of his memory. And it had been his hands on the wheel of the car he'd driven up to this place. To her.

It was time, he thought, to discover more about her.

"Bryna."

She paused in the act of spooning stew into thick white bowls. "Aye?"

"How long have you lived here, alone like this?"

"The last five years I've been alone. It was part of the pattern. The wineglasses are to the right of you there."

"How old are you?" He took down two crystal glasses, poured bloodred wine.

"Twenty-six. Four years less than you." She set the bowls on the table, took one of the glasses. "My first memory of you, this time, was of you riding a horse made out of a broom around a parlor with blue curtains. A little black dog chased you. You called him Hero."

She took a sip from her glass, set it down, then turned to take the warmed bread from the oven. "And when he died, fifteen years later on a hot summer day, you buried him in the backyard, and your parents helped you plant a rosebush over his grave. All of you wept, for he'd been very dear. Neither you nor your parents have had a pet since. You don't think you have the heart to lose one again."

He let out a long, uneasy breath, took a deep gulp of wine. None of that information, none of it, was in his official bio. And certainly none of the emotions were public fare. "Where is your family?"

"Oh, here and there." She bent to give Hecate an affectionate scratch between the ears. "It's difficult for them just now. There's nothing they can do to help. But I feel them close, and that's comfort enough."

"So . . . your parents are witches too?"

She heard the amusement in his voice and bristled. "I'm a hereditary witch. My power and my gift runs through the blood, generation to generation. It's not an avocation I have, Calin, nor is it a hobby or a game. It is my destiny, my legacy and my pride. And don't be insulting me when you're about to eat my food." She tossed her head and sat down.

He scratched his chin. "Yes, ma'am." He sat across from her, sniffed at the bowl. "Smells great." He spooned up some, sampled, felt the spicy warmth of it spread through his system. "Tastes even better."

"Don't flatter me, either. You're hungry enough to eat a plate of raw horsemeat."

"Got me there." He dug in with relish. "So, any eye of newt in here?"

Her eyes kindled. "Very funny."

"I thought so." It was either take the situation with humor or run screaming, he decided. "Anyway, what do you do up here alone?" No, he realized, he wasn't sure he wanted to know that. "I mean, what do you do for a living?"

It was no use being annoyed with him, she told herself. No use at all. "You're meaning to make money? Well, that's a necessary thing." She passed him the bread and salt butter. "I weave, and sell my wares. Sweaters, rugs, blankets, throws, and the like. It's a soothing art, and a solitary one. It gives me independence."

"The rugs in the other room? Your work?"

"They are, yes."

"They're beautiful—color, texture, workmanship." Remembering the spinning wheel, he blinked. "Are you telling me you spin your own wool?"

"It's an old and venerable art. One I enjoy."

Most of the women he knew couldn't even sew on a button. He'd never held the lack of domesticity against anyone, but he found the surplus of it intriguing in Bryna. "I wouldn't think a witch would . . . well, I'd think she'd just—you know—*poof.*"

"*Poof?*" Her brows arched high. "Saying if I wanted a pot of gold I'd just whistle up the wind and coins would drop into my hands?" She leaned forward. Annoyance spiked her voice. "Tell me why you use that camera with all the buttons and business when they make those tidy little things that all but think for you and snap the picture themselves?"

"It's hardly worthwhile if you automate the whole process. If it's to mean anything I have to be involved, in control, do the planning out, see the picture . . ." He trailed off, catching her slow, and smug, smile. "Okay, I get it. If you could just snap your fingers, it wouldn't be art."

"It wouldn't. And more, it's a pledge, you see. Not to abuse a gift or take it for granted. And most vital, never to use power to harm. You nearly believe me, Calin."

Stunned that she was right, he jerked back. "Just making conversation," he muttered, then rose to refill his empty bowl, the cat trailing him like a hopeful shadow. "When's the last time you were in the States?"

"I've never been to America." She picked up her wine after he topped it off. "It wasn't permitted for me to contact you, face-to-face, until you came here. It wasn't permitted for you to come until one month before the millennium passed."

Cal drummed his fingers on the table. She sure knew how to stick to a story. "So it's a month to the anniversary of . . . the spell casting."

"No, it's on the solstice. Tomorrow night." She picked up her wine again, but only turned the stem around and around in her fingers.

"Cutting it close, aren't you?"

"You didn't want to hear me—and I waited too long. It was pride. I was wanting you to call to me, just once." Defeated by her own heart, she closed her eyes. "Like some foolish teenage girl waiting by the phone for her boy to call her. You'd hurt me when you turned away from me." Her eyes opened again, pinned him with the sharp edge of her unhappiness. "Why did you turn from me, Calin? Why did you stop answering, stop hearing?"

He couldn't deny it. He was here, and so was she. He'd been pulled to her, and no matter how he struggled to refuse it, he could remember—the soft voice, the plea in it. And those eyes, so incredibly blue, with that same deep hurt glowing in them.

It was, he realized, accept this or accept insanity. "Because I didn't want to answer, and I didn't want to be here." His voice roughened as he shoved the bowl aside. "I wanted to be normal."

"So you rejected me, and the gift you'd been given, for what you see as normality?"

"Do you know what it's like to be different, to be odd?" he tossed back furiously. Then he hissed through his teeth. "I suppose you do," he muttered. "But I hated it, hated seeing how it worried my parents."

"It wasn't meant to be a burden but a joy. It was part of her, part of me that was passed to you, Calin, that small gift of sight. To protect you, not to threaten."

"I didn't want it!" He shoved back from the table. "Where are my rights in all this? Where's my choice?"

She wanted to weep for him, for the small boy who hadn't understood that his uniqueness had been a loving gift. And for the man who would reject it still. "The choice has always been yours."

"Fine. I don't want any of this."

"And me, Calin." She rose as well, slowly, pride in the set of her shoulders, the set of her head. "Do you not want me as well?"

"No." It was a lie, and it burned on his tongue. "I don't want you."

He heard the laughter, a nasty buzz on the air. Hecate hissed, arched her back, then growled out a warning. Cal saw fear leap into Bryna's eyes even as she whirled and flung herself in front of him like a shield.

"No!" Her voice boomed, power and authority.

"You are not welcome here. You have no right here."

The shadows in the doorway swirled, coalesced, formed into a man. He wore sorcerer's black, piped with silver, on a slender frame. A face as handsome as a fairy-tale prince was framed with golden hair and accented with eyes as black as midnight.

"Bryna, your time is short." His voice was smooth, laced with dark amusement. "There is no need for this war between us. I offer you such power, such a world. You've only to take my hand, accept."

"Do you think I would? That a thousand years, or ten thousand, would change my heart? Doomed you are, Alasdair, and the choice was your own."

"The wait's nearly at an end." Alasdair lifted a hand, and thunder crashed overhead like swords meeting. "Send him away and I will allow it. My word to you, Bryna. Send him away and he goes unharmed by me. If he stays, his end will be as it was before, and I will have you, Bryna, unbound or in chains. That choice is your own."

She lifted a hand, and light glinted off her ring of carved silver. "Come into my circle now, Alasdair." Her lips curved in a sultry dare, though her heart was pounding in terror, for she was not ready to meet him power to power. "Do you risk it?"

His lips thinned in a sneer, his dark eyes glittering with malicious promise. "On the solstice, Bryna." His gaze flickered to Cal, amusement shining dark. "You, warrior, remember death."

There was pain, bright and sharp and sudden, stabbing into Cal's belly. It burned through him like acid, cutting off his breath, weakening his knees, even as he gripped Bryna's shoulders and shoved her behind him.

"Touch her and die." He felt the words rise in his throat, heard them come through his lips. He felt the sweat pearl cold and clammy on his brow as he faced down the image.

And so it faded, leaving only a dark glint like a smudge, and an echo of taunting laughter.

5

CAL pressed a hand to his stomach, half expecting to find blood, and worse, dripping through his fingers. The pain had dulled to numbness, with a slick echo of agony.

"He can't harm you." Bryna's voice registered dimly, made him aware that he was still gripping her arm. "He can only make you remember, deceive you with the pain. It's all tricks and lies with him."

"I saw him." Dazed, Cal studied his own fingers. "I saw it."

"Aye. He's stronger than I'd believed, and more rash, to come here like this." Gently she put a hand over the one bruising her arm. "Alasdair is sly and full of lies. You must remember that, Calin. You must never forget it."

"I saw him," Cal repeated, struggling to absorb

the impossible into reality. "I could see through him, the table in the hall, the flowers on it."

"He wouldn't dare risk coming here in full form. Not as yet. Calin, you're hurting my arm."

His fingers jerked, dropped. "Sorry. I lost my head. Seeing ghosts does that to me."

"A ghost he isn't. But a witch, one who embraced the dark and closed out the light. One who broke every oath."

"Is he a man?" He whirled on her so abruptly that she caught her breath, then winced as his hands gripped her arms again. "He looked at you as a man would, with desire."

"We're not spirits. We have our needs, our weaknesses. He wants me, yes. He has broken into my dreams and shown me just what he wants from me. And rape in dreams is no less a rape." She trembled and her eyes went blind. For a moment she was only a woman, with a woman's fears. "He frightens me. Is that enough for you? Is it enough that I'd rather die than have his hands on me? He frightens me," she said again and pressed her face into Cal's shoulder. "Oh, Calin, his hands are cold, so cold."

"He won't touch you." The need to protect was too strong to deny. His arms tightened, brought her close. "He won't touch you. Bryna." His lips brushed over her hair, down her temple. Found hers. "Bryna," he said again. "Sweet God."

She melted into him, yielding like wax, giving like glory. All the confusion, the doubt, the fear slid away from him. Here was the woman, the only, the ever. His hands dived into her hair, fisted in those soft ropes of red silk, pulled her head back so that he could drive the kiss deeper.

Whatever had brought him here he would face. Whatever else he might continue to deny, there was no denying this. Need could be stronger than reason.

The sounds humming in her throat were both plea and seduction. Her heart hammered fast and hard against his, and her body shuddered lightly. She nipped at his lip, urging him on. He heard her sigh his name, moan it, then whisper words ripe with longing.

The words were in Gaelic, and that was what stopped him. He understood them as if he'd been speaking the language all his life.

"Love," she had said. "My love."

"Is this the answer?" The fury returned as he pushed her back against the wall. "Is this what you want?" Now his kiss tasted of violence, of desperation, nearly of punishment.

Her own fears sprang hot to her throat, taunting her to fight him, to reject the anger. But she offered no struggle, took the heat, the rough hands until he drew back and stared at her out of stormy eyes.

She took a steadying breath, waited until she was sure her voice would be strong and sure. "It's one answer. Yes, I want you." Slowly she unfastened the buttons running down the front of her dress. "I want you to touch me, to take me." Parted the material, let it slide to the floor so that she stood before him defenseless and naked. "Where you like, when you like, how you like."

He kept his eyes on hers. "You said that to me before, once before."

Emotions swirling, she closed her eyes, then opened them again. And smiled. "I did. A thousand years ago. More or less."

He remembered. She had stood facing him, flowers blooming at her feet. And she had undraped herself so that the pearly light had gleamed on her skin. She had offered herself without restrictions. He'd lost himself in her, flowers crushed and fragrant under their eager bodies.

He shook his head, and the image faded away. Memory or imagination, it no longer mattered. He knew only one vital thing. "This is now. This is you and me. Nothing else touches it. Whatever happened or didn't happen before, this is for us."

He scooped her into his arms. "That's the way I want it," he stated.

She stared at him, for she was spellbound now. She'd thought he would simply take her where they stood, seeking release, even oblivion. She'd tasted the sharp edge of his passion, felt the violence simmering under his skin. Instead, he carried her in his arms as if she were something he could cherish.

And when he laid her on the bed, stepped back to look at her, she felt a flush warm her cheeks. She managed a quick smile. "You'll be needing your clothes off," she said, tried to laugh and sit up, but he touched a hand to her shoulder.

"I'll do it. Lie back, Bryna. I want to see you with your hair burning over the pillows, and the sun on your skin." He would photograph her like this, he realized. Would be compelled to see if he could capture the magic of it, of her—long limbs, slender curves, eyes full of needs and nerves.

He watched her as he undressed, and his voice was quiet and serious when he spoke. "Are you afraid of me?"

"I wasn't. I didn't expect to be." But her heart was fluttering like birds' wings. "I suppose I am, yes. A little. Because it means . . . everything."

He tossed his clothes toward the little chair, never taking his eyes from hers. "I don't know what I believe, what I can accept. Except one thing." He lowered himself to her, kept his mouth a whisper from hers. "This matters. Here. Now. You. It matters."

"Love me." She drew his mouth down to hers. "I've ached for you so long."

It was slow and testing and sweet. Sighs and secrets, tastes and textures. He knew how her mouth would fit against his, knew the erotic slide of her tongue, the suggestive arch of her hips. He swallowed each catchy breath as he took his hands slowly, so slowly over her. Skimming curves, warming flesh. He filled his hands with her breasts, then his mouth, teasing her nipples with tongue and teeth until she groaned out his name like a prayer.

She took her hands over him, testing those muscles, tracing the small scars. Not a warrior's body, but a man's, she thought. And for now, hers. Her heart beat slow and thick as he used his mouth on her with a patience and concentration she knew now she'd been foolish not to expect.

Her heart beat thickly, the sun warmed her closed lids as pleasure swamped her. And love held so long in her heart bloomed like wild roses.

"Calin."

His name shuddered through her lips when he cupped her. He watched her eyes fly open, saw the deep-blue irises go glassy and blind in speechless arousal. He sent her over the edge, viciously delighted when she cried out, shuddered, when her hands fell weakly.

His, was all he could think as he blazed a hot trail down her thigh. His. His.

Blood thundered in his head as he slipped inside her, as she moaned in pleasure, arched in welcome. Now her eyes were open, vivid blue and intense. Now her arms were around him, a circle of possession. She mated with him, their rhythm ancient and sure.

His strokes went deep, deeper, and his mouth crushed down on hers in breathless, mutual pleasure. She flew, as she had waited a lifetime to fly, as he emptied himself into her.

She held him close as the tension drained from his body. Stroked his hair as he rested his head between her breasts. "It's new," she said quietly. "Ours. I didn't know it could be. Knowing so much, yet this I never knew."

He shifted, lifted his head so that he could see

her face. Her skin was soft, dewy, her eyes slumberous, her mouth rosy and swollen. "None of this should be possible." He cupped a hand under her chin, turned her profile just slightly, already seeing it in frame, in just that light. Black and white. And he would title it *Aftermath*. "I'm probably having a breakdown."

Her laugh was a quick, silly snort. Carefree, careless. "Well, your engine seemed to be running fine, Calin, if you're after asking me."

His mouth twitched in response. "We're pushing into the twenty-first century. I have a fax built into my car phone, a computer in my office that does everything but make my bed, and I'm supposed to believe I've just made love to a witch. A witch who makes fire burn out of thin air, calls up winds where there isn't a breeze in sight."

She combed her fingers through his hair as she'd dreamed of doing countless times. "Magic and technology aren't mutually exclusive. It's only that the second so rarely takes the first into account. Normality is only in the perspective." She watched his eyes cloud at that. "You had visions, Calin. As a child you had them."

"And I put away childish things."

"Visions? Childish?" Her eyes snapped once, then she closed them on a sigh. "Why must you think so? A child's mind and heart are perhaps more open to such matters. But you saw and you felt and you knew things that others didn't. It was a gift you were given."

"I'm no witch."

"No, that only makes the gift more special. Calin—"

"No." He sat up, shaking his head. "It's too much. Let it be for a while. I don't know what I feel." He scrubbed his hands over his face, into his hair. "All I know is that here was where I had to be—and you're who I had to be with. Let the rest alone for a while."

They had so little time. She nearly said it before she stopped herself. If time was so short, then what they had was precious. If she was damned for taking it for only the two of them, then she was damned.

"Then let it rest we will." She lay back, stretched out a hand for his. "Come kiss me again. Come lie with me."

He skimmed a hand up her thigh, watched her smile bloom slow. And the light. Oh, the light. "Stay right there." He bounded out of bed, grabbing his jeans on the run.

She blinked. "What? Where are you going?"

"Be right back. Don't move. Stay right there."

She huffed out a breath at the ceiling. Then her face softened again and she stretched her arms high. Oh, she felt well loved. Like a cat thoroughly stroked. Chuckling, she glanced over at Hecate, curled in front of the hearth and watching her.

"Aye, you know the feeling, don't you? Well, I like it." The cat only stared, unblinking. Ten seconds. Twenty. Bryna closed her eyes. "I need the time. Damn it, we need it. A few hours after so many years. Why should we be denied it? Why must there be a price for every joy? Go then, leave me be. If the fare comes due, I'll pay it freely."

With a swish of her tail, the cat rose and padded out of the room. Calin's footsteps sounded on the steps seconds later. Prepared to smile, Bryna widened her eyes instead. He'd snapped two quick pictures before she could push herself up and cross her arms over her breast.

"What do you think you're about? Taking photographs of me without my clothes. Put it away. You won't be hanging me on some art gallery wall."

"You're beautiful." He circled the bed, changing angles. "A masterpiece. Drop your left shoulder just a little."

"I'll do no such thing. It's outrageous." Shocked to the core, she tugged at the rumpled spread, pulled it up—and to Cal's mind succeeded only in looking more alluring and rumpled.

But he lowered the camera. "I thought witches were supposed to like to dance naked under the full moon."

"Going skyclad isn't an exhibition. And there's a time and place for such things. No one snaps pictures of private matters nor of rituals."

"Bryna." Using all his charm, he stepped closer, tugged gently at the sheet she'd pulled over her breasts. "You have a beautiful body, your coloring is exquisite, and the light in here is perfect. Unbelievable." He skimmed the back of his fingers over her nipple, felt her tremble. "I'll show them to you first."

She barely felt the sheet slip to her waist. "I know what I look like."

"You don't know how I see you. But I'll show you. Lie back for me. Relax." Murmuring, he spread her hair over the pillows as he wanted it. "No, don't cover yourself. Just look at me." He shot straight down, then moved back. "Turn your head, just a little. I'm touching you. Imagine my hands on you, moving over you. There. And there." He braced a knee on the foot of the bed, working quickly. "If I had a darkroom handy, I'd develop these tonight and you'd see what I see."

"I have one." Her voice was breathless, aroused.

"What?"

"I had one put in for you, off the kitchen." Her smile was hesitant when he lowered the camera and stared at her. "I knew you would come, and I wanted you to have what you needed, what would make you comfortable."

So you would stay with me, she thought, but didn't say it.

"You put in a darkroom? Here?"

"Aye, I did."

With a laugh, he shook his head. "Amazing. Absolutely amazing." Rising, he set the camera down on the bureau. "I think you need to be a little more . . . mussed before I shoot the rest of that roll." He climbed onto the bed. "The things I do for my art," he murmured and covered her laughing mouth with his.

6

LATER, in the breezy evening when the sun gilded the sky and polished the air, he walked with her toward the cliffs. Both his mind and his body were relaxed, limber.

Logically he knew he should be racing to the nearest psychiatric ward for a full workup. But a lonely cliffside, a ruined castle, a beautiful woman who claimed to be a witch—visions and sex and legends. It was a time and place to set logic aside, at least for a while.

"It's a beautiful country," he commented. "I'm still trying to adjust that I've only been here since this morning. Barely twelve hours."

"Your heart's been here longer." It was so simple to walk with him, fingers linked. So simple. So ordinary. So miraculous. "Tell me about New York. All the movies, the pictures I've seen have only made me wonder more. Is it like that, really? So fast and crowded and exciting?"

"It can be." And at that moment it seemed a world away. A thousand years away.

"And your house?"

"It's an apartment. It looks out over the park. I wanted a big space so I could have my studio right there. It's got good light."

"You like to stand on the balcony," she began, then rolled her eyes when he shot her a quick look. "I've peeked now and then."

"Peeked." He caught her chin in his hand before she could turn away. "At what? Exactly?"

"I wanted to see how you lived, how you worked."

She eased away and walked along the rocks, where the water spewed up, showered like diamonds in the sunlight. Then she turned her head, tilting it in an eerily feline movement.

"You've had a lot of women, Calin Farrell—coming and going at all hours in all manner of dress. And undress."

He hunched his shoulders as if he had an itch he couldn't scratch. "You watched me with other women?"

"I peeked," she corrected primly. "And never watched for long in any case. But it seemed to me that you often chose women who were lacking in the area of intelligence."

He ran his tongue around his teeth. "Did it?"

"Well . . ." A shrug, dismissing. "Well, so it

seemed." Bending, she plucked a wildflower that had forced its way through a split in the rock. Twirled it gaily under her nose. "Is it worrying you that I know of them?"

He hooked his thumbs in his pockets. "Not particularly."

"That's fine, then. Now, if I were the vindictive sort, I might turn you into an ass. Just for a short time."

"An ass?"

"Just for a short time."

"Can you do that sort of thing?" He realized when he asked it that he was ready to believe anything.

She laughed, the sound carrying rich music over wind and sea. "If I were the vindictive sort." She walked to him, handed him the flower, then smiled when he tucked it into her hair. "But I think you'd look darling with long ears and a tail."

"I'd just as soon keep my anatomy as it is. What else did you . . . peek at?"

"Oh, this and that, here and there." She linked her fingers with his and walked again. "I watched you work in your darkroom—the little one in the house where you grew up. Your parents were so proud of you. Startled by your talent, but very proud. I saw your first exhibition, at that odd wee gallery where everyone wore black—like at a wake."

"SoHo," he murmured. "Christ, that was nearly ten years ago."

"You've done brilliant things since. I could look

through your eyes when I looked at your pictures. And felt close to you."

The thought came abruptly, stunning him. He turned her quickly to face him, stared hard into her eyes. "You didn't have anything to do with . . . you haven't made what I can do?"

"Oh, Calin, no." She lifted her hands to cover the ones on her shoulders. "No, I promise you. It's yours. From you. You mustn't doubt it," she said, sensing that he did. "I can tell you nothing that isn't true. I'm bound by that. On my oath, everything you've accomplished is yours alone."

"All right." He rubbed his hands up and down her arms absently. "You're shivering. Are you cold?"

"I was for a moment." Bone-deep, harrowing. Alasdair. She cast it out, gripped his hand tightly and led him over the gentle slope of the hill. "Even as a child I would come here and stand and look out." Content again, she leaned her head against his shoulder, scanning hill and valley, the bright flash of river, the dark shadows cast by twisted trees. "To Ireland spread out before me, green and gold. A dreaming place."

"Ireland, or this spot?"

"Both. We're proud of our dreamers here. I would show you Ireland, Calin. The bank where the columbine grows, the pub where a story is always waiting to be told, the narrow lane flanked close with hedges that bloom with red fuchsia. The simple Ireland."

Tossing her hair back, she turned to him. "And more. I would show you more. The circle of stones where power sleeps, the quiet hillock where the faeries dance of an evening, the high cliff where a wizard once ruled. I would give it to you, if you'd take it."

"And what would you take in return, Bryna?"

"That's for you to say." She felt the chill again. The warning. "Now I have something else to show you, Calin." She glanced uneasily over her shoulder, toward the ruins. Shivered. "He's close," she whispered. "And watching. Come into the house."

He held her back. He was beginning to see that he had run from a good many things in his life. Too many things. "Isn't it better to face him now, be done with it?"

"You can't choose the time. It's already set." She gripped his hand, pulled. "Please. Into the house."

Reluctantly, Cal went with her. "Look, Bryna, it seems to me that a bully's a bully whatever else he might be. The longer you duck a bully, the worse he gets. Believe me, I've dealt with my share."

"Oh, aye, and had a fine bloody nose, as I remember, from one. The two of you, pounding on each other on the street corner. Like hoodlums."

"Hey, he started it. He tried to shake me down once too often, so I . . ." Cal trailed off, blew out a long breath. "Whoa. Too weird. I haven't thought about Henry Belinski in twenty years. Anyway, he may have bloodied my nose, but I broke his."

"Oh, and you're proud of that, are you now?

Breaking the nose of an eight-year-old boy."

"*I* was eight too." He realized that she had maneuvered him neatly into the house, turned the subject, and gotten her own way. "Very clever, Bryna. I don't see that you need magic when you can twist a conversation around like that."

"Just a small talent." She smiled and touched his cheek. "I was glad you broke his nose. I wanted to turn him into a toad—I had already started the charm when you dealt with it yourself."

"A toad?" He couldn't help it, the grin just popped out. "Really?"

"It would have been wrong. But I was only four, and such things are forgiven in the child." Then her smile faded, and her eyes went dark. "Alasdair is no child, Calin. He wants more than to wound your pride, skin your knees. Don't take him lightly."

Then she stepped back, lifting both hands. *I call the wind around my house to swirl.* She twisted a wrist and brought the wind howling against the windows. *Fists of fog against my windows curl. Deafen his ears and blind his eyes. Come aid me with this disguise. Help me guard what was trusted to me. As I will, so mote it be.*

He'd stepped back from her, gaping. Fog crawled over the windows, the wind howled like wolves. The woman before him glowed like a candle, shimmering with a power he couldn't understand. The fire she'd made out of air was nothing compared with this.

"How much am I supposed to believe? Accept?"

She lowered her hands slowly. "Only what you will. The choice will always be yours, Calin. Will you come with me and see what I would show you?"

"Fine." He blew out a breath. "And after, if you don't mind, I'd like a glass of that Irish of yours. Straight up."

She managed a small smile. "Then you'll have it. Come." As she started toward the stairs, she chose her words carefully. "We have little time. He'll work to break the spell. His pride will demand it, and my powers are more . . . limited than they were."

"Why?"

"It's part of it," was all she would say. "And so is what I have to show you. It isn't just me he wants, you see. He wants everything I have. And he wants the most precious treasure of the Castle of Secrets."

She stopped in front of a door, thick with carving. There was no knob, no lock, just glossy wood and that ornate pattern on it that resembled ancient writing. "This room is barred to him by power greater than mine." She passed a hand over the wood, and slowly, soundlessly, the door crept open.

" 'Open locks,' " Cal murmured, " 'whoever knocks.' "

"No, only I. And now you." She stepped inside, and after a brief hesitation, he crossed the threshold behind her.

Instantly the room filled with the light of a hundred candles. Their flames burned straight and true, illuminating a small, windowless chamber. The walls were wood, thickly carved like the door, the ceiling low, nearly brushing the top of his head.

"A humble place for such a thing," Bryna murmured.

He saw nothing but a simple wooden pedestal standing in a white circle in the center of the room. Atop the column was a globe, clear as glass.

"A crystal ball?"

Saying nothing, she crossed the room. "Come closer." She waited, kept her hands at her side until he'd walked up and put the globe between them.

"Alasdair lusts for me, envies you, and covets this. For all his power, for all his trickery, he has never gained what he craves the most. This has been guarded by a member of my blood since before time. Believe me, Calin, wizards walked this land while men without vision still huddled in caves, fearing the night. And this ancient ball was conjured by one of my blood and passed down generation to generation. Bryna the Wise held this in her hands a thousand years past and through her power, and her love, concealed it from Alasdair at the last. And so it remained hidden. No one outside my blood has cast eyes on it since."

Gently, she lifted the globe from its perch, raised it high above her head. Candlelight flickered over it, into it, seemed to trap itself inside until the ball burned bright. When she lowered it, it glowed still, colors dazzling, pulsing, beating.

"Look, my love." Bryna opened her hand so that the globe rolled to her fingertips, clung there in defiance of gravity. "Look, and see."

He couldn't stop his hands from reaching out, cupping it. Its surface was smooth, almost silky, and warmed in his hands like flesh. The pulse of it, the life of it, seemed to swim up his arms.

Colors shifted. The bright clouds they formed parted, a magic sea. He saw dragons spewing fire and a silver sword cleaving through scales. A man bedding a woman in a flower-strewn meadow under a bright white sun. A farmer plowing a rocky field behind swaybacked horses. A babe suckling at his mother's breast.

On and on it went, image after image in a blur of life. Dark oceans, wild stars, a quiet village as still as a photograph. An old woman's face, ravaged with tears. A small boy sleeping under the shade of a chestnut tree.

And even when the images faded into color and light, the power sang. It flooded him, a river of wine. Cool and clean. It hummed still when the globe was clear again, tossing the flames of the candles into his eyes.

"It's the world." Cal's voice was soft and thick. "Here in my hands."

"The heart of it. The hope for it. Power gleams there. In your hands now."

"Why?" He lifted his gaze to hers. "Why in my hands, Bryna?"

"I am the guardian of this place. My heart is in there as well." She took a slow breath. "I am in your hands, Calin Farrell."

"I can refuse?"

"Aye. The choice is yours."

"And if he—Alasdair—claims this?"

She would stop him. It would cost her life, but she would stop him. "Power can be twisted, abused—but what is used will turn on the abuser, ten times ten."

"And if he claims you?"

"I will be bound to him, a thousand years of bondage. A spell that cannot be broken." But with death, she thought. Only with death. "He is wicked, but not without weaknesses." She laid her hand on the globe so that they held it together. "He will not have this, Calin. Nor will he bring harm to you. That is my oath."

She stared hard into his eyes, murmuring. His vision blurred, his head spun. He lifted a hand as if to push back what he couldn't see. "No."

"To protect." She laid a hand on his cheek as she cast the charm. "My love."

He blinked, shook his head. For a moment his mind remained blank with some faint echo of words. "I'm sorry. What?"

Her lips curved. He would remember nothing, she knew. It was all she could do for him. "I said we need to go." She placed the globe back on the pedestal. "We're not to speak of this outside this room." She walked toward the door, held out a hand. "Come. I'll pour you that whiskey."

7

THAT night his dreams were restful, lovely. Bryna
had seen to that.

There was a man astride a gleaming black horse,
riding hard over hills, splashing through a bright
slash of river, his gray cape billowing in a brisk and
icy wind.

There was the witch who waited for him in a
silver castle atop a spearing cliff where candles and
torches burned gold.

There was a globe of crystal, clear as water,
where the world swam from decade to decade, century past century.

There was love sweet as honey and need sharp
as honed steel.

And when he turned to her in the night, lost in
dreams, she opened for him, took him in.

Bryna didn't sleep, nor did she dream. She lay in

the circle of his arms while the white moon rose and the shudders his hands had caused quieted.

Who had loved her? she wondered. Cal, or Caelan? She turned her face into his shoulder, seeking comfort, a harbor from fear on this last night before she would face her fate.

He would be safe, she thought, laying a hand over his heart. She had taken great pains, at great risk, to assure it. And her safety depended on the heart that beat quietly under her palm. If he did not choose to give it freely, to stand with her linked by love, she was lost.

So it had been ordained in fire and in blood, on that terrible night a millennium before.

For a thousand years we sleep, a hundred years times ten. But blood stays true and hearts are strong when we are born again. And in this place we meet, with love our lifted shield. In the shortest night the battle will rage and our destiny be revealed. My warrior's heart his gift to me, his sword bright as the moon. If he brings both here of his own free will, we will bring to Alasdair his doom. When the dawn breaks that longest day and his love has found a way, our lives will then be free of thee. As I will, so mote it be.

The words of Bryna the Wise, lifted high the blazing castle walls, echoed in her head, beat in her heart. When the moon rose again, it would be settled.

Bryna lay in the circle of Cal's arms, listened to the wind whisper, and slept not at all.

* * *

WHEN Cal woke, he was alone, and the sun was streaming. For a moment, he thought it had all been a dream. The woman—the witch—the ruined castle and tiny cottage. The globe that held the world. A hallucination brought on, he thought, by fatigue and stress and the breakdown he'd secretly worried about.

But he recognized the room—the flowers still fresh in the vases, the scent of them, and Bryna, on the air. True, then. He pressed his fingers to his eyes to rub away sleep. All true, and all unbelievable. And all somehow wonderful.

He got out of bed, walked into the charming little bathroom, stepped into the clawfoot tub, and twitched the circling curtain into place. He adjusted the shower for hot and let the steam rise.

He hadn't showered with her yet, Cal thought, grinning as he turned his face into the spray. Hadn't soaped that long, lovely body of hers until it was slick and slippery, hadn't seen the water run through that glorious mane of flame-red hair. Had yet to ease inside her while the water ran hot and the steam rose in clouds.

His grin winked off, replaced by a look of puzzlement. Had he turned to her in the night, in his dreams, seeking that tangle of tongues and limbs, that slow, satiny slide of bodies?

Why couldn't he remember? Why couldn't he be sure?

What did it matter? Annoyed with himself, he flicked off the water, snatched a towel from the heating rack. Whether it had been real or a dream, she was there for him as he'd wanted no one to be before.

Was it you, or another, she moved under in the night?

Cal's eyes went dark as the voice whispered slyly in his head. He toweled off roughly.

She uses you. Uses you to gain her own ends. Spellbinds you until she has what she seeks.

The room was suddenly airless, the steam thick and clogging his lungs. He reached blindly for the door, found only swirling air.

She brought you here, drew you into her web. Other men have been trapped in it. She seeks to possess you, body and soul. Who will you be when she's done with you?

Cal all but fell into the door, panicked for a shuddering instant when he thought it locked. But his slippery hands yanked it open and he stumbled into the cool, sun-washed air of the bedroom. Behind him the mists swirled dark, shimmered greedily, then vanished.

What the hell? He found himself trembling all over, like a schoolboy rushing out of a haunted house. It had seemed as if there had been . . . something, something cold and slick and smelling of death crowded into that room with him, hiding in the mists.

But when Cal turned and stepped back to the

door, he saw only a charming room, a fogged mirror, and the thinning steam from his shower.

Imagination working overtime, he thought, then let out half a laugh. Whose wouldn't, under the circumstances? But he shut the bathroom door firmly before he dressed and went down to find her.

She was spinning wool. Humming along with the quiet, rhythmic clacking of spindle and wheel. Her hands were as graceful as a harpist's on strings and her wool was as white as innocence.

Her dress was blue this morning, deep as her eyes. A thick silver chain carrying an ornately carved pendant hung between her breasts. Her hair was pinned up, leaving that porcelain face unframed.

Cal's hands itched for his camera. And for her.

She looked up, her hands never faltering, and smiled. "Well, did you decide to join the living, then?"

"My body clock's still in the States. Is it late?"

"Hmm, nearly half-ten. You'll be hungry, I'll wager. Come, have your coffee. I'll fix your breakfast."

He caught her hand as she rose. "You don't have to cook for me."

She laughed, kissed him lightly. "Oh, we'd have trouble soon enough if you thought I did. As it happens, it's my pleasure to cook for you this morning."

His eyes gleamed as he nibbled on her knuckles. "A full Irish breakfast? The works."

"If you like."

"Now that you mention it . . ." His voice trailed off as he took a long, thorough study of her face.

Her eyes were shadowed, her skin paler than it should have been. "You look tired. You didn't sleep well."

She only smiled and led him into the kitchen. "Maybe you snore."

"I do not." He nipped her at the waist, spun her around and kissed her. "Take it back."

"I only said maybe." Her brows shot up when his hands roamed around, cupped her bottom. "Are you always so frisky of a morning?"

"Maybe. I'll be friskier after I've had that coffee." He gave her a quick kiss before turning to pour himself a cup. "You know I noticed things this morning that I was too . . . distracted to take in yesterday. You don't have a phone."

She put a cast-iron skillet on a burner. "I have ways of calling those I need to call."

"Ah." He rubbed the chin he had neglected to shave. "Your kitchen's equipped with very modern appliances."

"If I choose to cook why would I use a campfire?" She sliced thick Irish bacon and put it on to sizzle and snap.

"Good point. You're out of sugar," he said absently when he lifted the lid on the bowl. "You spin your own wool, but you have a state-of-the-art stereo."

"Music is a comfort," she murmured, watching him go unerringly to the pantry and fetch the unmarked tin that held her sugar supply.

"You make your own potions, but you buy your

staples at the market." With quick efficiency, he filled her sugar bowl. "The contrast is fascinating. I wonder . . ." He stopped, stood with the sugar scoop in his hand, staring. "I knew where to find this," he said quietly. "I knew the sugar was on the second shelf in the white tin. The flour's in the blue one beside it. I knew that."

" 'Tis a gift. You've only forgotten to block it out. It shouldn't disturb you."

"Shouldn't disturb me." He neglected to add the sugar and drank his coffee black and bitter.

"It's yours to control, Cal, or to abjure."

"So if I don't want it, I can reject it."

"You've done so for half your life already."

It was her tone, bitter as the coffee, that had his eyes narrowing. "That annoys you."

She cut potatoes into quick slices, slid them into hot oil. "It's your choice."

"But it annoys you."

"All right, it does. You turn your back on it because you find it uncomfortable. Because it disturbs your sense of normality. As I do." She kept her back to him as she took the bacon out of the pan, set it to drain, picked up eggs. "You shut out your gift and me along with it because we didn't fit into your world. A tidy world where magic is only an illusion done with smoke and mirrors, where witches wear black hats, ride broomsticks, and cackle on All Hallows' Eve."

As the eggs cooked, she spooned up porridge, plopped the bowl on the table, and went back to slice bread. "A world where I have no place."

"I'm here, aren't I?" Cal said evenly. "Did I choose to be, Bryna, or did you will it?"

She uses you. She's drawn you into her web.

"Will it?" Insulted, struck to the bone, she whirled around to face him. "Is that what you think? After all I've told you, after all we've shared?"

"If I accept even half of what you've told me, if I put aside logic and my own sense of reality and accept that I'm standing in the kitchen with a witch, a stone's throw away from an enchanted castle, about to do battle of some kind with an evil wizard in a war that has lasted a millennium, I think it's a remarkably reasonable question."

"Reasonable?" With clenched teeth she swept back to the stove and shoveled eggs onto a platter. " 'It's reasonable,' says he. Have I pulled him in like a spider does a fly, lured him across an ocean and into my lair?" She thumped the laden platter down and glared at him. "For what, might I ask you, Calin Farrell? For a fine bout of sex, for the amusement of having a man for a night or two. Well, I needn't have gone to such trouble for that. There's men enough in Ireland. Eat your breakfast or you'll be wearing it on your head like a hat."

Another time he might have smiled, but that sly voice was muttering in his ear. Still he sat, picked up his fork, tapped it idly against the plate. "You didn't answer the question. If I'm to believe you can't lie to me, isn't it odd that you've circled around the question and avoided a direct answer?

Yes or no, Bryna. Did you will me here?"

"Yes or no?"

Her eyes were burning-dry, though her heart was weeping. Did he know he was looking at her with such doubt, such suspicion, such cool dispassion? There was no faith in the look, and none of the love she needed.

One night, she thought on a stab of despair, had not been enough.

"No, Calin, will you here I did not. If that had been my purpose, or in my power, would I have waited so long and so lonely for you? I asked you to come, begged without pride, for I needed you. But the choice to come or not was yours."

She turned away, gripping the counter as she looked out the window toward the sea. "I'll give you more," she said quietly, "as time is short." She inhaled deeply. "You broke my heart when you shut me out of yours. Broke it to pieces, and it's taken me years to mend it as best I could. That choice was yours as well, for the knowledge was there in your head, and again in your heart if you chose to see it. All the answers are there, and you have only to look."

"I want to hear them from you."

She squeezed her eyes tightly shut. "There are some I can't tell you, that you must find for yourself." She opened her eyes again, lifted her chin and turned back to him.

Her face was still pale, he noted, her eyes too dark. The hair she'd bundled up was slipping its pins, and her shoulders were stiff and straight.

"But there's something that's mine to tell, and I'll give you that. I was born loving you. There's been no other in my heart, even when you turned from me. Everything I am, or was, or will be, is yours. I cannot change my heart. I was born loving you," she said again. "And I will die loving you. There is no choice for me."

Turning, she bolted from the room.

8

SHE'D vanished. Cal went after her almost immediately but found no trace. He rushed through the house, flinging open doors, calling her. Then cursing her.

Damn temperamental female, he decided. The fury spread through him. That she would tell him she loved him, then leave him before he had even a moment to examine his own heart!

She expected too much, he thought angrily. Wanted too much. Assumed too much.

He hurried out of the house, raced for the cliffs. But he didn't find her standing out on the rocks, staring out to sea with the wind billowing her hair. His voice echoed back to him emptily, infuriating him.

Then he turned, stared at the scarred stone walls of the castle. And knew. "All right, damn it," he muttered as he strode toward the ruins. "We're going to talk this through, straight. No magic, no legends, no bullshit. Just you and me."

He stepped toward the arch and bumped into air that had gone solid. Stunned, he reached out, felt the shield he couldn't see. He could see through it to the stony ground, the fire-scored walls, the tumble of rock, but the clear wall that blocked him was cold and solid.

"What kind of game is this?" Eyes narrowed, he drove his shoulder against it, yielded nothing. Snarling, he circled the walls, testing each opening, finding each blocked.

"Bryna!" He pounded the solidified air with his fists until they ached. "Let me in. Goddamn it, let me pass!"

From the topmost turret, Bryna faced the sea. She heard him call for her, curse her. And oh, she wanted to answer. But her pride was scored, her power teetering.

And her decision made.

Perhaps she had made it during the sleepless night, curled against him, listening to him dream. Perhaps it had been made for her, eons before. She had been given only one single day with him, one single night. She knew, accepted, that if she'd been given more she might have broken her faith, let her fears and needs tumble out into his hands.

She couldn't tell him that her life, even her soul, was lost if by the hour of midnight his heart remained unsettled toward her. Unless he vowed his love, accepted it without question, there was no hope.

She had done all she could. Bryna turned her face to the wind, let it dry the tears that she was ashamed to have shed. Her charge would be protected, her lover spared, and the secrets of this place would die with her.

For Alasdair didn't know how strong was her will. Didn't know that in the amulet she wore around her neck was a powder of poison. If she should fail, and her love not triumph, then she would end her life before she faced one of bondage.

With Cal's voice battering the air, she closed her eyes, lifted her arms. She had only hours now to gather her forces.

She began the chant.

HUNDREDS of feet below, Cal backed away, panting. What the hell was he doing? he asked himself. Beating his head against a magic wall to get to a witch.

How had his life become a fairy tale?

Fairy tale or not, one thing was solid fact. Tick a woman off, and she sulks.

"Go on and sulk, then," he shouted. "When you're ready to talk like civilized people, let me know." His mood black, he stalked back to the house. He needed to get out, he told himself. To lose himself in work for a while, to let both of them cool off.

One day, he fumed. He'd had one day and she expected him to turn his life around. Pledge his undying love. The hell with that. She wasn't pushing him into anything he wasn't ready for. She could take her thousand-year-old spell and stuff it. He was a normal human being, and normal human beings didn't go riding off into the sunset with witches at the drop of a hat.

He shoved open the bedroom door, reached for his camera. Under it, folded neatly, was a gray sweater. He pulled his hand back and stared.

"That wasn't there an hour ago," he muttered. "Damn it, that wasn't there."

Gingerly he rubbed the material. Soft as a cloud, the color of storms. He remembered vaguely something about a cloak and a charm and wondered if this was Bryna's modern-day equivalent.

With a shrug, he peeled off his shirt and tried the sweater on. It fit as though it had been made for him. Of course it had, he realized. She'd spun the wool, dyed it, woven it. She'd known the length of his arms, the width of his chest.

She'd known everything about him.

He was tempted to yank it off, toss it aside. He was tired of his life and his mind being open to her when so much of hers was closed to him.

But as he started to remove the sweater, he thought he heard her voice, whispering.

A gift. Only a gift.

He lifted his head, looked into the mirror. His

face was unshaven, his hair wild, his eyes reflecting the storm-cloud color of the sweater.

"The hell with it," he muttered, and snatching up his camera and case, he left the house.

He wandered the hills for an hour, ran through roll after roll of film. Mockingbirds sang as he clambered over stone walls into fields where cows grazed on grass as green as emeralds. He saw farmers on tractors, tending their land under a cloud-thickened sky. Clothes flapping with whip snaps on the line, cats dozing in dooryards and sunbeams.

He wandered down a narrow dirt road where the hedgerows grew tall and thick. Through small breaks he spotted sumptuous gardens with flowers in rainbows of achingly beautiful colors. A woman with a straw hat over her red hair knelt by a flower bed, tugging up weeds and singing of a soldier gone to war. She smiled at him, lifted her hand in a wave as he passed by.

He wandered near a small wood, where leaves unfurled to welcome summer and a brook bubbled busily. The sun was straight up, the shadows short. Spending the morning in normal pursuits had settled his mood. He thought it was time to go back, see if Bryna had cooled down—perhaps try out the darkroom she had equipped.

A flash of white caught his eye, and he turned, then stared awestruck. A huge white stag stood at the edge of the leafy shadows, its blue eyes proud and wise.

Keeping his movements slow, controlled, Cal

raised his camera, then swore lightly when the stag lifted his massive head, whirled with impossible speed and grace, and bounded into the trees.

"No, uh-uh, I'm not missing that." With a quick glance at the ruins, which he had kept always just in sight, Cal dived into the woods.

He had hunted wildlife with his camera before, knew how to move quietly and swiftly. He followed the sounds of the stag crashing through brush. A bird darted by, a black bullet with a ringed neck, as Cal leaped over the narrow brook, skidded on the damp bank, and dug in for the chase.

Sun dappled through the leaves, dazzling his eyes, and sweat rolled down his back. Annoyed, he pushed the arms of the sweater up to his elbows and strained to listen.

Now there was silence, complete and absolute. No breeze stirred, no bird sang. Frustrated, he shoved the hair out of his eyes, his breath becoming labored in the sudden stifling heat. His throat was parchment-dry, and thinking of the cold, clear water of the brook, he backtracked.

The sun burned like a furnace through the sheltering leaves now. It surprised him that they didn't singe and curl under the onslaught. Desperate for relief, he pulled off the sweater, laid it on the ground beside him as he knelt by the brook.

He reached down to cup water in his hand. And pulled back a cup of coffee.

"Do you good to get away for a few days, change of scene."

"What?" He stared down at the mug in his hand, then looked up into his mother's concerned face.

"Honey, are you all right? You've gone pale. Come sit down."

"I . . . Mom?"

"Here, now, he needs some water, not caffeine." Cal saw his father set down his fishing flies and rise quickly. Water ran out of the kitchen faucet into a glass. "Too much caffeine, if you ask me. Too many late nights in the darkroom. You're wearing yourself out, Cal."

He sipped water, tasted it. Shuddered. "I—I had a dream."

"That's all right." Sylvia rubbed his shoulders. "Everybody has dreams. Don't worry. Don't think about them. We don't want you to think about them."

"No—I thought it was, it wasn't . . ." Wasn't like before? he thought. It was more than before. "I went to Ireland." He took a deep breath, tried to clear his hazy brain. Desperately, he wanted to turn, rest his head against his mother's breast like a child. "Did I go to Ireland?"

"You haven't been out of New York in the last two months, slaving to get that exhibition ready." His father's brow creased. Cal saw the worry in his eyes, that old baffled look of concern. "You need a rest, boy."

"I'm not going crazy."

"Of course you're not." Sylvia murmured it, but

Cal caught the faint uncertainty in her voice. "You're just imagining things."

"No, it's too real." He took his mother's hand, gripped it hard. He needed her to believe him, to trust him. "There's a woman. Bryna."

"You've got a new girl and didn't tell us." Sylvia clucked her tongue. "That's what this is about?"

Was that relief in her voice, Cal wondered, or doubt? "Bryna—that's an odd name, isn't it, John? Pretty, though, and old-fashioned."

"She's a witch."

John chuckled heartily. "They all are, son. Each and every one." John picked up one of his fishing lures. The black fly fluttered in his fingers, its wings desperate for freedom. "Don't you worry now."

"I—I need to get back."

"You need to sleep," John said, toying with the fly. "Sleep and don't give her a thought. One woman's the same as another. She's only trying to trap you. Remember?"

"No." The fly, alive in his father's fingers. No, no, not his father's hand. Too narrow, too long. His father had workingman's hands, callused, honest. "No," Cal said again, and as he scraped back his chair, he saw cold fury light his father's eyes.

"Sit down."

"The hell with you."

"Calin! Don't you speak to your father in that tone."

His mother's voice was a shriek—a hawk's call to prey—cutting through his head. "You're not real." He was suddenly calm, deadly calm. "I reject you."

He was running down a narrow road where the hedgerows towered and pressed close. He was breathless, his heart hammering. His eyes were focused on the ruined walls of the castle high on the cliff—and too far away.

"Bryna."

"She waits for you." The woman with the straw hat over her red hair looked up from her weeding and smiled sadly. "She always has, and always will."

His side burned from cramping muscles. Gasping for air, Cal pressed a hand against the pain. "Who are you?"

"She has a mother who loves her, a father who fears for her. Do you think that those who hold magic need family less than you? Have hearts less fragile? Needs less great?"

With a weary sigh, she rose, walked toward him and stepped into the break in the hedge. Her eyes were green, he saw, and filled with worry, but the mouth with its serious smile was Bryna's.

"You question what she is—and what she is bars you from giving your heart freely. Knowing this, and loving you, she has sent you away from danger and faces the night alone."

"Sent me where? How? Who are you?"

"She's my child," the woman said, "and I am helpless." The smile curved a little wider. "Almost helpless. Look to the clearing, Calin Farrell, and take what is offered to you. My daughter waits. Without you, she dies this night."

"Dies?" Terror gripped his belly. "Am I too late?"

She only shook her head and faded back into air.

He awoke, drenched with sweat, stretched out on the cool, damp grass of the bank. And the moon was rising in a dark sky.

"No." He stumbled to his feet, found the sweater clutched in his hand. "I won't be too late. I can't be too late." He dragged the sweater over his head as he ran.

Now the trees lashed, whipped by a wind that came from nowhere and howled like a man gone mad. They slashed at him, twined together like mesh to block his path with gnarled branches armed with thorns. He fought his way through, ignored the gash that sliced through denim into flesh.

Overhead, lighting cut like a broadsword and dimmed the glow of the full white moon.

Alasdair. Hate roiled up inside him, fighting against the love he'd only just discovered. Alasdair would not win, if he had to die to prevent it.

"Bryna." He lifted his head to the sky as it exploded with wild, furious rain. "Wait for me. I love you."

The stag stood before him, white as bone, its patient eyes focused. Cal rushed forward as it turned and leaped into the shadows. With only instinct to trust, he plunged into the dark to follow the trail. The ground trembled under his feet, thorns ripped his clothes to tatters as he raced to keep that flash of white in sight.

Then it was gone as he fell bleeding into a clearing where moonlight fought through the clouds to beam on a jet-black horse.

Without hesitation, Calin accepted the impossible. Taking the reins, he vaulted into the saddle, his knees vising as the stallion reared and trumpeted a battle cry. As he rode, he heard the snap of a cloak flying and felt the hilt of a sword gripped in his own hand.

9

THE Castle of Secrets glimmered with the light of a thousand torches. Its walls glinted silver and speared up toward the moon. The stone floor of the great hall was smooth as marble. In the center of the charmed circle cast by the ancients, Bryna stood in a robe of white, her hair a fall of fire, her eyes the blue of heated steel.

Here she would make her stand.

"Do you call the thunder and whistle up the winds, Alasdair? Such showmanship."

In a swirl of smoke, a sting of sulphur, he appeared before her. Solid now, his flesh as real as hers. He wore the robes of crimson, of blood and power. His golden looks were beautiful, an angel's face but for the contrast of those dark, damning eyes.

"And an impressive, if overdone entrance," Bryna

said lightly, though her pulse shuddered.

"Your trouble, my darling, is that you fail to appreciate the true delights of power. Contenting yourself with your woman's charms and potions when worlds are at your mercy."

"I take my oath, and my gifts, to heart, Alasdair. Unlike you."

"My only oath is to myself. You'll belong to me, Bryna, body and soul. And you will give me what I want the most." He flung up a hand so that the walls shook. "Where is the globe?"

"Beyond you, Alasdair, where it will remain. As I will." She gestured sharply, shot a bolt of white light into the air to land and burn at his feet. A foolish gesture, she knew, but she needed to impress him.

He angled his head, smiled indulgently. "Pretty tricks. The moon is rising to midnight, Bryna. The time of waiting is ending. Your warrior has deserted you once again."

He stepped closer, careful not to test the edge of the circle and his voice became soft, seductive. "Why not accept—even embrace—what I offer you? Lifetimes of power and pleasure. Riches beyond imagination. You have only to accept, to take my hand, and we will rule together."

"I want no part of your kingdom, and I would rather be bedded by a snake than have your hands on me."

Murky blue fire gleamed at his fingertips, his anger taking form. "You've felt them on you in your dreams. And you'll feel them again. Gentle I can be, or punishing, but you'll never feel another's hand but mine. He's lost to you, Bryna. And you are lost to me."

"He's safe from you." She threw up her head. "So I have already won." Lifting her hands, she loosed a whip of power, sent him flying back. "Be gone from this place." Her voice filled the great hall, rang like bells. "Or face the death of mortals."

He wiped a hand over his mouth, furious that she'd drawn first blood. "A battle, then."

At his vicious cry, a shadow formed at his feet, and the shadow took the shape of a wolf, black-pelted, red-eyed, fangs bared. With a snarl, it sprang, leaping toward Bryna's throat.

CAL pounded up the cliff, driving his mount furiously. The castle glowed brilliant with light, its walls tall and solid again, its turrets shafts of silver that nicked the cloud-chased moon. With a burst of knowledge, he thrust a hand inside the cloak and drew out the globe that waited there.

It swam red as blood, fire sparks of light piercing the clouds. He willed them to clear, willed himself to see as he thundered higher toward the crest of the cliff.

Visions came quickly, overlapping, rushing. Bryna weeping as she watched him sleep. The dark chamber with the globe held between them and her whispering her spell.

You will be safe, you will be free. There is nothing, my love, you cannot ask of me. Follow the stag whose pelt is white, if your heart is not open come not back in the night. This gift and this duty I trust unto you. The globe of hope and visions true. Live, and be well, and remember me not. What cannot be held is best forgot. What I do I do free. As I will, so mote it be.

And terror struck like a snake, its fangs plunging deep into the heart. For he knew what she meant to do.

She meant to die.

SHE wanted to live, and fought fiercely. She sliced the wolf, cleaving its head from its body with one stroke of will. And its blood was black.

She sent her lights blazing, the burning cold that would scorch the flesh and freeze the bone.

And knew she would lose when midnight rang.

Alasdair's robes smoked from the violence of her power. And still he could not break the circle and claim her.

He sent the ground heaving under her feet, watched her sway, then fall to her knees. And his smile bloomed dark when her head fell weakly and that fiery curtain of hair rained over the shuddering stones.

"Will you ask for pain, Bryna?" He stepped closer, felt the hot licks when his soft boots skimmed the verge of the circle. Not yet, he warned himself, inching back. But soon. Her spell was waning. "Just take my hand, spare yourself. We will forget this battle and rule. Give me your hand, and give me the globe."

Her breath was short and shallow. She whispered words in the old tongue, the secrets of magic, incantations that flickered weakly as her power slipped like water through her fingers.

"I will not yield."

"You will." He inched closer again, pleased when he met with only faint resistance. "You have no choice. The charm was cast, the time has come. You belong to me now."

He reached down, and her shoulder burned where his fingers brushed. "I belong to Calin." She gripped the amulet, steeling herself, then flipped its poison chamber open with her thumb. She whipped her head up and, with a last show of defiance, smiled. "You will never have what is his."

She brought the amulet to her lips, prepared to take the powder.

The horse and rider burst into the torchlight in a flurry of black, storm-gray, and bright steel.

"Would you rather die than trust me?" Cal demanded furiously.

The amulet slipped through her fingers, the powder sifted onto the stones. "Calin."

"Touch her, Alasdair"—Cal controlled the restless horse as if he'd been born astride one—"and I'll cut off your hands at the wrists."

Though there was alarm, and there was shock,

Alasdair straightened slowly. He would not lose
now. The woman was already defeated, he calculated, and the man was, after all, only a foolish mortal. "You were a warrior a thousand years ago,
Caelan of Farrell. You are no warrior tonight."

Cal vaulted from the horse, and his sword sang
as he pulled it from its scabbard. "Try me."

Unexpected little flicks of fear twisted in Alasdair's belly. But he circled his opponent, already
plotting. "I will bring such fury raining down on
your head . . ." He crossed his arms over his chest,
then flung them to the side. Black balls of lightning
shot out, hissing trails of snaking sparks.

Instinctively Cal raised the sword. Pain and
power shot up his arm as the charges struck, ca-
reened away, and crashed smoking into stone.

"Do you think such pitiful weapons can defend
against a power such as mine?" Arrogance and rage
rang in Alasdair's voice as he hurled arrows of
flame. His cry echoed monstrously as the arrows
struck Cal's cloak and melted into water.

"Your power is nothing here."

Bryna was on her feet again, her white robe swirling like foam. And her face so glowed with beauty
that both men stared in wonder.

"I am the guardian of this place." Her voice was
deeper, fuller, as if a thousand voices joined it. "I
am a witch whose power flows clean. I am a woman
whose heart is bespoken. I am the keeper of all you
will never own. Fear me, Alasdair. And fear the warrior who stands with me."

"He will not stand with you. And what you guard,

I will destroy." With fists clenched, he called the flames, shot the torches from their homes to wheel and burn and scorch the air. "You will bow yet to my will."

With lifted arms, Bryna brought the rain, streaming pure and cool through the flames to douse them. And felt as the damp air swirled, the power pour through her, from her, as rich and potent as any she'd known.

"Save this place," Alasdair warned, "and lose the man." He whirled on Cal, sneered at the lifted sword. "Remember death."

Like a blade sliced through the belly, the agony struck. Blood flowed through his numbed fingers, and the sword clattered onto the wet stone. He saw his death, leaping like a beast, and heard Bryna's scream of fear and rage.

"You will not harm him. It's trickery only, Calin, hear me." But her terror for him was so blinding that she ran to him, leaving the charm of the circle.

The bolt of energy slapped her like a jagged fist, sent her reeling, crumbling. Paralyzed, she fought for her strength but found the power that had flowed so pure and true now only an ebbing flicker.

"Calin." The hand she'd flung out to shield him refused to move. She could only watch as he knelt on the stones, unarmed, bleeding, beyond her reach. "You must believe," she whispered. "Trust. Believe or all is lost."

"He loses faith, you lose your power." Robes singed and smoking, Alasdair stood over her. "He is weak and blind, and you have proven yourself more woman than witch to trade your power for his life."

Reaching down, he grabbed her hair and dragged her roughly to her knees. "You have nothing left," he said to her. "Give me the globe, come to me freely, and I will spare you from pain."

"You will have neither." She gripped the amulet, despairing that its chamber was empty. She bit off a cry as icy fingers squeezed viciously around her heart.

"From this time and this place, you are in bondage to me for a hundred years times ten. And this pain you feel will be yours to keep until you bend your will to mine."

He lowered his gaze to her mouth. "A kiss," he said, "to seal the spell."

She was wrenched out of his arms, her fingers locked with Cal's. Even as she whispered his name, he stepped in front of her, raised the sword in both hands so that it shimmered silver and sharp.

"Your day is done." Cal's eyes burned and the pain swirling through him only added to his strength. "Can you bleed, wizard?" he demanded and brought the sword down like fury.

There was a cry, ululating, inhuman, a stench of sulphur, a blinding flash. The ground heaved, the stones shook, and lightning, cold and blue, speared out of the air and struck.

The explosion lifted him off his feet. Even as he grabbed for Bryna, Cal felt the hot, greedy hand of it hurl him into the whirling air, into the dark.

10

VISIONS played through his head. Too many to count. Voices hummed and murmured. Women wept. Charms were chanted. He swam through them, weighed down with weariness.

Someone told him to sleep, to be easy, but he shook off the words and the phantom hands that stroked his brow.

He had slept long enough.

He came to, groggy, aching in every bone. The thin light of pre-dawn filtered the air. He thought he heard whispering, but decided it was just the beat of the sea and the flow of the wind through grass.

He could see the last of the stars just winking out. And with a moan, he turned his head and tried to shake off the dream.

The cat was watching him, sitting patiently, her eyes unblinking. Dazed, he pushed himself up on his elbows, wincing from the pain, and saw that he was lying on the ground outside the ruins.

Gone were the tall silver spears, the glowing torches that had lighted the great hall. It was, as it had been when he'd first seen it, a remnant of what it once had been, a place where the wind wound about and the grass and wildflowers forced their way through stony ground.

But the scent of smoke and blood still stung the air.

"Bryna." Panicked, he heaved himself to his feet. And nearly stumbled over her.

She was sprawled on the ground, one arm out-flung. Her face was pale, bruised, her white robe torn and scorched. He fell to his knees, terrified that he would find no pulse, no spark of life. But he found it, beating in her throat, and shuddering with relief, he lowered his lips to hers.

"Bryna," he said again. "Bryna."

She stirred, her lashes fluttering, her lips moving against his. "Calin. You came back. You fought for me."

"You should have known I would." He lifted her so that he could cradle her against him, resting a cheek on her hair. "How could you have kept it from me? How could you have sent me away?"

"I did what I thought best. When it came to facing it, I couldn't risk you."

"He hurt you." He squeezed his eyes tight as he remembered how she'd leaped from safety and been struck down.

"Small hurts, soon over." She turned, laid her hands on his face. There were bruises there as well, cuts and burns. "Here." Gently, she passed her hands over them, took them away. Her face knit in concentration, she knelt and stroked her fingers over his body, skimming where the cloak hadn't shielded until every wound was gone. "There. No pain," she murmured. "No more."

"You're hurt." He lifted her as he rose.

"It's a different matter to heal oneself. I have what I need in the cupboard, in the kitchen."

"We weren't alone here. After?"

"No." Oh, she was so weary, so very weary. "Family watches over. The white bottle," she told him as he carried her through the kitchen door and sat her at the table. "The square one, and the small green one with the round stopper."

"You have explaining to do, Bryna." He set the bottles on the table, fetched her a glass. "When you're stronger."

"Yes, we've things to discuss." With an expert hand, an experienced eye, she mixed the potions into the glass, let them swirl and merge until the liquid went clear as plain water. "But would you mind, Calin, I'd like a bath and a change of clothes first."

"Conjure it," he snapped. "I want this settled."

"I would do that, but I prefer the indulgence. I'll ask you for an hour." She rose, cupping the glass in both hands. "It's only an hour, Calin, after all."

"One thing." He put a hand on her arm. "You

told me you couldn't lie to me, that it was forbidden."

"And never did I lie to you. But I came close to the line with omission. One hour," she said on a sigh that weakened him. "Please."

He let her go and tried to soothe his impatience by brewing tea. His cloak was gone, he noted, and the sweater she'd woven for him stank of smoke and blood. He stripped it off, tossed it over the back of a chair, then glanced down as the cat came slinking into the room.

"So how do I handle her now?" Cal cocked his head, studied those bland blue eyes. "Any suggestions? You'd be her familiar, wouldn't you? Just how familiar are you?"

Content with the cat for company, he crouched down and stroked the silky black fur. "Are you a shape-shifter too?" He tilted the cat's head up with a finger under the chin. "Those eyes looked at me from out of the face of a white stag."

Letting out a breath, he simply sat on the floor, let the cat step into his lap and knead. "Let me tell you something, Hecate. If a two-headed dragon walked up and knocked on the kitchen door, I wouldn't blink an eye. Nothing is ever going to surprise me again."

BUT he was wrong about that. He was stunned with surprise when Bryna came downstairs again. She was as he'd seen her the night before, when her power had glowed in her face, striking it with impossible beauty.

"You were beautiful before," he managed, "but now . . . Is this real?"

"Everything's real." She smiled, took his hand. "Would you walk with me, Cal? I'm wanting the air and the sun."

"I have questions, Bryna."

"I know it," she said as they stepped outside. Her body felt light again, free of aches. Her mind was clear. "You're angry because you feel I deceived you, but it wasn't deception."

"You sent the white stag to lure me into the woods, away from you."

"I did, yes. I see now that Alasdair knew, and he used it against me. I wanted you safe. Knowing you now—the man you are now—that became more important than . . ." She looked at the castle. "Than the rest. But he tricked you into removing the protection I'd given you, then sent you into dreams to cloud your mind and make you doubt your reason."

"There was a woman . . . she said she was your mother."

"My mother." Bryna blinked once, then her lips curved. "Was she in her garden, wearing a foolish hat of straw?"

"Yes, and she had your mouth and hair."

Clucking her tongue, Bryna strolled toward the ruins. "She wasn't meant to interfere. But perhaps it was permitted, as I bent the rules a bit myself. The air's clearing of him," she added as she stepped under the arch. "The flowers still bloom here."

He saw the circle of flowers, untouched, unscarred. "It's over, then. Completely?"

Completely, she thought and fought to keep her smile in place. "He's destroyed. Even at the moment of his destruction he tried to take us with him. He might have done it if you hadn't been quick, if you hadn't been willing to risk."

"Where's the globe now?"

"You know where it is. And there it stays. Safe."

"You trusted me with that, but you didn't trust me with you."

"No." She looked down at the hands she'd linked together. "That was wrong of me."

"You were going to take poison."

She bit her lip at the raw accusation in his voice. "I couldn't face what he had in mind for me. I couldn't bear it, however weak it makes me. I couldn't bear it."

"If I'd been a moment later, you would have done it. Killed yourself. Killed yourself," he repeated, jerking her head up. "You couldn't trust me to help you."

"No, I was afraid to. I was afraid and hurt and desperate. Have I not the right to feelings? Do you think what I am strips me of them?"

Her mother had asked almost the same of him, he remembered. "No." He said it very calmly, very clearly. "I don't. Do you think what I'm not makes me less?"

Stunned, she shook her head, and pressing a hand to her lips, turned away. It wasn't only he who had questioned, she realized. Not only he who had lacked faith.

"I've been unfair to you, and I'm sorry for it. You came here for me and learned to accept the impossible in only one day."

"Because part of me accepted it all along. Burying something doesn't mean it ceases to exist. We were born for what happened here." He let out an impatient breath. Why were her shoulders slumped, he wondered, when the worse of any life was behind them? "We've done what we were meant to do, and maybe it was done as it was meant to be."

"You're right, of course." Her shoulders straightened as she turned, and her smile was bright. And false, he realized as he looked into her eyes.

"He can't come back and touch you now."

"No." She shook her head, laid a hand briefly on his. "Nor you. He was swallowed by his own. His kind are always here, but Alasdair is no more."

Then with a laugh she brought his hand to her cheek. "Oh, Cal, if I could give you a picture, as fine and bold as any of your own. How you looked when you hefted that sword over your head, the light in your eyes, the strength rippling in waves around you. I'll carry that with me, always."

She turned then, walked regally to the circle of flowers. In the center she turned, faced him, held out her hands. "Calin Farrell, you met your fate. You came to me when my need was great, when my life was imperiled. In this place you stood between me and the unbearable, fought against magic dark and deadly, wielded sword for me. You've saved my life and in so doing saved this place and all I guard in it."

"Quite a speech," he murmured and stepped closer.

She only smiled. "You're brave and true of heart. And from this hour, from this place you are free."

"Free?" Understanding was dawning, and he angled his head. "Free from you, Bryna?"

"Free from all and ever. The spell is broken, and you have no debt to pay. But a debt is owed. Whatever you ask that is in my power you shall have. Whatever boon you wish will be yours."

"A boon, is it?" He tucked his tongue in his cheek. "Oh, let's say, like immortality?"

Her eyes flickered—disappointment quickly masked. "Such things aren't within the power I hold."

"Too tough for you, huh?" With a nod, he circled around her as if considering. "But if I decided on, say, unlimited wealth or incredible sexual powers, you could handle that."

Her chin shot up another inch, went rigid. "I could, if it's what you will. But a warning before you choose. Be wary and sure of what you wish for. Every gift, even given freely, has a price."

"Yeah, yeah. I've heard that. Let's think about it.

Money? Sex? Power, maybe. Power's good. I could have a nice island in the Caribbean, be a benign despot. I could get into that."

"This offer was not made for your amusement," she said stiffly.

"No? Well, it tickles the hell out of me." Rocking back on his heels, he tucked his hands into his pockets. "All I had to do was knock off an evil wizard and save the girl, and I can have whatever I want. Not a bad deal, all in all. So, just what do I want?"

He narrowed his eyes in consideration, then stepped into the circle. "You."

Eyes widening, she jerked back. "What?"

"You. I want you."

"To—to do what?" she said stupidly, then blinked when he roared with laughter. "Oh, you've no need to waste a boon there." She lifted her hands to unfasten her dress, and found them caught in his.

"That, too," he said, walking her backward out of the circle, keeping her arms up, her hands locked behind her head. "Yeah, in fact, I look forward to quite a bit of that."

The warrior was back, she thought dizzily. There, the glint of battle and triumph in his eyes. "What are you doing?"

"I'm holding you to your boon. You, Bryna, all of you, no restrictions. For better or worse," he continued until he had her backed against the wall. "For richer or poorer. That's the deal."

She couldn't get her breath, couldn't keep her balance. "You want . . . me?"

"I'm not getting down on one knee when it's my boon."

"But you're free. The spell is broken. I have no hold on you."

"Don't you?" He lowered his mouth, buckling her knees with his kiss. "You can't lie to me." He crushed his lips to hers again, pulling her closer. "You were born loving me." He swallowed her moan and dived deeper. "You'll die loving me."

"Yes." Powerless, she flexed the hands he held above her head.

"Look at me," he murmured, easing back as she trembled. "And see." He gentled his hands, lowered them to stoke her shoulders. "Beautiful Bryna. Mine. Only mine."

"Calin." Her heart wheeled when his lips brushed tenderly over hers. "You love me. After it's done, after it's only you and only me. You love me."

"I was born loving you." The kiss was deep and sweet. "I'll die loving you." He sipped the tears from her cheeks.

"This is real," she said in a whisper. "This is true magic."

"It's real. Whatever came before, this is what's real. I love you, Bryna. You," he repeated. "The woman who puts whiskey in my tea, and the witch who weaves me magic sweaters. Believe that."

"I do." Her breath released on a shudder of joy. She felt it. Love. Trust. Acceptance. "I do believe it."

"It's time we made a home together, Bryna. We've waited long enough."

"Calin Farrell." She wound her arms around his neck, pressed her cheek against his. "Your boon is granted."

EVER AFTER

To my sisters in magic—
Ruth, Marianne, and Jill

1

"This," the old woman said, "is for you."

Allena studied the pendant that swung gently from the thickly braided links of a silver chain. Really, she'd only come in to browse. Her budget didn't allow for impulse buys—which were, of course, the most fun and the most satisfying. And her affection for all things impulsive was the very reason she couldn't afford to indulge herself.

She shouldn't have entered the shop at all. But who could resist a tiny little place tucked into the waterfront of a charming Irish village? Especially a place called Charms and Cures.

Certainly not Allena Kennedy.

"It's beautiful, but I—"

"There's only one." The woman's eyes were faded and blue, like the sea that slapped and spewed against the stone wall barely a stone's throw from the door. Her hair was steel gray and bundled into a bun that lay heavy on her thin neck.

She wore a fascinating rattle of chains and pins, but there was nothing, Allena thought, like the pendant she held in her bony fingers. "Only one?"

"The silver was cured in Dagda's Cauldron over the Midsummer's fire and carved by the finger of Merlin. He that was Arthur's."

"Merlin?"

Allena was a sucker for tales of magic and heroics. Her stepsister Margaret would have sniffed and said no, she was simply a sucker.

"The high king's sorcerer wandered through Ireland in his time. It was here he found the Giant's Dance, and coveting it for Arthur, floated it away over the Irish Sea to Britain. But while he took magic from this land, some he also left." Watching Allena, she set the pendant swaying. "Here is some, and it belongs to you."

"Well, I really can't . . ." But Allena trailed off, her gaze locked on the pendant. It was a long oval, dulled and tarnished a bit, and centered in it was a carving in the shape of a bursting star.

It seemed to catch the murky, cloud-filtered light coming through the small shop window, hold it, expand it, so that it glittered hypnotically in Allena's eyes. It seemed the star shimmered.

"I just came in to look around."

"Sure and if you don't look, you can't find, can you? You came looking, all the way from America."

She'd come, Allena tried to remember, to assist

Margaret with the tour group. Margaret's business, A Civilized Adventure, was very successful—and very regimented. Everyone said that Allena needed some regimentation. And Margaret had been clear, brutally clear, that this opportunity was her last chance.

"Be organized, be prepared, and be on time," Margaret had told her as she'd sat behind her polished desk in her perfectly terrifying and perfectly ordered office in New York. "If you can manage that, there might be a chance for you. If you can't, I wash my hands of you, Lena."

It wouldn't be the first time someone had washed their hands of her. In the past three years she'd lost three jobs. Well, four, but it didn't seem necessary to count those hideous two days she'd spent as assistant to her uncle's mother-in-law's sister.

It wasn't as if she'd spilled ink on the white Valentino gown on purpose. And if the Social Dragon hadn't insisted that she use a fountain pen—I mean, really—for all correspondence, there wouldn't have been ink to spill.

But that wasn't the point, she reminded herself as she stared at the pendant. She'd lost that job and all the others, and now Margaret was giving her a chance to prove she wasn't a complete moron.

Which, Allena feared, she probably was.

"You need to find your place."

Blinking, Allena managed to tear her gaze away from the pendant and look back into the old woman's eyes. They seemed so kind and wise. "Maybe I don't have one."

"Oh, there now, each of us has one, but there are those who don't fit so easily into the world the way others see it. And us. You've only been looking in the wrong places. Till now. This," she said again, "belongs to you."

"I really can't afford it." There was apology in her voice, even as she reached out. Just to touch. And touching, she felt heat from the silver, and terrible longing inside her. A thrill raced up her spine even as something heavy seemed to settle over her heart.

It couldn't hurt to try it on. Surely there was no harm in just seeing how it looked on her, how it felt.

As if in a dream, she took the chain from the old woman, slipped it around her neck. The heaviness in her heart shifted. For a moment, the light through the window strengthened, beamed brilliantly over the trinkets and pots of herbs and odd little stones crammed on the shelves and counters.

An image swam into her mind, an image of knights and dragons, of wild wind and water, of a circle of stones standing alone under a black and raging sky.

Then a shadow that was a man, standing still as the stones, as if waiting.

In her heart she knew he waited for her, as no one had before and no one would after. And would wait, eternally.

Allena closed her hand over the pendant, ran her

thumb over the star. Joy burst through her, clear as the sunlight. Ah, she thought. Of course. It's mine. Just as I'm his, and he's mine.

"How much is it?" she heard herself say, and knew no price would be too dear.

"Ten pounds, as a token."

"Ten?" She was already reaching for her purse. "It has to be worth more." A king's ransom, a sorcerer's spell, a lover's dream.

"It is, of course." But the woman merely held out her hand for the single note. "And so are you. Go on your journey, a *chuid*, and see."

"Thank you."

"You're a good lass," the woman said as Allena walked to the door. And when it shut, her smile turned bright and crafty. "He won't be pleased, but you'll bring him 'round by Midsummer's Eve. And if you need a bit of help, well, that will be my pleasure."

Outside, Allena stared at the sea wall, the dock, the line of cottages as if coming out of a dream. Odd, she thought, hadn't that all been wonderfully odd? She traced a finger over the pendant again. Only one, cast in Dagda's Cauldron, carved by Merlin.

Of course, Margaret would sneer and tell her that the old woman had a dozen more in the stockroom ready to pass them off to birdbrained tourists. And Margaret, as always, was probably right. But it didn't matter.

She had the pendant and a wonderful story to go

with it. And all for ten pounds. Quite a bargain.

She glanced up now, wincing. The sky was heavy with clouds, and all of them were thick and gray. Margaret would not be pleased that the weather wasn't falling in line with today's plans. The ferry ride to the island had been meticulously arranged.

Tea and scones would be served on the trip over, while Margaret lectured her twenty-person group on the history of the place they were about to visit. It had been Allena's job to type up Margaret's notes and print the handouts.

First stop would be the visitors' center for orientation. There would be a tour of a ruined abbey and graveyard, which Allena looked forward to, then lunch, picnic style, which the hotel had provided in hampers. Lunch was to last precisely sixty minutes.

They would then visit the beehive cottages, and Margaret would deliver a lecture on their history and purpose. The group would be allotted an hour to wander on their own, into the village, the shops, down to the beach, before gathering at four-thirty on the dot for high tea at the restored castle, with, naturally, another lecture on that particular spot.

It was Allena's job to keep all of Margaret's lecture notes in order, to help herd the group, to watch valuables, to haul parcels should there be any, and to generally make herself available for any and all menial chores.

For this she would be paid a reasonable salary by Margaret's definition. But, more important, it was explained, she would receive training and experience that, her family hoped, would teach her responsibility and maturity. Which, by the age of twenty-five, she should have learned already.

There was no point in explaining that she didn't want to be responsible and mature if it turned her into another Margaret. Here she was, four days into her first tour and already something inside her was screaming to run away.

Dutifully, she quashed the rebellion, glanced at her watch. Stared at it, dumbfounded.

That couldn't be. It was impossible. She'd only meant to slip into the shop for a few minutes. She couldn't possibly have spent an hour in there. She couldn't—oh, God, she *couldn't* have missed the ferry.

Margaret would murder her.

Gripping the strap of her bag, she began to run.

She had long, dancer's legs and a slim build. The sturdy walking shoes Margaret had ordered her to buy slapped pavement on her race to the ferry dock. Her bag bounced heavily against her hip. Inside was everything ordered from the Civilized Adventure directive and a great deal more.

The wind kicked in from the sea and sent her short blond hair into alarmed spikes around her sharp-boned face. The alarm was in her eyes, gray as the clouds, as well. It turned quickly to despair and self-disgust when she reached the dock and saw the ferry chugging away.

"Damn it!" Allena grabbed her own hair and pulled viciously. "That's it and that's all. I might as well jump in and drown myself." Which would be more pleasant, she had no doubt, than the icy lecture Margaret would deliver.

She'd be fired, of course, there was no doubt of it. But she was used to that little by-product of her professional endeavors. The method of termination would be torture.

Unless . . . There had to be another way to get to the island. If she could get there, throw herself on Margaret's stingy supply of mercy, work like a dog, forfeit her salary. Make an excuse. Surely she'd be able to come up with some reason for missing the damn ferry.

She looked around frantically. There were boats, and if there were boats, there were people who drove boats. She'd hire a boat, pay whatever it cost.

"Are you lost, then?"

Startled, she lifted a hand, closed it tight over her pendant. There was a young man—hardly more than a boy, really, she noted—standing beside a small white boat. He wore a cap over his straw-colored hair and watched her out of laughing green eyes.

"No, not lost, late. I was supposed to be on the ferry." She gestured, then let her arms fall. "I lost track of time."

"Well, time's not such a matter in the scheme of things."

"It is to my sister. I work for her." Quickly now, she headed down toward him where the sea lapped the shore. "Is this your boat, or your father's?"

"Aye, it happens it's mine."

It was small, but to her inexperienced eye looked cheerful. She had to hope that made it seaworthy. "Could you take me over? I need to catch up. I'll pay whatever you need."

It was just that sort of statement, Allena thought the minute the words left her mouth, that would make Margaret cringe. But then bargaining wasn't a priority at the moment. Survival was.

"I'll take you where you need to be." His eyes sparkled as he held out a hand. "For ten pounds."

"Today everything's ten pounds." She reached for her purse, but he shook his head.

"It was your hand I was reaching for, lady, not payment. Payment comes when you get where you're going."

"Oh, thanks." She put her hand in his and let him help her into the boat.

She sat starboard on a little bench while he cast off. Closing her eyes with relief, she listened to the boy whistle as he went about settling to stern and starting the motor. "I'm very grateful," she began. "My sister's going to be furious with me. I don't know what I was thinking of."

He turned the boat, a slow and smooth motion. "And couldn't she have waited just a bit?"

"Margaret?" The thought made Allena smile. "It wouldn't have occurred to her."

The bow lifted, and the little boat picked up speed. "It would have occurred to you," he said, and then they were skimming over the water.

Thrilled, she turned her face to the wind. Oh, this

was better, much better, than any tame ferry ride, lecture included. It was almost worth the price she would pay at the end, and she didn't mean the pounds.

"Do you fish?" she called out to him.

"When they're biting."

"It must be wonderful to do what you want, when you want. And to live so near the water. Do you love it?"

"I've a fondness for it, yes. Men put restrictions on men. That's an odd thing to my way of thinking."

"I have a terrible time with restrictions. I can never remember them." The boat leaped, bounced hard and made her laugh. "At this rate, we'll beat the ferry."

The idea of that, the image of her standing on shore and giving Margaret a smug look when the ferry docked, entertained Allena so much she didn't give a thought to the shiver of lightning overhead or the sudden, ominous roar of the sea.

When the rain began to pelt her, she looked around again, shocked that she could see nothing but water, the rise and fall of it, the curtain that closed off light.

"Oh, she won't like this a bit. Are we nearly there?"

"Nearly, aye, nearly." His voice was a kind of crooning that smoothed nerves before they could fray. "Do you see there, through the storm? There, just ahead, is where you need to be."

She turned. Through the rain and wind, she saw

the darker shadow of land, a rise of hills, the dip of valley in shapes only. But she knew, she already knew.

"It's beautiful," she murmured.

Like smoke, it drifted closer. She could see the crash of surf now and the cliffs that hulked high above. Then in the flash of lightning, she thought, just for an instant, she saw a man.

Before she could speak, the boat was rocking in the surf, and the boy leaping out into the thrashing water to pull them to shore.

"I can't thank you enough, really." Drenched, euphoric, she climbed out onto the wet sand. "You'll wait for the storm to pass, won't you?" she asked as she dug for her wallet.

"I'll wait until it's time to go. You'll find your way, lady. Through the rain. The path's there."

"Thanks." She passed the note into his hand. She'd go to the visitors' center, take shelter, find Margaret and do penance. "If you come up with me, I'll buy you some tea. You can dry off."

"Oh, I'm used to the wet. Someone's waiting for you," he said, then climbed back into his boat.

"Yes, of course." She started to run, then stopped. She hadn't even asked his name. "I'm sorry, but—" When she rushed back, there was nothing there but the crash of water against the shore.

Alarmed that he'd sailed back into that rising storm, she called out, began to hurry along what she could see of the shore to try to find him. Lightning flashed overhead, more vicious than exciting now, and the wind slapped at her like a furious hand.

Hunching against it, she jogged up the rise, onto a path. She'd get to shelter, tell someone about the boy. What had she been thinking of, not insisting that he come with her and wait until the weather cleared?

She stumbled, fell, jarring her bones with the impact, panting to catch her breath as the world went suddenly mad around her. Everything was howling wind, blasting lights, booming thunder. She struggled to her feet and pushed on.

It wasn't fear she felt, and that baffled her. She should be terrified. Why instead was she exhilarated? Where did this wicked thrill of anticipation, of *knowledge*, come from?

She had to keep going. There was something, someone, waiting. If she could just keep going.

The way was steep, the rain blinding. Somewhere along the way she lost her bag, but didn't notice.

In the next flash of light, she saw it. The circle of stones, rising out of the rough ground like dancers trapped in time. In her head, or perhaps her heart, she heard the song buried inside them.

With something like joy, she rushed forward, her hand around the pendant.

The song rose, like a crescendo, filling her, washing over her like a wave.

And as she reached the circle, took her first step inside, lightning struck the center, the bolt as clear and well defined as a flaming arrow. She watched the blue fire rise in a tower, higher, higher still, until it seemed to pierce the low-hanging clouds. She felt the iced heat of it on her skin, in her bones. The power of it hammered her heart.

And she fainted.

2

THE storm made him restless. Part of the tempest seemed to be inside him, churning, crashing, waiting to strike out. He couldn't work. His concentration was fractured. He had no desire to read, to putter, to simply be. And all of those things were why he had come back to the island.

Or so he told himself.

His family had held the land, worked it, guarded it, for generations. The O'Neils of Dolman had planted their seed here, spilled their blood and the blood of their enemies for as far back as time was marked. And further still, back into the murky time that was told only in songs.

Leaving here, going to Dublin to study, and to work, had been Conal's rebellion, his escape from what others so blithely accepted as his fate. He would not, as he'd told his father, be the passive pawn in the chess game of his own destiny.

He would make his destiny.

And yet, here he was, in the cottage where the O'Neils had lived and died, where his own father had passed the last day of his life only months before. Telling himself it had been his choice didn't seem quite so certain on a day where the wind lashed and screamed and the same violence of nature seemed to thrash inside him.

The dog, Hugh, which had been his father's companion for the last year of his life, paced from window to window, ears pricked up and a low sound rumbling in his throat, more whimper than growl.

Whatever was brewing, the dog sensed it as well, so that his big gray bulk streamed through the cottage like blown smoke. Conal gave a soft command in Gaelic, and Hugh came over, bumping his big head under Conal's big hand.

There they stood, watching the storm together, the large gray dog and the tall, broad-shouldered man, each with a wary expression. Conal felt the dog shudder. Nerves or anticipation? Something, all Conal could think, was out there in the storm.

Waiting.

"The hell with it. Let's see what it is."

Even as he spoke, the dog leaped toward the door, prancing with impatience as Conal tugged a long black slicker off the peg. He swirled it on over rough boots and rougher jeans and a black sweater that had seen too many washings.

When he opened the door, the dog shot out,

straight into the jaws of the gale. "Hugh! *Cuir uait!*"

And though the dog did stop, skidding in the wet, he didn't bound back to Conal's side. Instead he stood, ears still pricked, despite the pounding rain, as if to say *hurry!*

Cursing under his breath, Conal picked up his own pace, and let the dog take the lead.

His black hair, nearly shoulder-length and heavy now with rain, streamed back in the wind from a sharply honed face. He had the high, long cheekbones of the Celts, a narrow, almost aristocratic nose, and a well-defined mouth that could look, as it did now, hard as granite. His eyes were a deep and passionate blue.

His mother had said they were eyes that saw too much, and still looked for more.

Now they peered through the rain, and down, as Hugh climbed, at the turbulent toss of the sea. With the storm, the day was almost black as night, and he cursed again at his own foolishness in being out in it.

He lost sight of Hugh around a turn on the cliff path. More irritated than alarmed, he called the dog again, but all that answered was the low-throated, urgent bark. Perfect, was all Conal could think. Now the both of us will likely slip off the edge and bash our brains on the rocks.

He almost turned away, at that point very nearly retreated, for the dog was surefooted and knew his way home. But he wanted to go on—too much wanted to go on. As if something was tugging him forward, luring him on, higher and higher still, to where the shadow of the stone dance stood, singing through the wind.

Because part of him believed it, part of him he had never been able to fully quiet, he deliberately turned away. He would go home, build up the fire, and have a glass of whiskey in front of it until the storm blew itself out.

Then the howl came, a wild and primitive call that spoke of wolves and eerie moonlight. The shudder that ran down Conal's spine was as primal as the call. Grimly now, he continued up the path to see what caused young Hugh to bay.

The stones rose, gleaming with wet, haloed by the lightning strikes so that they almost seemed to glow. A scent came to him, ozone and perfume. Hot, sweet, and seductive.

The dog sat, his handsome head thrown back, his great throat rippling with his feral call. There was something in it, Conal thought, that was somehow triumphant.

"The stones don't need guarding," Conal muttered. He strode forward, intending to grab the dog by the collar and drag them both back to the warmth of the cottage.

And saw that it wasn't the stones Hugh guarded, but the woman who lay between them.

Half in and half out of the circle, with one arm stretched toward the center, she lay on her side almost as if sleeping. For a moment he thought he imagined her, and wanted to believe he did. But when he reached her side, his fingers instinctively going to her throat to check her pulse, he felt the warm beat of life.

At his touch her lashes fluttered. Her eyes opened. They were gray as the stones and met his with a sudden and impossible awareness. A smile curved her lips, parted them as she lifted a hand to his cheek.

"There you are," she said, and with a sigh closed her eyes again. Her hand slid away from his cheek to fall onto the rain-trampled grass.

Delirious, he told himself, and most likely a lunatic. Who else would climb the cliffs in a storm? Ignoring the fact that he'd done so himself, he turned her over, seeing no choice but to cart her back to the cottage.

And when he started to gather her into his arms, he saw the pendant, saw the carving on it in another spit of lightning.

His belly pitched. His heart gave one violent knock against his chest, like an angry fist.

"Damn it."

He stayed crouched as he was, closing his eyes while the rain battered both of them.

SHE woke slowly, as if floating lazily through layers of thin, white clouds. A feeling of well-being cushioned her, like satin pillows edged with the softest of lace. Savoring it, she lay still while sunlight played on her eyelids, cruised warm over her face.

She could smell smoke, a pleasant, earthy scent, and another fragrance, a bit darker, that was man.

She enjoyed that mix, and when she opened her eyes, her first thought was she'd never been happier in her life.

It lasted seconds only, that sensation of joy and safety, of contentment and place. Then she shot up in bed, confused, alarmed, lost.

Margaret! She'd missed the ferry. The boat. The boy in the boat. And the storm. She'd gotten caught in it and had lost her way. She couldn't quite remember, couldn't quite separate the blurry images.

Stones, higher than a man and ringed in a circle. The blue fire that burned in the center without scorching the grass. The wild scream of the wind. The low hum of the stones.

A wolf howling. Then a man. Tall, dark, fierce, with eyes as blue as that impossible fire. Such anger in his face. But it hadn't frightened her. It had amused her. How strange.

Dreams, of course. Just dreams. She'd been in some sort of accident.

Now she was in someone's house, someone's bed. A simple room, she thought, looking around to orient herself. No, not simple, she corrected, spartan. Plain white walls, bare wood floor, no curtains at the window. There was a dresser, a table and lamp and the bed. As far as she could tell, there was nothing else in the room but herself.

Gingerly now, she touched her head to see if there were bumps or cuts, but found nothing to worry her. Using the same caution, she turned back the sheet, let out a little sigh of relief. Whatever sort of accident there'd been, it didn't appear to have hurt her.

Then she gaped, realizing she wore nothing but a shirt, and it wasn't her own. A man's shirt, faded blue cotton, frayed at the cuffs. And huge.

Okay, that was okay. She'd been caught in the storm. Obviously she had gotten soaked. She had to be grateful that someone had taken care of her.

When she climbed out of bed, the shirt hung halfway to her knees. Modest enough. At her first step, the dog came to the door. Her heart gave a little hitch, then settled.

"So at least you're real. Aren't you handsome?" She held out a hand and had the pleasure of him coming to her to rub his body against her legs. "And friendly. Good to know. Where's everyone else?"

With one hand on the dog's head, she walked to the bedroom door and discovered a living area that was every bit as spartan. A couch and chair, a low burning fire, a couple of tables. With some relief she saw her clothes laid over a screen in front of the fire.

A check found them still damp. So, she hadn't been asleep—unconscious—for long. The practical thing to do, now that she'd apparently done everything impractical, was to find her rescuer, thank him, wait for her clothes to dry, then track down Margaret and beg for mercy.

The last part would be unpleasant, and probably fruitless, but it had to be done.

Bolstering herself for the task, Allena went to the door, opened it. And let out a soft cry of sheer delight.

The watery sunlight shimmered over the hills, and the hills rolled up green in one direction, tumbled down in the other toward the rock-strewn shore. The sea reared and crashed, the walls of waves high and wonderful. She had an urge to rush out, to the edge of the slope, and watch the water rage.

Just outside the cottage was a garden gone wild so that flowers tangled with weeds and tumbled over themselves. The smell of them, of the air, of the sea had her gulping in air, holding her breath as if to keep that single sharp taste inside her forever.

Unable to resist, she stepped out, the dog beside her, and lifted her face to the sky.

Oh, this place! Was there ever a more perfect spot? If it were hers, she would stand here every morning and thank God for it.

Beside her, the dog let out one quiet woof, at which she rested her hand on his head again and glanced over at the little building, with its rough stone, thatched roof, wide-open windows.

She started to smile, then the door of it opened. The man who came out stopped as she did, stared as she did. Then with his mouth hard set, he started forward.

His face swam in front of her. The crash of the sea filled her head with roaring. Dizzy, she held out a hand to him, much as she had to the dog.

She saw his mouth move, thought she heard him swear, but she was already pitching forward into the dark.

3

SHE looked like a faerie, standing there in a wavery sunbeam. Tall and slender, her bright hair cropped short, her eyes long-lidded, tilted at the tips, and enormous.

Not a beauty. Her face was too sharp for true beauty, and her mouth a bit top-heavy. But it was an intriguing face, even in rest.

He'd thought about it even after he'd dumped her in bed after carrying her in from the storm. Undressing her had been an annoying necessity, which he'd handled with the aloof detachment of a doctor. Then, once she was dry and settled, he'd left her, without a backward glance, to burn off some of the anger in work.

He worked very well in a temper.

He didn't want her here. He didn't want her. And,

he told himself, he wouldn't have her, no matter what the fates decreed.

He was his own man.

But now when he came out, saw her standing in the doorway, in the sunlight, he felt the shock of it sweep through him—longing, possession, recognition, delight, and despair. All of those in one hard wave rose inside him, swamped him.

Before he could gain his feet, she was swaying.

He didn't manage to catch her. Oh, in the storybooks, he imagined, his feet would have grown wings and he'd have flown across the yard to pluck her nimbly into his arms before she swooned. But as it was, she slid to the ground, melted wax pooling into the cup and taking all the candle as well, before he'd closed half the distance.

By the time he reached her, those long gray eyes were already opening again, cloudy and dazed. She stared at him, the corners of her mouth trembling up.

"I guess I'm not steady yet," she said in that pretty American voice. "I know it's a cliché and predictable, but I have to say it—where am I?"

She looked ridiculously appealing, lying there between the flowers, and made him all too aware she wore nothing but one of his shirts. "You're on O'Neil land."

"I got lost—a bad habit of mine. The storm came up so fast."

"Why are you here?"

"Oh, I got separated from the group. Well, I was

late—another bad habit—and missed the ferry. But the boy brought me in his boat." She sat up then. "I hope he's all right. He must be, as he seemed to know what he was doing and it was such a quick trip anyway. Is the visitors' center far?"

"The visitors' center?"

"I should be able to catch up with them, though it won't do me a lot of good. Margaret'll fire me, and I deserve it."

"And who is Margaret?"

"My stepsister. She owns A Civilized Adventure. I'm working for her—or I did work for her for the last twenty-three days." She let out a breath, tried the smile again. "I'm sorry. I'm Allena Kennedy, the moron. Thank you for helping me."

He glanced down at the hand she held out, then with some reluctance took it. Instead of shaking it, he pulled her to her feet. "I've a feeling you're more lost than you know, Miss Kennedy, as there's no visitors' center here on Dolman Island."

"Dolman? But that's not right." The hand in his flexed, balled into a little fist of nerves. "I'm not supposed to be on Dolman Island. Oh, damn it. Damn it! It's my fault. I wasn't specific with the boy. He seemed to know where I was going, was supposed to be going. Or maybe he got turned around in the storm, too. I hope he's all right."

She paused, looked around, sighed. "Not just fired," she murmured. "Disinherited, banished, and mortified all in one morning. I guess all I can do is go back to the hotel and wait to face the music."

"Well, it won't be today."

"Excuse me?"

Conal looked out to sea, studying the crashing wall of waves. "You won't find your way back today, and likely not tomorrow, as there's more coming our way."

"But—" She was talking to his back as he walked inside as though he hadn't just sealed her doom. "I have to get back. She'll be worried."

"There'll be no ferry service in these seas, and no boatman with a brain in his head would chance the trip back to the mainland."

She sat on the arm of a chair, closed her eyes. "Well, that caps it. Is there a phone? Could I use your phone to call the hotel and leave a message?"

"The phones are out."

"Of course they are." She watched him go to the fire to add some bricks of turf. Her clothes hung on the screen like a recrimination. "Mr. O'Neil?"

"Conal." He straightened, turned to her. "All the women I undress and put into bed call me Conal."

It was a test, deliberately provocative. But she didn't flush or fire. Instead her eyes lit with humor. "All the men who undress me and put me into bed call me Lena."

"I prefer Allena."

"Really? So do I, but it seems to be too many syllables for most people. Anyway, Conal, is there a hotel or a bed-and-breakfast where I can stay until the ferry's running again?"

"There's no hotel on Dolman. It's a rare tourist

who comes this far. And the nearest village, of which there are but three, is more than eight kilometers away."

She gave him a level look. "Am I staying here?"

"Apparently."

She nodded, rubbing her hand absently over Hugh's broad back as she took stock of her surroundings. "I appreciate it, and I'll try not to be a nuisance."

"It's a bit late for that, but we'll deal with it." When her only response was to lift her eyebrows and stare steadily, he felt a tug of shame. "Can you make a proper pot of tea?"

"Yes."

He gestured toward the kitchen that was separated from the living area by a short counter. "The makings are in there. I've a few things to see to, then we'll talk this out over a cup."

"Fine." The word was rigidly and properly polite. Only the single gunshot bang of a cupboard door as he started out again told him she was miffed.

She'd make the damn tea, she thought, jerking the faucet on to fill the kettle, which was no easy matter since the cast-iron sink was loaded with dishes. And she'd be grateful for Conal O'Neil's hospitality, however reluctantly, however *rudely* given.

Was it her fault she'd ended up on the wrong island? Was it her fault she'd gotten turned around in a storm and passed out and had to be carted back to his house? Was it her fault she had nowhere else to go?

Well, yes. She rolled her eyes and began to empty the dishes out of the sink so that she could fill it with soapy water and wash them. Yes, technically it *was* her fault. Which just made it all the more annoying.

When she got back to New York she would be jobless. Again. And once more she'd be the object of pity, puzzlement, and pursed lips. And that was her fault, too. Her family expected her to fail now— flighty, scatterbrained Lena.

Worse, she realized, was that she expected it, too.

The problem was she wasn't particularly good at anything. She had no real skill, no craft, and no driving ambitions.

She wasn't lazy, though she knew Margaret would disagree. Work didn't frighten her. Business did.

But that was tomorrow's problem, she reminded herself as she dealt with the dishes and waited for the kettle to boil. Today's problem was Conal O'Neil and how to handle the situation she'd put them both into.

A situation, she thought, as she went about stacking dishes, wiping counters, heating the teapot, that should have been thrilling. A storm-swept island; a handsome, brooding man; a cozy, if rustic, cottage isolated from the world.

This, she decided, perking up, was an adventure.

She was going to find a way to enjoy it before the axe fell.

When Conal came back in, the old teapot was sitting snugly in a frayed and faded cozy. Cups and saucers were set on the table, and the table scrubbed clean. The sink was empty, the counters sparkling, and the chocolate biscuits he'd had in a tin were arranged prettily on a plate.

"I was hungry." She was already nibbling on one. "I hope you don't mind."

"No." He'd nearly forgotten what it was like to sit down and have tea in tidiness. Her little temper snap appeared to be over as well, he noted. She looked quietly at home in his kitchen, in his shirt.

"So." She sat down to pour. The one thing she was good at was conversation. She'd often been told she was too good at it. "You live here alone?"

"I do."

"With your dog."

"Hugh. He was my father's. My father died some months back."

She didn't say she was sorry, as so many—too many—would have. But her eyes said it, and that made it matter more. "It's a beautiful spot. A perfect spot. That's what I was thinking before I fell into your garden. You grew up here?"

"I did."

"I grew up in New York, in the city. It never fit, somehow." She studied him over her teacup. "This fits you. It's wonderful to find the right fit. Everyone in my family fits except me. My parents and Margaret and James—my brother and sister. Their mother died when Margaret was twelve and James ten. Their father met my mother a couple of years later, then they married and had me."

"And you're Cinderella?"

"No, nothing as romantic as that." But she sighed and thought how lovely it would be. "Just the misfit. They're all brilliant, you see. Every one of them. My father's a doctor, a surgeon. My mother's a lawyer. James is a wildly successful cosmetic surgeon, and Margaret has her own business with A Civilized Adventure."

"Who would want an adventure civilized?"

"Yes." Delighted, Allena slapped a palm on the table. "That's exactly what I thought. I mean, wouldn't regimenting it mean it wasn't an adventure at all? But saying that to Margaret earned me a twenty-minute lecture, and since her business is thriving, there you go."

The light was already shifting, he noted, as a new sea of clouds washed in. But there was enough of the sun yet to sprinkle over her hair, into her eyes. And make his fingers itch for a pencil.

He knew just what he would do with her, exactly how it would be. Planning it, he let his gaze wander over her. And nearly jolted when he saw the pendant. He'd all but forgotten it.

"Where did you get that?"

She'd seen those vivid blue eyes travel down, had felt a shiver of response, and now another of relief that—she hoped—it was the pendant that interested him.

"This? It's the heart of my problem."

She'd meant it as a joke, but his gaze returned to her face, all but seared the flesh with the heat of it. "Where did you get it?"

Though the edge to his voice puzzled her, she shrugged. "There was a little shop near the waterfront. The display window was just crammed with things. Wonderful things. Magic."

"Magic."

"Elves and dragons, books and jewelry in lovely, fascinating shapes. A hodgepodge, but a crafty one. Irresistible. I only meant to go in for a minute. I had time before we were to meet at the ferry. But the old woman showed me this, and somehow while we were talking, time just went away. I didn't mean to buy it, either. But I do a lot of things I don't mean to do."

"You don't know what it is?"

"No." She closed her hand over it, felt that low vibration that couldn't be there, blinked as something tried to slide in on the edge of her vision. "It feels old, but it can't be old, not valuably old, because it only cost ten pounds."

"Value's different for one than for another." He reached out. It was irresistible. With his eyes steady and level he closed his hand over hers that held the pendant.

The jolt snapped into her, sharp as an electric current. The air seemed to turn the blue of lightning.

She was on her feet, her head tipping back to keep her eyes locked with his as he shoved back from the table with enough violence to send his chair crashing.

That same violence was in him when his mouth crushed hers. The need, so bright, so strong, so right, whipped through her even as the wind rushed sudden and sharp through the window at her back. Her hand fisted in his hair, her body lifted itself to his.

And fit.

The pounding of her heart was like a song, each note a thrill. Here, with him, it was enough, even if the world crumbled to dust around them.

He couldn't stop. The taste of her was like water, cool and clean, after a lifetime of thirst. Empty pockets he hadn't known he carried inside him filled, bulged, overflowed. His blood was a rage of heat, his body weak with wanting. He gathered the back of the shirt in his bunched fingers, prepared to rip.

Then they dropped the pendant they held between them to reach for each other. And he snapped back as if from a blow.

"This is not what I want." He took her shoulders, intending to shake her, but only held her. She looked dazed. Faerie-struck. "This is not what I'll accept."

"Would you let me go?" Her voice was low, but it didn't quaver. When he did, and stepped back, she let out a short, quiet breath. There was no point in being a coward, she told herself.

"I have a couple of choices here," she began.

"One is I hit my head when I fell and I have a concussion. The other is that I just fell in love with you. I think I prefer the concussion theory, and I imagine you do, too."

"You didn't hit your head." He jammed his hands in his pockets and strode away from her. The room was suddenly too small. "And people don't fall in love in an instant, over one kiss."

"Sensible ones don't. I'm not sensible. Ask anyone." But if there was ever a time to try to be, it was now.

"I think I should get dressed, take a walk, clear my head or whatever."

"Another's storm's brewing."

Allena tugged her clothes off the screen. "You're telling me," she muttered and marched into the bedroom.

4

CONAL wasn't in the cottage when she came out again, but Hugh sat by the fire as if waiting for her. He got up as she came through and pranced to the door, turning his big head so that his eyes met hers.

"Want a walk? Me, too."

It was a pity about the gardens, Allena thought as she paused between them. She'd have enjoyed getting down into them, yanking out those choking weeds, pinching off deadheads. An hour's pleasant work, she thought, maybe two, and instead of looking wild and neglected, those tumbling blossoms would just look wild. Which is what was needed here.

Not her job, she told herself, not her home, not her place. She cast an eye at the little outbuilding. He was probably in there doing . . . whatever the hell he did. And doing it, she imagined, angrily.

Why was there so much anger in him?

Not her problem, she thought, not her business, not her man.

Though for a moment, when their hands and mouths were joined, he had seemed to be.

I don't want this. I don't want you.

He'd made himself very clear. And she was tired of finding herself plopped down where she wasn't wanted.

The wind raced in off the sea, driving thick, black-edged clouds toward the island. As she began to walk, she could see the pale and hopeful blue being gradually, inevitably consumed.

Conal was right. A storm was coming.

Walking along the shoreline couldn't do any harm. She wouldn't climb the hills, though she longed to. She would just stick to the long curve of surf and sand and enjoy the jittery thrill of watching the fierce waves crash.

Hugh seemed content to walk at her side. Almost, she thought, like a guard.

Eight kilometers to the nearest village, she remembered. That wasn't so very far. She could wait for the weather to clear, then walk it if Conal wouldn't drive her. There'd been a truck parked between the cottage and the outbuilding, a sleek and modern thing, anachronistic but surely serviceable.

Why had he kissed her like that?

No, that wasn't right. It hadn't been his doing. It had simply happened, to both of them. For both of them. There'd been a roar in her head, in her blood, that she'd never experienced before. More than passion, she thought now, more than lust. It was a kind of desperate recognition.

There you are. Finally. At last.

That, of course, was ridiculous, but she had no other way to explain what had spurted to life inside her. And what had spread from that first hot gush felt like love.

You couldn't love what you didn't know. You couldn't love where there was no understanding, no foundation, no history. Her head told her all these sensible, rational things. And her heart laughed at them.

It didn't matter. She could be conflicted, puzzled, annoyed, even willing to accept. But it didn't matter when he didn't want her or what had flamed to life between them.

She stopped, let the wind beat its frantic wings over her, let the spray from the waves fly on her. Overhead a gull, white as the moon, let out its triumphant scream and streamed off in the current of electric air.

Oh, she envied that freedom, for the heart of flight was inside her. To simply fly away, wherever the wind took her. And to know that when she landed, it would be her place, her time, her triumph.

But you have to live in the present, don't you, Lena? Her mother's patient and puzzled voice murmured in her ear. *You have to apply yourself, to pay attention. You can't keep drifting this way and make something of yourself. It's time you focused on a career, put your considerable energy into making your mark.*

And under that voice, unsaid, was *You disappoint me.*

"I know it. I'm sorry. It's awful. I wish I could tell you how awful it is to know I'm your only failure."

She would do better, Allena promised herself. She'd talk Margaret into giving her a second chance. Somehow. Then she'd work harder, pay more attention, be responsible, be practical.

Be miserable.

The dog bumped his head against her leg, rubbed his warm fur against her. The small gesture comforted her and turning away from the water, she continued to walk along its verge.

She'd come out to clear her head, she reminded herself, not to fill it with more problems. Surely there couldn't be a more perfect spot for easing heart and mind. Under those threatening skies, the rough hills shone, the wicked cliffs gleamed. Wildflowers, dots and splashes of color, tangled in the green and gray, and she saw a shadowy spread of purple that was heather.

She wanted to gather it, fill her arms with it, bury her face in the scent. Delighted with the idea, she turned to scramble over rocks where sprigs of it thrived in the thin soil, then higher to mounds bumpy and thick until the fragrance of it overpowered even the primitive perfume of the sea.

When her arms were full, she wanted more.

Laughing, she hurried along a narrow path. Then stopped dead. Startled, she shook her head. She heard the oddest hum. She started to step forward again, and couldn't. Simply couldn't. It was as if a wall of glass stood between her and the next slope of rock and flowers.

"My God, what is this?"

She lifted a trembling hand, sending sprigs of heather falling, then flying free in the wind. She felt no barrier, but only a kind of heat when her hand pressed the air. And try as she might, she couldn't push through it.

Lightning burst. Thunder rolled. Through it, she heard the sound of her name. She looked down to the beach, half expecting to see dragons or sorcerers. But it was only Conal, standing with his legs spread, his hair flying, and his eyes annoyed.

"Come down from there. You've no business clambering up the rocks when a storm's breaking."

What a picture she made. He'd come after her out of responsibility, he liked to think. But he'd been dumbstruck when he'd seen her walking the cliff path in the eerie light, her hair fluttering, her arms overflowing with flowers. It made him want to climb after her, to whirl her and her flowers into his arms, to press his mouth to hers again while the wind whipped savagely over them.

Because he wanted it, could all but taste her, his tone was blade-sharp when she met him on the beach. "Have you no more sense than to pick flowers in such weather?"

"Apparently not. Would you walk down there?"

"What?"

"Just humor me, and walk down the beach five more feet."

"Maybe you did rattle your brains." He started to grab her hand, pull her away, but she took a nimble step aside.

"Please. It'll only take you a minute."

He hissed out an oath, then strode off, one foot, two, three. His abrupt halt had Allena closing her eyes, shivering once. "You can't do it, can you? You can't go any farther than that. Neither could I." She opened her eyes again, met his furious ones when he turned. "What does it mean?"

"It means we deal with it. We'll go back. I've no desire to find myself drenched to the skin a second time in one day."

He said nothing on the way back, and she let him have his silence. The first fat drops of rain splattered as they reached the cottage door.

"Do you have anything to put these in?" she asked him. "They'll need water, and I'd like to keep my hands busy while you explain things to me."

He shrugged, made a vague gesture toward the kitchen, then went to add more turf to the fire.

It was a downpour. The wind rose to a howl, and she began to gather vases and bottles and bowls. When he remained silent, scowling into the fire, she heated up the tea.

He glanced over when she poured the cups, then went into the kitchen himself to take out a bottle of whiskey. A healthy dollop went into his own tea, then he lifted a brow, holding the bottle over hers.

"Well, why not?"

But when it was laced, she picked up the flowers instead of the cup and began to tuck them into vases. "What is this place? Who are you?"

"I've told you that already."

"You gave me names." The homey task calmed her, as she'd known it would. When her gaze lifted to his again, it was direct and patient. "That's not what I meant."

He studied her, then nodded. Whether she could handle it or not, she deserved to know. "Do you know how far out in the sea you are?"

"A mile, two?"

"More than ten."

"Ten? But it couldn't have taken more than twenty minutes to get here—and in rough weather."

"More than ten miles out is Dolman Island from the southwest coast of Ireland. Here we straddle the Atlantic and Celtic Seas. Some say the silkies come here, to shed their hides and sun on the rocks in human form. And the faeries come out of their rafts under the hills to dance in the moonlight."

Allena slipped the stems of shorter blossoms into a squat bottle. "Do you say it?"

"Some say," he continued without answering, "that my great-grandmother left her raft, her palace under the hill, and pledged herself to my great-grandfather on the night of the summer solstice while they stood by the king stone of the dance on the cliffs. One hundred years ago. As a hundred years before, another with my blood stood with his woman in that same place to pledge. And a century before that as well, and always on that same night in that same place when the star shows itself."

She touched her pendant. "This star?"

"They say."

"And in two days it's the solstice, and your turn?"

"If I believed my great-grandmother was other than a simple woman, that I have elfin blood in my veins and could be directed to pledge to a woman because of the way a star shines through the stones, I wouldn't be in this place."

"I see." She nodded and carried one of the vases into the living room to set it on a table. "So you're here to prove that everything you've just told me is nonsense."

"Can you believe otherwise?"

She had no idea what she believed, but had a feeling there was a great deal, a very great deal, that she *could* believe. "Why couldn't I walk away from here, Conal? Why couldn't you?"

She left the question hanging, walked back into the kitchen. She took a sip of her tea, felt the hot flow of whiskey slide into her, then began to select her other arrangements and put them where she liked. "It would be hard for you, being told this story since you were a child, being expected to accept it."

"Can you accept it?" he demanded. "Can you just shrug off education and reason and accept that you're to belong to me because a legend says so?"

"I would've said no." Pleasing herself, she set bottles of heather on the narrow stone mantel over the simmering fire. "I would have been intrigued, amused, maybe a little thrilled at the idea of it all. Then I would have laughed it off. I would have," she said as she turned to face him. "Until I kissed you and felt what I felt inside me, and inside you."

"Desire's an easy thing."

"That's right, and if that had been it, if that had been all, we'd both have acted on it. If that had been all, you wouldn't be angry now, with yourself and with me."

"You're awfully bloody calm about it."

"I know." She smiled then, couldn't help herself. "Isn't that odd? But then, I'm odd. Everyone says so. Lena, the duck out of water, the square peg, the fumbler always just off center. But I don't feel odd or out of place here. So it's easier for me to be calm."

Nor did she look out of place, he thought, wandering through the cottage placing her flowers. "I don't believe in magic."

"And I've looked for it all my life." She took a sprig of heather, held it out to him. "So, I'll make you a promise."

"You don't owe me promises. You don't owe me anything."

"It's free. I won't hold you with legends or magic. When I can leave, if that's what you want, I'll go."

"Why?"

"I'm in love with you, and love doesn't cling."

Humbled, he took the heather, slipped it into her hair. "Allena, it takes clear eyes to recognize what's in the heart so easily. I don't have them. I'll hurt you." He skimmed his fingers down her cheek. "And I find I'd rather not."

"I'm fairly sturdy. I've never been in love before, Conal, and I might be terrible at it. But right now it suits me, and that's enough."

He refused to believe anything could be so simple. "I'm drawn to you. I want my hands on you. I want you under me. If that's all, it might not be enough for you, or for me in the end. So it's best to stand back."

He walked to the peg, tugged down his slicker. "I need to work," he said, and went out into the rain.

It would be more than she'd had, she realized, and knew that if necessary, she could make it enough.

THE storm was only a grumble when he came back. Evening was falling, soft and misty. The first thing he noticed when he stepped inside, was the scent. Something hot and rich that reminded his stomach it was empty.

Then he noticed the little changes in the living room. Just a few subtle touches: a table shifted, cushions smoothed. He wouldn't have noticed the dust, but he noticed the absence of it, and the faint tang of polish.

She'd kept the fire going, and the light, mixed with that of the candles she'd found and set about, was welcoming. She'd put music on as well and was humming along to it as she worked in the kitchen.

Even as he hung up his slicker, the tension he'd carried through his work simply slid off his shoulders.

"I made some soup," she called out. "I hunted up some herbs from the kitchen bed, foraged around in here. You didn't have a lot to work with, so it's pretty basic."

"It smells fine. I'm grateful."

"Well, we have to eat, don't we?"

"You wouldn't say that so easy if I'd been the one doing the cooking." She'd already set the table, making the mismatched plates and bowls look cheerful and clever instead of careless. There were candles there, too, and one of the bottles of wine he'd brought from Dublin stood breathing on the counter.

She was making biscuits.

"Allena, you needn't have gone to such trouble."

"Oh, I like puttering around. Cooking's kind of a hobby." She poured him wine. "Actually, I took lessons. I took a lot of lessons. This time I thought maybe I'd be a chef or open my own restaurant."

"And?"

"There's a lot more to running a restaurant than cooking. I'm horrible at business. As for the chef idea, I realized you had to cook pretty much the same things night after night, and on demand, to suit the menu, you know? So, it turned into one of my many hobbies." She slipped the biscuits into the oven. "But at least this one has a practical purpose. So." She dusted her hands on the dishcloth she'd tucked into her waistband. "I hope you're hungry."

He flashed a grin that made her heart leap. "I'm next to starving."

"Good." She set out the dish of cheese and olives she'd put together. "Then you won't be critical."

Where he would have ladled the soup straight from the kettle, she poured it into a thick white bowl. Already she'd hunted out the glass dish his mother had used for butter and that he hadn't seen for years. The biscuits went in a basket lined with a cloth of blue and white checks. When she started to serve the soup, he laid a hand over hers.

"I'll do it. Sit."

The scents alone were enough to make him weep in gratitude. The first taste of herbed broth thick with hunks of vegetables made him close his eyes in pleasure.

When he opened them again, she was watching him with amused delight. "I like your hobby," he told her. "I hope you'll feel free to indulge yourself with it as long as you're here."

She selected a biscuit, studied it. It was so gratifying to see him smile. "That's very generous of you."

"I've been living on my own poor skills for some months now." His eyes met hers, held. "You make me realize what I've missed. I'm a moody man, Allena."

"Really?" Her voice was so mild the insult nearly slipped by him. But he was quick.

He laughed, shook his head, and spooned up more soup. "It won't be a quiet couple of days, I'm thinking."

5

HE slept in his studio. It seemed the wisest course.

He wanted her, and that was a problem. He had
no doubt she would have shared the bed with him,
shared herself with him. As much as he would have
preferred that to the chilly and narrow cot crammed
into his work space, it didn't seem fair to take ad-
vantage of her romantic notions.

She fancied herself in love with him.

It was baffling, really, to think that a woman
could make such a decision, state it right out, in a
fingersnap of time. But then, Allena Kennedy wasn't
like any of the other women who'd passed in and
out of his life. A complicated package, she was, he
thought. It would have been easy to dismiss her as
a simple, almost foolish sort. At a first and casual
glance.

But Conal wasn't one for casual glances. There

were layers to her—thoughtful, bubbling, passionate, and compassionate layers. Odd, wasn't it? he mused, that she didn't seem to recognize them in herself.

That lack of awareness added one more layer, and that was sweetness.

Absently, with his eyes still gritty from a restless night, he began to sketch. Allena Kennedy from New York City, the square peg in what appeared to be a family of conformists. The woman who had yet to find herself, yet seemed perfectly content to deal with where she'd landed. A modern woman, certainly, but one who still accepted tales of magic.

No, more than accepted, he thought now. She embraced them. As if she'd just been waiting to be told where it was she'd been going all along.

That he wouldn't do, refused to do. All his life he'd been told this day would come. He wouldn't passively fall in, give up his own will. He had come back to this place at this time to prove it.

And he could almost hear the fates giggling.

Scowling, he studied what he'd drawn. It was Allena with her long eyes and sharp bones, the short and shaggy hair that suited that angular face and slender neck. And at her back, he'd sketched in the hint of faerie wings.

They suited her as well.

It annoyed the hell out of him.

Conal tossed the pad aside. He had work to do, and he'd get to it as soon as he'd had some tea.

The wind was still up. The morning sun was slipping through the stacked clouds to dance over the water. The only thunder now was the crash and boom of waves on the shore. He loved the look of it, that changing and capricious sea. His years in Dublin hadn't been able to feed this single need in him, for the water and the sky and the rough and simple land that was his.

However often he left, wherever he went, he would always be drawn back. For here was heart and soul.

Turning away from the sea, he saw her.

She knelt in the garden, flowers rioting around her and the quiet morning sun shimmering over her hair. Her face was turned away from him, but he could see it in his mind. She would have that half-dreaming, contented look in her eyes as she tugged away the weeds he'd ignored.

Already the flowers looked cheerful, as if pleased with the attention after weeks of neglect.

There was smoke pluming from the chimney, a broom propped against the front wall. She'd dug a basket out of God knew where, and in this she tossed the weeds. Her feet were bare.

Warmth slid into him before he could stop it and murmured *welcome* in his ear.

"You don't have to do that."

She looked up at his voice, and she was indeed happy. "They needed it. Besides, I love flowers. I have pots of them all over my apartment, but this is so much better. I've never seen snapdragons so big." She traced a finger on a spike of butter-yellow blooms. "They always make me think of Alice."

"Alice?"

"In Wonderland. I've already made tea." She got to her feet, then winced at the dirt on the knees of her trousers. "I guess I should've been more careful. It's not like I have a vast wardrobe to choose from at the moment. So. How do you like your eggs?"

He started to tell her she wasn't obliged to cook his breakfast. But he remembered just how fine the soup had been the night before. "Scrambled would be nice, if it's no trouble."

"None, and it's the least I can do for kicking you out of your own bed." She stepped up to the door, then turned. Her eyes were eloquent, and patient. "You could have stayed."

"I know it."

She held his gaze another moment, then nodded. "You had some bacon in your freezer. I took it out last night to thaw. Oh, and your shower dripped. It just needed a new washer."

He paused at the doorway, remembered, as he hadn't in years, to wipe his feet. "You fixed the shower?"

"Well, it dripped." She was already walking into the kitchen. "You probably want to clean up. I'll get breakfast started."

He scratched the back of his neck. "I'm grateful."

She slanted him a look. "So am I."

When he went into the bedroom, she did a quick dance, hugged herself. Oh, she loved this place. It was a storybook, and she was right in the middle of it. She'd awakened that morning half believing it had all been a dream. But then she'd opened her eyes to that misty early light, had smelled the faint drift of smoke from the dying fire, the tang of heather she'd put beside the bed.

It was a dream. The most wonderful, the most real dream she'd ever had. And she was going to keep it.

He didn't want it, didn't want her. But that could change. There were two days yet to open his heart. How could his stay closed when hers was so full? Love was nothing like she'd expected it to be.

It was so much more brilliant.

She needed the hope, the faith, that on one of the days left to her he would wake up and feel what she did.

Love, she discovered, was so huge it filled every space inside with brightness. There was no room for shadows, for doubts.

She was in love, with the man, with the place, with the promise. It wasn't just in the rush of an instant, though there was that thrill as well. But twined with it was a lovely, settled comfort, an ease of being, of knowing. And that was something she wanted for him.

For once in her life, she vowed, she wouldn't fail. She would not lose.

Closing her eyes, she touched the star that hung between her breasts. "I'll make it happen," she whispered, then with a happy sigh, she started breakfast.

* * *

HE didn't know what to make of it. He couldn't have said just what state the bathroom had been in before, but he was dead certain it hadn't sparkled. There may or may not have been fresh towels out the last time he'd seen it. But he thought not. There hadn't been a bottle of flowers on the windowsill.

The shower had dripped, that he remembered. He'd meant to get to that.

He could be certain that it was a great deal more pleasant to shower and shave in a room where the porcelain gleamed and the air smelled faintly of lemon and flowers.

Because of it, he guiltily wiped up after himself and hung the towel to dry instead of tossing it on the floor.

The bedroom showed her touch as well. The bed was tidily made, the pillows fluffed up. She'd opened the windows wide to bring in the sun and the breeze. It made him realize he'd lived entirely too long with dust and dark.

Then he stepped out. She was singing in the kitchen. A pretty voice. And the scents that wafted to him were those of childhood. Bread toasting, bacon frying.

There was a rumble he recognized as the washer spinning a load. He could only shake his head.

"How long have you been up and about?" he asked her.

"I woke up at dawn." She turned to pass him a

mug of tea over the counter. "It was so gorgeous I couldn't get back to sleep. I've been piddling."

"You've a rare knack for piddling."

"My father calls it nervous energy. Oh, I let Hugh out. He bolted to the door the minute my feet hit the floor, so I figured that was the routine."

"He likes to run around in the mornings. Dog piddling, I suppose."

It made her laugh as she scooped his eggs from skillet to plate. "He's terrific company. I felt very safe and snug with him curled up at the foot of the bed last night."

"He's deserted me for a pretty face." He sat, then caught her hand. "Where's yours?"

"I had something earlier. I'll let you eat in peace. My father hates to be chattered at over breakfast. I'll just hang out the wash."

"I'm not your father. Would you sit? Please." He waited until she took a seat and for the first time noticed nerves in the way she linked her fingers together. Now what was that about? "Allena, do you think I expect you to cater to me this way? Cook and serve and tidy?"

"No, of course not." The lift had gone out of her voice, out of her eyes. "I've overstepped. I'm always doing that. I didn't think."

"That's not what I meant. Not at all." His eyes were keen, part of his gift, and they saw how her shoulders had braced, her body tensed. "What are you doing? Waiting for the lecture?" With a shake of his head, he began to eat. "They've done what they could, haven't they, to stifle you? Why is it people are always so desperate to mold another into their vision, their way? I'm saying only that you're not obliged to cook my meals and scrub my bath. While you're here you should do what pleases you."

"I guess I have been."

"Fine. You won't hear any complaints from me. I don't know what you've done with these humble eggs unless it's magic."

She relaxed again. "Thyme and dill, from your very neglected herb bed. If I had a house, I'd plant herbs, and gardens." Imagining it, she propped her chin on her fist. "I'd have stepping-stones wandering through it, with a little bench so you could just stop and sit and look. It would be best if it was near the water so I could hear the beat of it the way I did last night. Pounding, like a quickened heart."

She blinked out of the image, found him staring at her. "What? Oh, I was running on again." She started to get up, but he took her hand a second time.

"Come with me."

He got to his feet, pulled her to hers. "The dishes—"

"Can wait. This can't."

He'd already started it that morning with the sketch. In his head, it was all but finished, and the energy of it was driving him, so he strode quickly out of the house, toward his studio. She had to run to keep up.

"Conal, slow down. I'm not going anywhere."

Ignoring her, he shoved open the door, pulled her in after him. "Stand by the window."

But she was already moving in, eyes wide and delighted. "You're an artist. This is wonderful. You sculpt."

The single room was nearly as big as the main area of the cottage. And much more cramped. A worktable stood in the center, crowded with tools and hunks of stone, pots of clay. A half dozen sketch pads were tossed around. Shelves and smaller tables were jammed with examples of his work. Mystical, magical creatures that danced and flew.

A blue mermaid combed her hair on a rock. A white dragon breathed fire. Faeries no bigger than her thumb ringed in a circle with faces sly. A sorcerer nearly as tall as she, held his arms high and wept.

"They're all so alive, so vivid." She couldn't help herself, she had to touch, and so she ran her finger down the rippling hair of the mermaid. "I've seen this before," she murmured. "Not quite this, but the same feeling of it, but in bronze. At a gallery in New York."

She looked over then where he was impatiently flipping through a sketch pad. "I've seen your work in New York. You must be famous."

His answer was a grunt.

"I wanted to buy it—the mermaid. I was with my mother, and I couldn't because she'd have reminded me I couldn't afford the price. I went back the next day, because I couldn't stop thinking about it, but it was already sold."

"In front of the window, turn to me."

"That was two years ago, and I've thought about her a dozen times since. Isn't it amazing that she was yours?"

Muttering an oath, he strode to her, pulled her to the window. "Lift your head, like that. Hold it there. And be quiet."

"Are you going to draw me?"

"No, I'm after building a boat here. Of course I'm drawing you. Now be quiet for one bloody minute."

She shut her mouth, but couldn't do anything about the grin that trembled on her lips. And that, he thought, was precisely what he wanted. Just that trace of humor, of energy, of personal delight.

He would do a clay model, he thought, and cast her in bronze. Something that gleamed gold and warmed to the touch. She wasn't for stone or wood. He did three quick studies of her face, moving around her for a change of angle. Then he lowered his pad.

"I need the line of your body. Your shape. Take off your clothes."

"Excuse me?"

"I have to see how you're made. The clothes are in the way of you."

"You want me to pose nude?"

With an effort, he brought himself back from his plans, met her eyes. "If this was a matter of sex, I wouldn't have slept on that rock in the corner last night. You've my word I won't touch you. But I have to see you."

"If this was a matter of sex, I wouldn't be so nervous. Okay." She shut her eyes a minute, bolstered her courage. "I'm like a bowl of fruit," she told herself and unbuttoned her shirt.

When she slipped it off, folded it, set it aside, Conal lifted a brow. "No, you're like a woman. If I wanted a bowl of fruit, I'd get one."

6

SHE was slim, leaning toward angular, and exactly right. Eyes narrowed, mind focused, he flipped up a fresh page and began.

"No, keep your head up," he ordered, faintly irritated that she should be so exactly right. "Hold your arms back. Just a bit more. Palms down and flat. No, you're not a flaming penguin, spread your fingers a little. Ah."

It was then he noticed the faint flush spreading over her skin, the stiffness in her movements. Moron, he told himself and bit back a sigh. Of course she was nervous and embarrassed. And he'd done nothing to put her at ease.

He'd grown too used, he supposed, to professional models who undraped without a thought. She liked to talk, so he would let her talk.

"Tell me about these lessons of yours."

"What?"

"The lessons. You said you'd taken a number of lessons on this and that. What was it you studied?"

She pressed her lips together, fought back the foolish urge to cross her arms over her breasts. "I thought you said I wasn't supposed to talk."

"Now I'm saying you can."

She heard the exasperation, rolled her eyes. What was she, a mind reader? "I, ah, took art lessons."

"Did you now? Turn to the right just a bit. And what did you learn from them?"

"That I'm not an artist." She smiled a little. "I'm told I have a good eye for color and shapes and aesthetics, but no great skill with the execution."

Yes, it was better when she talked. Her face became mobile again. Alive again. "That discouraged you?"

"Not really. I draw now and then when I'm in the mood."

"Another hobby?"

"Oh, I'm loaded with them. Like music. I took music lessons."

Ah, she was relaxing. The doe-in-the-crosshairs look was fading from her eyes. "What's your instrument?"

"The flute. I'm reasonably adept, but I'm never going to have a chair with the Philharmonic."

She shrugged, and he bit back a sharp order for her not to change the line.

"I took a course in computer programming, and that was a complete wash. As most of my business courses were, which scuttled the idea I had of opening a little craft shop. I could handle the craft part, but not the shop part."

Her gaze was drawn back to the mermaid. She coveted that, not just the piece itself, but the talent and vision that had created it.

"Stand on your toes. That's it, that's lovely. Hold a minute. Why don't you take on a partner?"

"For what?"

"The shop, if it's what you want. Someone business-minded."

"Mostly because I have enough business sense to know I could never afford the rent in New York, the start-up costs." She moved a shoulder. "Overhead, equipment, stock. I guess running a business is a study in stress. Margaret always says so."

Ah, he thought, the inestimable Margaret, whom he'd already decided to detest. "What do you care what she says? No, that's not right. It's not quite right. Turn around. You have a beautiful back."

"I do?" Surprise had her turning her head to look at him.

"There! Hold that. Lower your chin a little more to your shoulder, keep your eyes on me."

That was what he wanted. No shyness here. Coyness was something different altogether. There was a hint of that in the upward angle of her gaze, the tilt of her head. And just a bit of smugness as well, in the slight curve of her lips.

Allena of the Faeries, he thought, already eager

to begin in clay. He ripped the sheets off the pad, began tacking them to the wall.

"I'll do better with you as well as the sketches. Relax a minute while I prep the clay." As he passed, he touched a hand absently to her shoulder. He stopped. "Christ, you're cold. Why didn't you say something?"

She was turning toward him, a slow shift of her body. "I didn't notice."

"I didn't think to keep the fire going." His hand skimmed over her shoulder, fingers tracing the blade where he imagined wings. "I'll build one now." Even as he spoke he was leaning toward her, his eyes locked on hers. Her lips parted, and he could feel the flutter of her breath.

He jerked back, like a man snapping out of a dream. Lifted his hand, then held them both up, away from her. "I said I wouldn't touch you. I'm sorry."

The rising wave of anticipation in her broke, then vanished as he walked away to yank a blanket from the cot. "I wish you weren't. Sorry, I mean."

He stood with the table between them, the blanket in his hands, and felt like a man drowning. There was no shyness in her now, nor coyness. But the patience was there, and the promise.

"I don't want this need for you. Do you understand?"

"You want me to say yes." She was laid bare now, she realized. Much more than her body laid bare. "It would make it easier if I said that I understand. But I can't, I don't. I want that need, Conal. And you."

"Another place, another time," he murmured. "There'd be no need to understand. Another place, another time, I'd want it as well."

"This is here," she said quietly. "And this is now. It's still your choice."

He wanted to be sure of it, wanted to know there was nothing but her. "Will you take that off?"

She lifted a hand to the pendant, her last shield. Saying nothing, she slipped the chain over her head, then walked to the table, set it down. "Do you think I'll feel differently without it?"

"There's no magic between us now. We're only who and what we are." He stepped to her, swept the blanket around her shoulders. "It's as much your choice as mine, Allena. You've a right to say no."

"Then . . ." She laid her hands on his shoulders, brought her lips to within a breath of his. "I've also a right to say yes."

It was she who closed that tenuous distance so mouths and bodies met. And she who let the blanket drop when her arms went around him.

She gave, completely, utterly. All the love, so newly discovered in her heart, poured out for him. Her lips seduced, her hands soothed, her body yielded.

There was a choice. She had made hers, but he still had his own. To draw back, step away and refuse. Or to gather close and take. Before his blood could take over, before it was all need and heat, he took her face in his hands until their eyes met again.

"With no promises, Allena."

He suffered. She could see the clouds and worry in his eyes, and said what she hoped would comfort. And be the truth as well. "And no regrets."

His thumbs skimmed over her cheeks, tracing the shape of her face as skillfully as he'd drawn it on paper. "Be with me, then."

The cot was hard and narrow, but might have been a bed of rose petals as they lay on it. The air was chill, still damp from the storm, but she felt only warmth when his body covered hers.

Here. At last.

He knew his hands were big, the palms rough and callused from his work, and very often careless. He would not be careless with her, would not rush through the moment they offered each other. So he touched her, gently, giving himself the pleasure of the body he'd sketched. Long limbs, long bones, and soft white skin. Her sigh was like music, the song his name.

She tugged off his sweater, sighing again when flesh met flesh, and again murmuring his name against the pulse of his own throat. With only that, she gave him the sweetness he'd denied himself. Whatever he had of that simple gift inside him, he offered back.

Under him she lifted and moved as if they'd danced this dance together for a lifetime. Flowed with and against him, now fluid, now strong. And the quickening pulse that rose in her was like his own.

Her scent was soap, her taste fresh as rain.

He watched her glide up, the faerie again, soaring on one long spread of wings. As she crested, her eyes opened, met his. And she smiled.

No one had brought her so much, or shown her how much she had to offer. Her body quivered from the thrill of it, and in her heart was the boundless joy of finding home.

She arched up, opened so he would fill her. As he slid inside her, the beauty dazzled, and the power hummed.

While they took each other, neither noticed the star carved in silver, glowing blue as flame.

SHE lay over him now, snug under his arm with her cheek upon his chest. It was lovely to hear how his heart still pounded. A kind of rage, she thought, though he'd been the most tender of lovers.

No one could have shown her that kind of caring if there wasn't caring inside. And that, she thought, closing her eyes, was enough.

"You're cold," he murmured.

"Am not." She snuggled against him and would have frozen to the bone before she let him move. But she lifted her head so she could grin at him.

"Allena Kennedy." His fingers trailed lightly down the back of her neck. "You look smug."

"I feel smug. Do you mind?"

"I would be a foolish man to mind."

She bent down to kiss his chin, a sweet and casual gesture that moved him. "And Conal O'Neil is not a foolish man. Or is he?" She angled her head. "If we can't go beyond a certain point and walk to the village, wouldn't it follow that no one from the village can come here?"

"I suppose it would."

"Then let's do something foolish. Let's go swim naked in the sea."

"You want to swim naked in the sea?"

"I've always wanted to. I just realized it this minute." She rolled off the cot and tugged at his hand. "Come be foolish with me, Conal."

"*Leannan*, the first wave'll flatten you."

"Will not." *Leannan*. She had no idea what it meant, but it sounded tender, and made her want to dance. She raked both hands through her hair, then the light of challenge lighted her eyes. "Race you."

She darted off like a rabbit and had him scrambling up. "Wait. Damn it, the seas are too rough for you."

Bird bones, he thought, snatching up the blanket on his way. She would crack half a dozen of them in minutes.

No, she didn't run like a rabbit, he realized. She ran like a bloody gazelle, with long, loping strides that had her nearly at the foaming surf. He called out her name, rushing after her. His heart simply stopped when she raced into the water and dived under its towering wall.

"Sweet Jesus."

He'd gotten no farther than the beach when she surfaced, laughing. "Oh, it's cold!" She struggled to the shallows, slicking her hair back, lifted her face, her arms. For the second time his heart stopped, but now it had nothing to do with alarm.

"You're a vision, Allena."

"No one's ever said that to me before." She held out a hand. "No one's ever looked at me the way you do. Ride the sea with me."

It had been, he decided, much too long since he'd been foolish. "Hold on, then."

It tossed them up, a rush of power. It sucked them down into a blind, thundering world. The tumult of it was freedom, a cocky dare to fate. Wrapped around each other, they spun as the waves rolled over them.

Breathless, they surfaced, only to plunge in again. Her scream wasn't one of fear, but a cry of victory as, latched around him, she was swept into the air again.

"You'll drown us both!" he shouted, but his eyes were lit with wicked humor.

"I won't. I can't. Nothing but wonders today. Once more." She locked her arms around his neck. "Let's go under just once more."

To her shrieking delight, he snatched her off her feet and dived into the cresting wave with her.

When they stumbled out, panting, their hands were linked.

"Your teeth are chattering."

"I know. I loved it." But she snuggled into the blanket he wrapped around them both. "I've never done anything like that. I guess you've done it dozens of times."

"Not with the likes of you."

It was, she thought, the perfect thing to say. She held the words to her for a moment even as she held him. Hard against her heart.

"What does *leannan* mean?"

"Hmm?" Her head was on his shoulder, her arms linked around his waist. Everything inside him was completely at peace.

"*Leannan.* You said that to me, I wondered what it means."

His hand paused in midstroke on her hair. "It's a casual term," he said carefully. "A bit of an endearment, is all. 'Sweetheart' would be the closest."

"I like it."

He closed his eyes. "Allena, you ask for too little."

And hope for everything, she thought. "You shouldn't worry, Conal. I'm not. Now, before we both turn blue out here, I'll make fresh tea, and you'll build up the fire." She kissed him. "Right after I pick up some of these shells."

She wiggled away, leaving him holding the blanket and shaking his head. Most of the shells that littered the beach had been broken by the waves, but that didn't appear to bother her. He left her to it and went into the studio to tug on his jeans.

She had a pile of shells when he came back, offering her his sweater and her pendant.

"I won't wear it if it bothers you."

"It's yours." Deliberately, as if challenging the fates, he slipped it around her neck. "Here, put this on before you freeze."

She bundled into it, then crouched to put the shells into the blanket. "I love you, Conal, whether I'm wearing it or not. And since loving you makes me happy, it shouldn't worry you."

She rose. "Don't spoil it," she murmured. "Let's just take today, then see about tomorrow."

"All right." He took her hand, brought it to his lips. "I'll give you a promise after all."

"I'll take it."

"Today will always be precious to me, and so will you."

7

SHE dug out an ancient pair of Conal's jeans, found a hunk of frayed rope, and went to work with scissors. As a fashion statement the chopped jeans, rough belt, and baggy sweater said Island Shipwreck, but they did the job.

As he insisted on making the tea this time around, she busied herself hanging the wash. And dreaming.

It could be just this way, she thought. Long, wonderful days together. Conal would work in his studio, and she'd tend the house, the gardens . . . and, oh, the children when they came along.

She would paint the shutters and the little back porch. She'd put an arbor in front, plant roses—the only roses she would have—so that they'd climb up and twine and ramble and it would be like walking through a fairy tale every time she went into the house.

And it would be her fairy tale, ever after.

They would need to add rooms, of course, for those children. A second floor, she imagined, with dormer windows. Another bath, a bigger kitchen, but nothing that would take away from the lovely cottage-by-the-sea feeling.

She'd make wonderful meals, keep the windows sparkling, sew curtains that would flutter in the breeze.

She stopped, pegging a sheet that flapped wetly. Her mother would be appalled. Household chores were something you hired other people to do because you had a career. You were a professional . . . something.

Of course, it was all just fantasy, she told herself as she moved down the clothesline. She had to make a living somehow. But she'd worry about that later. For now, she was going to enjoy the moment, the thrilling rush of being in love, the jittery ache of waiting to be loved in return.

They would have today, and their tomorrow. Whatever happened after, she'd have no regrets.

With the last of the laundry hung, she stepped back, lifted the basket to rest it on her hip. She saw Hugh prancing down the hill.

"Well, so you decided to come home. What have you got there?" Her eyes widened as she recognized the brown bulk he carried in his mouth. "My bag!"

She dropped the basket and rushed to him. And Hugh, sensing a game, began to race in circles around her.

Conal watched from the doorway. The tea was steeping in the pot, and he'd been about to call to her. Now he simply stood.

Sheets billowed like sails in the wind. He caught the clean, wet scent of them, and the drift of rosemary and lemon balm from the herb bed she'd weeded that morning. Her laughter lifted up, bright and delighted, as she raced with the dog.

His tattered old jeans hung on her, though she'd hacked them off to above her ankles. She'd rolled up the cuffs, pushed up the sleeves on his sweater, but now as she ran around with Hugh, they'd come down again and fell over her hands. She hadn't put on her shoes.

She was a joy to watch. And when, he wondered, had he stopped letting joy into his life? The shadow of his fate had grown longer with each passing year. He'd huddled under it, he thought now, telling himself he was standing clear.

He had let no one touch him, let nothing be important to him but his work. He had estranged himself from his father and his home. Those had been his choices, and his right. Now, watching Allena play tug-of-war with the big dog in a yard filled with sun and sailing white sheets, he wondered for the first time what he'd missed along the way.

And still, whatever he'd missed, she was here.

The pendant was here.

The solstice was closing in.

He could refuse it. He could deny it. However much this woman called to his blood, he would, at the end of that longest day, determine his own fate.

It would not be magic that forced his destiny, but his own will.

He saw Allena yank, Hugh release. She stumbled back, clutching something to her chest, then landed hard on her back. Conal was out the door and across the yard in a single skipping heartbeat.

"Are you hurt?" He issued one sharp order to the dog in Gaelic that had Hugh hanging his head.

"Of course not." She started to sit up, but Conal was already gathering her, stroking, murmuring something in Gaelic that sounded lovely. Loving. Her heart did one long, slow cartwheel. "Conal."

"The damn dog probably outweighs you, and you've bones like a bird."

"We were just playing. There, now, you've hurt Hugh's feelings. Come here, baby, it's okay."

While Conal sat back on his heels and scowled, she hugged and cuddled the dog. "It's all right. He didn't mean it, whatever it was. Did you, Conal?"

Conal caught the sidelong glance the dog sent him, and had to call it smug. "I did."

She only laughed and kissed Hugh's nose. "Such a smart dog, such a good dog," she crooned. "He found my bag and brought it home. I, on the other hand, am a moron. I forgot all about it."

Conal studied the oversized purse. It was wet, filthy, and now riddled with teeth marks. That didn't seem to bother her a bit. "It's taken a beating."

"I must've dropped it in the storm. Everything's in here. My passport, my credit cards, my ticket. My makeup." She hugged the bag, thrilled to have her lipstick back. "Oh, and dozens of things. Including my copy of Margaret's itinerary. Do you think the phone's working now?"

Without waiting for him to answer, she leaped up. "I can call her hotel, let her know I'm all right. She must be frantic."

She dashed into the house, clutching the bag, and Conal stayed as he was.

He didn't want the phones to be working. He didn't want that to break their bubble. Realizing it left him shaken. Here, he thought, at the first chance to reach out of their world, she'd run to do it.

Of course she had. He pressed his fingers to his eyes. Wouldn't he have done the same? She had a life beyond this, beyond him. The romance of it had swept her away for a while, just as it had nearly swept him. She would get her feet back under her and move on. That was as it should be. And what he wanted.

But when he rose to go after her, there was an ache inside him that hadn't been there before.

"I got through." Allena sent him a brilliant smile. She stood by the counter, the phone in her hand and what appeared to be half her worldly goods dumped on the table. "She's checked in, and they're going to ring her room. I only hope she didn't call my parents. I'd hate to think they'd—Margaret! Oh, I'm so glad you're—"

She broke off again, and Conal watched the light

in her eyes go dim. "Yes, I know. I'm so sorry. I missed the ferry and . . ."

Saying nothing, he moved past her and got down mugs for tea. He had no intention of leaving her to her privacy.

"Yes, you're right, it was irresponsible. Inexcusable, yes, that, too, to leave you shorthanded this way. I tried to . . ."

He saw the moment she gave up, when her shoulders slumped and her face went carefully blank. "I understand. No, of course, you can't be expected to keep me on after this. Oh, yes, I know it was against your better judgment in the first place. You were very clear about that. I'm sorry I let you down. Yes, again."

Shame, fatigue, resignation closed in on her, a dingy fog of failure. She shut her eyes. "No, Margaret, excuses don't matter when people are depending on you. Did you call Mom and Dad? No, you're right. What would have been the point?"

"Bloody bitch," Conal muttered. They'd just see how Margaret liked being on the other end of a tongue-lashing, he decided, and grabbed the phone out of Allena's hand. The buzz of the dial tone left him no victim for his outrage.

"She had to go," Allena managed. "Schedule. I should—Excuse me."

"No, damned if I will." He took her shoulders in a firm grip before she could escape. There were tears on her lashes. He wanted Margaret's neck in his hands. "You'll not go off to lick your wounds. Why did you take that from her?"

"She was right. I was irresponsible. She has every reason to fire me. She'd never have taken me on in the first place without family pressure."

"Family pressure? Bugger it. Where was her family concern? Did she ask if you were all right? What had happened? Where you were? Did she once ask you why?"

"No."

A tear spilled over, slid down her cheek and inflamed him. "Where is your anger?" he demanded.

"What good does it do to be angry?" Wearily, she brushed the tear away. "I brought it on myself. I don't care about the job. That's the problem, really. I don't care about it. I wouldn't have taken it if I'd had a choice. Margaret's probably right. I bungle this way on purpose."

"Margaret is a jackass."

"No, really, she's not." She managed a wobbly grin. "She's just very disciplined and goal-oriented. Well, there's no use whining about it." She patted his hand, then moved away to pour the tea. "I'll call my parents after I've settled down a little, explain . . . oh, God."

Pressing her palms to the counter, she squeezed her eyes shut. "I *hate* disappointing them this way. Over and over, like a cycle I can't break. If I could just do something, if I could just be good at something."

Shaking her head, she went to the refrigerator to

take out last night's soup to heat for lunch. "You
don't know how much I envy you your talent and
your confidence in it. My mother always said if I'd
just focus my energies instead of scattering them a
dozen different ways, I'd move beyond mediocre."

"It should have shamed her to say such a thing
to you."

Surprised by the violence in his tone, she turned
back. "She didn't mean it the way I made it sound.
You have to understand, they're all so smart and
clever and, well, dedicated to what they do. My father's chief of surgery, my mother's a partner in one
of the most prestigious law firms on the East Coast.
And I can't do *anything*."

There was the anger. It whipped through her as
she slammed the pot on the stove. Pleased to see it,
Conal folded his arms, leaned back, and watched it
build.

"There's James with his glossy practice and his
gorgeous trophy wife and certified genius child,
who's a complete brat, by the way, but everyone
says she's simply precocious. As if precocious and
rude are synonymous. And Margaret with her perfect office and her perfect wardrobe and her perfect
home and her perfectly detestable husband, who
won't see anything but art films and collects coins."

She dumped soup into the pot. "And every
Thanksgiving they all sit around patting each other
on the back over how successful and brilliant they
are. Then they look at me as if I'm some sort of
alien who got dumped on the doorstep and had to

be taken in for humanitarian purposes. And I can't be a doctor or a lawyer or a goddamn Indian chief no matter how hard I try because I just can't *do* anything."

"Now *you* should be ashamed."

"What?" She pressed her fingers to her temples. Temper made her dizzy, and fuzzy-headed, which is why she usually tried to avoid it. "What?"

"Come here." He grabbed her hand, pulled her into the living room. "What did you do here?"

"About what?"

"What are the things you did in here?"

"I . . . dusted?"

"To hell and back again with the dust, Allena. Look here at your flowers and candles and your bowl of broken shells. And out here."

He dragged her to the door, shoved it open. "Here's a garden that was suffering from neglect until the morning. Where's the sand that was all over the walk that I didn't even notice until it was gone? There are sheets drying in the wind out back and soup heating in the kitchen. The bloody shower doesn't drip now. Who did those things?"

"Anyone can sweep a walk, Conal."

"Not everyone thinks to. Not everyone cares to. And not everyone finds pleasure in the doing of it. In one day you made a home out of this place, and it hasn't been one in too long, so that I'd all but forgotten the feel of a home around me. Do you think that's nothing? Do you think there's no value in that?"

"It's just . . . ordinary," she said for lack of a better word. "I can't make a career out of picking wild-flowers."

"A living can be made where you find it, if a living must be made. You've a need to pick wild-flowers and seashells, Allena. And there are those who are grateful for it, and notice the difference you make."

If she hadn't loved him already, she would have fallen at that moment with his words still echoing and his eyes dark with impatience. "That's the kindest thing anyone's ever said to me." She laid her hands on his cheeks. "The very kindest." Softly, she touched her lips to his. "Thank you."

Before he could speak, she shook her head, then rested it on his shoulder.

8

THEY shut out the world. Turned off time. Conal would have bristled at the idea that they were making a kind of magic, but for Allena there was no other word for it.

She posed for him again, in the studio where the afternoon sun slanted through the windows. And she watched herself be born in clay.

Because she asked, he told her of his years in Dublin. His studies and his work. The lean student years when he'd lived on tinned food and art. Then the recognition that had come, like a miracle, in a dingy gallery.

The first sale had given him the luxury of time, room to work without the constant worry of paying the rent. And the sales that followed had given him the luxury of choice, so that he'd been able to afford a studio of his own.

Still, though he spoke of it easily, she noticed that when he talked of Dublin, he didn't refer to it as home. But she said nothing.

Later, when he'd covered the clay with a damp cloth and washed in the little sink, they went for a walk along the shore. They spoke of a hundred things, but never once of the star she wore against her heart, or the stone circle that threw its shadows from the cliff.

They made love while the sun was still bright, and the warmth of it glowed on her skin when she rose over him.

As the day moved to evening, the light remained, shimmering as though it would never give way to night. She entertained herself mending the old lace curtains she'd found on a shelf in the closet while Conal sketched and the dog curled into a nap on the floor between them.

She had the most expressive face, he thought. Dreamy now as she sat and sewed. Everything she felt moved into her eyes of soft, clear gray. The witch behind those eyes had yet to wake. And when she did, he imagined that any man she cast them on would be spellbound.

How easily she had settled in—to him, his home, his life. Without a break of rhythm, he thought, and with such contentment. And how easy it would be to settle in to her. Even with these edgy flashes of need and desire, there was a comfort beneath.

What was he to do about her? Where was he to put these feelings she'd brought to life inside him?

And how was he to know if they were real?

"Conal?" She spoke quietly. His troubled thoughts were like a humming in the air, a warning. "Can't you put it aside for now? Can't you be content to wait and see?"

"No." It irritated him that she'd read his mood in his silence. "Letting others shape your life is your way, not mine."

Her hand jerked, as if it had been slapped, then continued to move smoothly. "Yes, you're right. I've spent my life trying to please people I love and it hasn't gotten me anywhere. They don't love me enough to accept me."

He felt a hitch in his gut, as if he'd shoved her away when he should have taken hold. "Allena."

"No, it's all right. They do love me, under it all, just not as much, or in the same way, or . . . however I love them. They want things for me that I'm not capable of—or that I just don't want for myself enough to make a real effort. I can't put restrictions on my feelings. I'm not made that way."

"And I can." He rose, paced. "It's not a matter of feelings, but of being. I can't and won't be led. I care for you more than should be possible in this short a time."

"And because of that you don't trust what's happened, what's happening between us." She nodded and, clipping the thread, set her needle aside. "That's reasonable."

"What do you know of reason?" he demanded.

"You're the damnedest, most irrational woman I've ever met."

She smiled at that, quick and bright. "It's so much easier to recognize reason when you have so little yourself."

His lips twitched, but he sat down. "How can you be so calm in the middle of all this?"

"I've had the most amazing two days of my life, the most exciting, the most beautiful." She spread her hands. "Nothing can ever take that away from me now that I've had it. And I'll have one more. One more long and wonderful day. So . . ." She got to her feet, stretched. "I think I'll get a glass of wine and go outside and watch the stars come out."

"No." He took her hand, rose. "I'll get the wine."

It was a perfect night, the sky as clear as glass. The sea swept in, drew back, then burst again in a shower of water that caught those last shimmers of day and sparkled like jewels.

"You should have benches," Allena began. "Here and here, with curved seats and high backs, in cedar that would go silver in the weather."

He wondered why he hadn't thought of it himself, for he loved to sit and watch the sea. "What else would you have, were you me?"

"Well, I'd put big pots near the benches and fill them with flowers that spilled out and spiked up. Dark blue crocks," she decided, then slanted him a look. "You could make them."

"I suppose I could. Flowerpots." The idea was amusing. No one had ever expected flowerpots from him before. He skimmed a hand over her hair as he sipped his wine and realized he would enjoy making them for her, would like to see her pleasure in them.

"Dark blue," she repeated, "to match the shutters when they're fixed up with the paint I found in the laundry room."

"Now I'm painting shutters?"

"No, no, no, your talents are much too lofty for such mundane chores. You make the pots, sturdy ones, and I'll paint the shutters."

"I know when someone's laughing at me."

She merely sent him a sly wink and walked down toward the water. "Do you know what I'm supposed to be doing tonight?"

"What would that be?"

"I should be manning the slide projector for Margaret's after-dinner lecture on megalithic sites."

"Well, then, you've had a narrow escape, haven't you?"

"You're telling me. Do you know what I'm going to do instead?"

"Ah, come back inside and make wild love with me?"

She laughed and spun in a circle. "I'm definitely putting that on the schedule. But first, I'm going to build a sand castle."

"A sand castle, is it?"

"A grand one," she claimed and plopped down on the beach to begin. "The construction of sand castles is one of my many talents. Of course, I'd do better work if I had a spade and a bucket. Both of which," she added, looking up at him from under her lashes, "can be found in the laundry room."

"And I suppose, as my talent for this particular art is in doubt, I'm delegated to fetch."

"Your legs are longer, so you'll get there and back faster."

"Can't argue with that."

He brought back the garden spade and the mop bucket, along with the bottle of wine.

As the first bold stars came to life, he sat and watched her build her castle of sand.

"You need a tower on that end," he told her. "You've left it undefended."

"It's a castle, not a fortress, and my little world here is at peace. However, I'd think a famous artist could manage to build a tower if he saw the need for one."

He finished off his glass of wine, screwed the stem in the sand, and picked up the challenge.

She added more turrets, carefully shaping, then smoothing them with the edge of her spade. And driven by his obviously superior talent with his hands, began to add to the structure, elaborately.

"And what, I'd like to know, is that lump you've got there?"

"It's the stables, or will be when I'm finished."

"It's out of proportion." He started to reach over to show her, but she slapped his hand away. "As you like, but your horses would have to be the size of Hugh to fit in there."

She sniffed, rocked back on her heels. Damn it, he was right. "I'm not finished," she said coolly. She scooped up more sand and worked it in. "And what is that supposed to be?"

"It will be the drawbridge."

"A drawbridge?" Delighted, she leaned over to study the platform he fashioned with his quick, clever hands. "Oh, that's wonderful. You're definitely sand castle-skilled. I know just what it needs."

She scrambled up and raced to the house. She came back with some wooden kitchen matches and a bit of red ribbon that she'd cut in a triangle.

"Chain would be better, but we'll be innovative." She poked the tip of the long match into the side of the drawbridge, slid the other end into the castle wall. "Fortunately, the royal family here is having a ball, so the drawbridge stays down." She set a second match in the other side.

She broke a third match, looped her ribbon around it, then hoisted her makeshift flag on the top-most tower. "Now that's a sand castle."

She plucked up the bottle of wine and poured for both of them. "To Dolman Castle." A dream, she thought, they'd made together.

After clinking her glass to his, she drew up her knees and looked out to sea. "It's a beautiful night. So many stars. You can't see sky like this in New York, just slices of it, pieces between buildings, so you forget how big it is."

"When I was a boy, I used to come out at night and sit here."

She turned her head, rested her cheek on her knee. "What else did you do when you were a boy?"

"Climbed the cliffs, played with my friends in the village, worked very hard to get out of chores that would have taken less time and less effort than the eluding of them took. Fished with my father."

He fell into silence, and the depth of it had Allena reaching out to take his hand. "You miss him."

"I left him, alone. I didn't know he was ill that last year. He never told me, never once asked me to come back and tend to him. He died by himself rather than ask me for that."

"He knew you'd come back."

"He should have told me. I could've brought him to Dublin, gotten him to hospital, for treatments, specialists."

"It's always so much harder on the ones who're left behind," she murmured. "He wanted to be here, Conal. To die here."

"Oh, aye, to die here, that was his choice. And knowing he was ill, and frail, he climbed the cliffs. And there at the stone dance is where his heart gave out. That was his choice."

"It makes you angry."

"It makes me helpless, which is the same thing to me. So I miss him, and I regret the time and distance that was between us—the time and distance I put between us. I sent him money instead of myself. And he left me all he had. The cottage, and Hugh."

He turned to her then and pulled the chain at her neck until the pendant slid clear. "And this. He left this for me in that small wood box you see on the dresser in the bedroom."

The shiver raced over her skin, chill and damp. "I don't understand."

"His mother had given it to him on his eighteenth birthday, as it had been given to her. And he gave it to my mother on the day he asked her to marry him, at the stone circle, as is the O'Neil tradition. She wore it always. And gave it back to him, to hold for me, on the night she died."

Cured in Dagda's Cauldron. Carved by the finger of Merlin. "It's yours," she murmured.

"No. No longer mine, never mine as I refused it. The day I buried my father, I came here and I threw this into the sea. That, I told myself, was the end of things."

There's only one, the old woman had told her. It belonged to her. She had found it, or it had found her. And led her, Allena thought, to him. How could she feel anything but joy at knowing it? And how, being who he was, could Conal feel anything but anger?

For her it was a key. For him a lock.

Allena touched his cheek. "I don't know how to comfort you."

"Neither do I." He rose, pulled her to her feet. "No more of this tonight. No more castles and stars. I want what's real. My need is real enough." He swept her up. "And so are you."

9

SHE couldn't sleep. No matter how short the night, she couldn't bear to waste it in dreams. So she lay quiet, and wakeful, reliving every moment of the day that had passed.

They'd ended it, she thought now, with love. Not the slow and tender sort they'd brought each other the first time. There'd been a desperation in Conal when he carried her into bed from the beach. A kind of fierce urgency that had streaked from him and into her so that her hands had been as impatient as his, her mouth as hungry.

And her body, she thought, oh, her body had been so very alive.

That kind of craving was another sort of beauty, wasn't it? A need that deep, that strong, that *willful* could dig deep and lasting roots.

Why wouldn't he let himself love her?

She turned to him, and in sleep he drew her against him. *I'm here*, she wanted to say. *I belong here. I know it.*

But she kept the words inside her, and simply took his mouth with hers. Soft, seductive, drawing what she needed and giving back. Slow and silky, a mating of lips and tongues. The heat from bodies wrapped close weighing heavy on the limbs.

He drifted into desire as a man drifts through mists. The air was thick, and sweet, and she was there for him. Warm and willing. And real.

He heard her breath catch and sigh out, felt her heart beat to match the rhythm of his own. And she moved against him, under him, bewitching in the dark.

When he slid into her, she took him in with a welcome that was home. Together they lifted and fell, steady and smooth. Mouths met again as he felt her rise up to peak, as he lost himself, gave himself. And emptied.

"Allena." He said her name, only her name as he once more gathered her against him. Comforted, settled, he slipped back into sleep never knowing that she wept.

Before dawn she rose, afraid that if she stayed beside him any longer in the dark she would ask— more afraid that if he offered some pale substitute for love and lifetimes, she would snatch at it, pitifully.

She dressed in silence and went out to wait for the dawn of the longest day.

There was no moon now, and no stars, nothing to break that endless, spreading dark. She could see the fall of land, the rise of sea, and to the west the powerful shadows of the jagged cliffs where the stone circle stood, and waited.

The pendant weighed heavy on her neck.

Only hours left, she thought. She wouldn't lose hope, though it was hard in this dark and lonely hour to cling to it. She'd been sent here, brought here, it didn't matter. What mattered was that she was here, and here she had found all the answers she needed.

She had to believe that Conal would find his in the day that was left to them.

She watched dawn break, a slow, almost sly shifting of light that gave the sky a polish. Mists slipped and slid over the ground, rose into the air like a damp curtain. And there, in the east, it flamed, gold, then spread to red over sky and water, brighter, and brighter still, until the world woke.

The air went from gray to the shimmer of a pearl.

On the beach, the castle had been swamped by the tide. And seeing what could be so easily washed away broke her heart a little.

She turned away from it and went back inside.

She needed to keep her hands busy, her mind busy. She could do nothing about the state of her heart, but she wouldn't mope, today of all days.

When Hugh came padding out, she opened the door so he could race through. She put on the kettle for tea. She already knew how Conal liked his, almost viciously strong with no sugar or cream to dilute the punch.

While it steeped, she got a small pot from a cupboard. Conal had mentioned there were berries ripening this time of year. If she could find them, and there were enough, they'd have fresh fruit for breakfast.

She went out the back, past the herb garden and a huge shrub covered with dozens of conical purple blossoms that smelled like potpourri. She wondered how they would look dried and spearing out of a big copper urn.

Ground fog played around her ankles as she walked and made her think it was something like wading in a shallow river. The wind didn't reach it, but fluttered at her hair as she climbed the gentle rise behind the cottage. Far off was the sound of Hugh's deep-throated bark, and somewhere nearer, the liquid trill of a bird. Over it all was the forever sound of the sea.

On impulse, she slipped off her shoes to walk barefoot over the cool, wet grass.

The hill dipped, then rose again. Steeper now, with the mist thickening like layers of filmy curtain. She glanced back once, saw the cottage was merely a silhouette behind the fog. A prickle over her skin had her pausing, nearly turning back. Then she heard the dog bark again, just up ahead.

She called out to him, turned in the direction of his bark, and kept climbing. On the top of the next rise was a scattering of trees sculpted by wind, and with them the bushes, brambles, and berries she hunted.

Pleased with her find, she set down her shoes and began to pick. And taste. And climb still higher to where the ripest grew. She would make pancakes, she thought, and mix the berries in the batter.

Her pot was half full when she scrambled up on a rock to reach a solitary bush pregnant with fat fruit of rich and deep purple.

"The most tempting are always the ones just out of reach."

Allena's breath caught, and she nearly overturned her pot when she saw the woman standing on the rough track on the other side of the bush.

Her hair was dark and hung past her waist. Her eyes were the moody green of the ocean at dawn. She smiled and rested her hand on Hugh's head as he sat patiently beside her.

"I didn't know anyone was here." Could be here, she thought. "I—" She looked back now, with some alarm, and couldn't see the cottage. "I walked farther than I realized."

"It's a good morning for a walk, and for berry picking. Those you have there'd make a fine mixed jam."

"I've picked too many. I wasn't paying attention."

The woman's face softened. "Sure, you can never pick too many as long as someone eats them. Don't fret," she said quietly. "He's sleeping still. His mind's quiet when he sleeps."

Allena let out a long breath. "Who are you?"

"Whoever you need me to be. An old woman in a shop, a young boy in a boat."

"Oh." Surrendering to shaky legs, she sat on the rock. "God."

"It shouldn't worry you. There's no harm meant. Not to you, or to him. He's part of me."

"His great-grandmother. He said—they say—"

The woman's smile widened. "They do indeed."

Struggling for composure, Allena reached under her sweater, drew out the pendant. "This is yours."

"It belongs to whom it belongs to . . . until it belongs to another."

"Conal said he threw it into the sea."

"Such a temper that boy has." Her laugh was light and rich as cream over whiskey. "It does me proud. He could throw it to the moon, and still it would come to whom it belongs to when it was time. This time is yours."

"He doesn't want to love me."

"Oh, child." She touched Allena's cheek, and it was like the brush of wings. "Love can't be wanted away. It simply is, and you already know that. You have a patient heart."

"Sometimes patience is just cowardice."

"That's wise." The woman nodded, obviously pleased, and helped herself to one of the berries in the pot. "And true as well. But already you understand him, and are coming to understand yourself, which is always a more difficult matter. That's considerable for such a short time. And you love him."

"Yes, I love him. But he won't accept love through magic."

"Tonight, when the longest day meets the shortest night, when the star cuts through with power and light, the choice you make, both you and he, will be what was always meant to be."

Then she took Allena's face in her hands, kissed both her cheeks. "Your heart will know," she said and slipped into the mist like a ghost.

"How?" Allena closed her eyes. "You didn't give us enough time."

When Hugh bumped his head against her legs, she bent down to bury her face in his neck. "Not enough time," she murmured. "Not enough to mope about it, either. I don't know what to do, except the next thing. I guess that's breakfast."

She wandered back the way she had come, with Hugh for company on this trip. The fog was already burning off at the edges and drawing into itself. It seemed that fate had decreed one more clear day for her.

When the cottage came into view, she saw Conal on the little back porch, waiting for her.

"You worried me." He walked out to meet her, knowing his sense of relief was out of proportion. "What are you doing, roaming away in the mist?"

"Berries." She held up the pot. "You'll never guess what I . . ." She trailed off as his gaze tracked down to the pendant.

"I'll never guess what?"

No, she thought, she couldn't tell him what had

happened, whom she had seen. Not when the shadows were in his eyes, and her heart was sinking because of them. "What I'm going to make for breakfast."

He dipped a hand into the pot. "Berries?"

"Watch," she told him and took her gatherings into the house. "And learn."

He did watch, and it soothed him. He'd wakened reaching for her, and that had disturbed him. How could a man spend one night with a woman, then find his bed so cold, so empty when she wasn't in it? Then that panic, that drawing down in the gut, when he hadn't been able to find her. Now she was here, mixing her batter in a bowl, and the world was right again.

Was there a name for this other than love?

"You really need a griddle." She set the bowl aside to heat a skillet. "But we'll make do."

"Allena."

"Hmm?" She glanced back. Something in his eyes made her dizzy. "Yes?" When she turned, the pendant swung, and caught at the sunlight.

The star seemed to flash straight into his eyes, taunting him. Without moving, Conal took a deliberate step back. No, he would not speak of love.

"Where are your shoes?"

"My shoes?" He'd spoken with such gentle affection that her eyes stung as she looked down at her own bare feet. "I must have left them behind. Silly of me."

"So you wander barefoot through the dew, pretty Allena?"

Words strangled in her throat. She threw her arms around him, burying her face at his shoulder as emotions whirled inside her.

"Allena." He pressed his lips to her hair and wished, for both of them, he could break this last chain that held his heart. "What am I to do about you?"

Love me. Just love me. I can handle all of the rest. "I can make you happy. If only you'd let me, I can make you happy."

"And what of you? There are two of us here. How can you believe, and accept, all I've told you and be willing to change your life for it?" He drew her back, touched a fingertip to the pendant. "How can you, Allena, so easily accept this?"

"Because it belongs to me." She let out a shaky breath, then took one in, and her voice was stronger. "Until it belongs to another."

Steadier, she took a ladle from a drawer and spooned batter into the skillet. "You think I'm naive, and gullible, and so needy for love that I'll believe anything that offers the possibility of it?"

"I think you have a soft heart."

"And a malleable one?" The cool gaze she sent him was a surprise, as was her nod. "You may be right. Trying to fit yourself into forms so that the people you love will love you back the way you want keeps the heart malleable. And while I hope to be done with that, while I'm going to try to be done with that, I prefer having a heart that accepts imprints from others."

A patient heart, she thought, but by God if it was a cowardly one.

Deftly, she flipped the pancakes. "What hardened yours, Conal?"

"You've good aim when you decide to notch the arrow."

"Maybe I haven't reached into the quiver often enough." But she would now. Movements smooth and unhurried, she turned the pancakes onto a platter, spooned more batter into the pan. "Why don't you ever speak of your mother?"

Bull's-eye, he thought, and said nothing as she set him a place at the table.

"I have a right to know."

"You do, yes."

She got out honey, cinnamon, poured the tea. "Sit down. Your breakfast will get cold."

With a half laugh, he did as she asked. She was a puzzle, and why had he believed he'd already solved her? He waited until she'd emptied the skillet, turned it off, and come to the table to join him.

"My mother was from the near village," he began. "Her father was a fisherman, and her mother died in childbirth when my own mother was a girl. The baby died as well, so my mother was the youngest and the only daughter and pampered, she told me, by her father and brothers."

"You have uncles in the village?"

"I do. Three, and their families. Though some of

the younger have gone to the mainland or beyond. My father was an only child."

She drizzled honey on her pancakes, passed the bottle to Conal. He had family, she thought, and still kept so much alone. "So you have cousins here, too?"

"Some number of them. We played together when I was a boy. It was from them that I first heard of what runs in me. I thought it a story, like others you hear, like silkies and mermaids and faerie forts."

He ate because it was there and she'd gone to the trouble to make it. "My mother liked to draw, to sketch, and she taught me how to see things. How to make what you see come out in pencil and chalk. My father, he loved the sea, and thought I would follow him there. But she gave me clay for my eighth birthday. And I . . ."

He paused, lifted his hands, stared at them through narrowed eyes. They were very like his father's. Big, blunt, and with strength in them. But they had never been made for casting nets.

"The shaping of it, the finding what was inside it . . . I was compelled to see. And wood, carving away at it until you could show others what you'd seen in it. She understood that. She knew that."

"Your father was disappointed?"

"Puzzled more, I think." Conal moved his shoulders, picked up his fork again. "How could a man make a living, after all, whittling at wood or chipping at hunks of rock? But it pleased my mother, so he let it be. For her, and I learned later, because in his mind my fate was already set. So whether I sculpted or fished wouldn't matter in the end."

When he fell silent, looked back at the pendant, Allena slipped it under her sweater. And feeling the quiet heat of it against her heart, waited for him to continue.

10

"After me, my parents tried for more children. Twice my mother miscarried, and the second, late in her term . . . damaged her. I was young, but I remember her having to stay in bed a long time and how pale she was even when she could get up. My father set a chair out for her, so she could be outside and watch the sea. She was never well after that, but I didn't know."

"You were just a boy." When she touched a hand to his, he looked down, smiled a little.

"Soft heart, Allena." He turned his hand over, squeezed hers once, then released. "She was ill the summer I was twelve. Three times that spring, my father took her on the ferry, and I stayed with my cousins. She was dying, and no one could find a way to save her. Part of me knew that, but I pushed it out of my mind. Every time she came home again, I was certain it was all right."

"Poor little boy," Allena murmured.

"He doesn't deserve as much sympathy as you think. That summer, when I was twelve, she walked down to the sea with me. She should've been in bed, but she wouldn't go. She told me of the stone dance and the star and my place in it. She showed me the pendant you're wearing now, though I'd seen it countless times before. She closed my hand around it with her own, and I felt it breathe.

"I was so angry. I wasn't different from the other lads I knew, no different from my cousins and play-mates. Why would she say so? She told me I was young to have it passed on to me, but she and my father had discussed it. He'd agreed to let her do it, in her time and her own way. She wanted to give me the pendant before she left us."

"You didn't want it."

"No, by God, I didn't. I wanted her. I wanted things to be as they were. When she was well and I was nothing more than a lad running over the hills. I wanted her singing in the kitchen again, the way she did before she was ill."

Everything inside her ached for him, but when she reached out, Conal waved her off. "I shouted at her, and I ran from her. She called after me, and tried to come after me, but I was strong and healthy and she wasn't. Even when I heard her weeping, I didn't look back. I went and hid in my uncle's boat shed. It wasn't till the next morning that my father found me.

"He didn't take a strap to me as I might have expected, or drag me home by the ear as I deserved. He just sat down beside me, pulled me against him, and told me my mother had died in the night."

His eyes were vivid as they met Allena's. She wondered that the force of them didn't burn away the tears that swam in her own. "I loved her. And my last words to her were the bitter jabs of an angry child."

"Do you think—oh, Conal, can you possibly believe those words are what she took with her?"

"I left her alone."

"And you still blame a frightened and confused twelve-year-old boy for that? Shame on you for your lack of compassion."

Her words jolted him. He rose as she did. "Years later, when I was a man, I did the same with my father."

"That's self-indulgent and untrue." Briskly, she stacked plates, carried them to the sink. It wasn't sympathy he needed, she realized. But plain, hard truth. "You told me yourself you didn't know he was ill. He didn't tell you."

She ran the water hot, poured detergent into it, stared hard at the rising foam. "You curse the idea you have—what did you call it—elfin blood—but you sure as hell appear to enjoy the notion of playing God."

If she'd thrown the skillet at his head he'd have

been less shocked. "That's easy for you to say, when you can walk away from all of this tomorrow."

"That's right, I can." She turned the faucet off and turned to him. "I can, finally, do whatever I want to do. I can thank you for that, for helping me see what I was letting happen, for showing me that I have something of value to give. And I want to give it, Conal. I want to make a home and a family and a life for someone who values me, who understands me and who loves me. I won't take less ever again. But you will. You're still hiding in the boat shed, only now you call it a studio."

Vile and hateful words rose up in his throat. But he was no longer a young boy, and he rejected them for the sharper blade of ice. "I've told you what you asked to know. I understand what you want, but you have no understanding of what I need."

He walked out, letting the door slap shut behind him.

"You're wrong," she said quietly. "I do understand."

SHE kept herself busy through the morning. If she did indeed go away the next day, she would leave something of herself behind. He wouldn't be allowed to forget her.

She hung the curtains she'd mended, pleased when the sunlight filtered through the lace into patterns on the floor. In the laundry room she found tools and brushes and everything she needed. With a kind of defiance she hauled it all outside. She was going to scrape and paint the damn shutters.

The work calmed her, and that malleable heart she'd spoken of began to ache. Now and then she glanced over at the studio. He was in there, she knew. Where else would he be? Though part of her wanted to give up, to go to him, she did understand his needs.

He needed time.

"But it's running out," she murmured. Stepping back, she studied the results of her labors. The paint gleamed wet and blue, and behind the windows the lace fluttered in the breeze.

Now that it was done and there was nothing else, her body seemed to cave in on itself with fatigue. Nearly stumbling with it, she went into the house. She would lie down for a little while, catch up on the sleep she'd lost the night before.

Just an hour, she told herself and, stretching out on the bed, went under fast and deep.

CONAL stepped back from his own work. His hands were smeared with clay to the wrists, and his eyes half blind with concentration.

Allena of the Faeries. She stood tall, slim, her head cocked slyly over one shoulder, her eyes long and her mouth bowed with secrets. She wasn't beautiful, nor was she meant to be. But how could anyone look away?

How could he?

Her wings were spread as if she would fly off at any moment. Or fold them again and stay, if you asked her.

He wouldn't ask her. Not when she was bound by something that was beyond both of them.

God, she'd infuriated him. He went to the sink, began to scrub his hands and arms. Snipping and sniping at him that way, telling him what he thought and felt. He had a mind of his own and he'd made it up. He'd done nothing but tell her the truth of that, of everything, from the beginning.

He wanted peace and quiet and his work. And his pride, he thought, as his hands dripped water. The pride that refused to accept that his path was already cut. In the end, would he be left with only that?

The emptiness stretched out before him, staggeringly deep. Were these, then, after all, his choices? All or nothing? Acceptance or loneliness?

Hands unsteady, he picked up a towel, drying off as he turned and studied the clay figure. "You already know, don't you? You knew from the first."

He tossed the towel aside, strode to the door. The light shifted, dimmed even as he yanked it open. Storm clouds crept in, already shadowing the sea.

He turned for the cottage, and what he saw stopped him in his tracks. She'd painted the shutters, was all he could think. The curtains she'd hung danced gaily in the rising wind. She'd hung a basket beside the door and filled it with flowers.

How was a man to resist such a woman?

How could it be a trap when she'd left everything, even herself, unlocked and unguarded?

All or nothing? Why should he live with nothing?

He strode toward the cottage and three steps from the door found the way barred to him. "No." Denial, and a lick of fear, roughened his voice as he shoved uselessly at the air. "Damn you! You'd keep me from her now?"

He called out to her, but her name was whisked away by the rising wind, and the first drops of rain pelted down.

"All right, then. So be it." Panting, he stepped back. "We'll see what comes at the end of the day."

So he went through the storm to the place that called to his blood.

SHE woke with a start, the sound of her own name in her ears. And woke in the dark.

"Conal?" Disoriented, she climbed out of bed, reached for the lamp. But no light beamed when she turned the switch. A storm, she thought blearily. It was storming. She needed to close the windows.

She fumbled for the candle, then her hand jerked and knocked it off the little table.

Dark? How could it be dark?

Time. What time was it? Frantically she searched for the candle, found a match. Before she could light it, lightning flashed and she saw the dial of the little wind-up clock.

Eleven o'clock.

No! It was impossible. She'd slept away all but the last hour of the longest day.

"Conal?" She rushed out of the room, out of the house, into the wind. Rain drenched her as she ran to his studio, fought to open the door.

Gone. He was gone. Struggling against despair, she felt along the wall for the shelves, and on the shelves for the flashlight she'd seen there.

The thin beam made her sigh with relief, then her breath caught again at what stood in the line of that light.

Her own face, her own body, made fanciful with wings. Did he see her that way? Clever and confident and lovely?

"I feel that way. For the first time in my life, I feel that way."

Slowly, she shut the light off, set it aside. She knew where he'd gone, and understood, somehow that she was meant to find her own way there, as he had, in the dark.

The world went wild as she walked, as wild as the day she had come to this place. The ground shook, and the sky split, and the sea roared like a dragon.

Instead of fear, all she felt was the thrill of being part of it. This day wouldn't pass into night without her. Closing her hand over the star between her breasts, she followed the route that was clear as a map in her head.

Steep and rough was the path that cut through rock, and slippery with wet. But she never hesitated, never faltered. The stones loomed above, giants dancing in the tempest. In its heart, the Midsummer fire burned, bright and gold, despite the driving rain.

And facing it, the shadow that was a man.

Her heart, as she'd been told, knew.

"Conal."

He turned to her. His eyes were fierce as if whatever wild was in the night pranced in him as well. "Allena."

"No, I've something to say." She walked forward, unhurried though the air trembled. "There's always a choice, Conal, always another direction. Do you think I'd want you without your heart? Do you think I'd hold you with this?"

In a violent move she pulled the pendant from around her neck and threw it.

"No!" He grabbed for it, but the star only brushed his fingertips before it landed inside the circle. "Can you cast it off so easily? And me with it?"

"If I have to. I can go, make a life without you, and part of me will always grieve. Or I can stay, make a home with you, bear your children, and love you for everything you are. Those are my choices. You have yours."

She held out her arms. "There's nothing but me here to hold you. There never was."

Emotions tumbled through him, end over end. "Twice I've let the people I loved go without telling them. Even when I came here tonight I thought I might do so again."

He pushed dripping hair away from his face. "I'm a moody man, Allena."

"So you told me once before. I never would have known it otherwise."

His breath came out in a half laugh. "You'd slap at me at such a time?" He took a step toward her. "You painted the shutters."

"So what?"

"I'll make you pots in dark blue, to fill with your flowers."

"Why?"

"Because I love you."

She opened her mouth, closed it again, took a careful breath. "Because I painted the shutters?"

"Yes. Because you would think to. Because you mended my mother's curtains. Because you pick berries. Because you swim naked in the sea. Because you look at me and see who I am. Whatever brought you here, brought us here, doesn't matter. What I feel for you is all there is. Please, God, don't leave me."

"Conal." The storm, inside her and around her, quieted. "You only have to ask."

"They say there's magic here, but it's you who brought it. Would you take me, Allena?" He reached for her hand, clasped it. "And give yourself to me. Make that home and that life and those children with me. I pledge to you I'll love you, and I'll treasure you, ever hour of every day." He lifted her hand, pressed his lips to it. "I'd lost something, and you brought it back to me. You've brought me my heart."

So, she thought, he'd found the key after all. "I'll take you, Conal, and give myself to you." Her eyes were dry and clear and steady. "And everything we make, we'll make together. I promise to love you now and ever after."

As she wrapped her arms around him, the mists cleared. In the dark sea of the sky a star began to pulse. The fire shimmered down to a pool of gold flame, tipped red as ruby. The air went sharp and cool so the stones stood out like a carving in glass.

And they sang in whispers.

"Do you hear it?" Allena murmured.

"Yes. There." He turned her, held her close to his side as the shimmering beam from the midsummer star shot through the stones and like an arrow pinned its light to its mate on the ground.

The pendant burst blue, a clean fire, star-shaped and brilliant. While star joined star, the circle was the world, full of light and sound and power.

Then the longest day passed, slipping into the shortest night. The light rippled, softened, faded. The stones sighed to silence.

Conal drew her farther into the circle. The fire rose up again, and shot sparks into her eyes, stroked warmth over his skin. He bent to pick up the pendant, and slipping the chain around her neck, sealed the promise.

"This belongs to you, and so do I."

"It belongs to me." She pressed their joined hands

against it. "Until it belongs to another. I'll always be yours."

She kissed him there, inside the echo of magic, then stepped back. "Come home," she said.

SOME say that the faeries came out of their raft to celebrate and danced round the Midsummer fire while the star showered the last of its light. But those who had magic in their hearts and had pledged it left the circle, walked from the cliffs and along the quiet beach to the cottage with dark blue shutters that waited by the sea.

IN DREAMS

For those who believe in magic

PROLOGUE

ALL he had were the dreams. Without them he was alone, always and ever alone. For the first hundred years of his solitude, he lived on arrogance and temper. He had plenty of both to spare.

For the second, he lived on bitterness. Like one of his own secret brews, it bubbled and churned inside him. But rather than healing, it served as a kind of fuel that pushed him from day to night, from decade to decade.

In the third century, he fell into despair and self-pity. It made him miserable company, even for himself.

His stubbornness was such that it took four hundred years before he began to make a home for himself, to struggle to find some pleasure, some beauty, some satisfaction in his work and his art. Four hundred years before his pride made room for the admission that he may have been, perhaps, just slightly and only partially responsible for what had become of him.

Still, had his actions, his attitude, deserved such a harsh judgment from the Keepers? Did his mistake, if indeed it had been a mistake, merit centuries of imprisonment, with only a single week of each hundred-year mark in which to really live?

When half a millennium had passed, he surrendered to the dreams. No, it was more than surrender. He embraced them, survived on them. Escaped into them when his soul cried out for the simple touch of another being.

For she came to him in dreams, the dark-haired maid with eyes like blue diamonds. In dreams she would run through his forest, sit by his fire, lie willing in his bed. He knew the sound of her voice, the warmth of it. He knew the shape of her, long and slender as a boy. He knew the way the dimple would wink to life at the corner of her mouth when she laughed. And the exact placement of the crescent moon birthmark on her thigh.

He knew all of this, though he had never touched her, never spoken to her, never seen her but through the silky curtain of dreams.

Though it had been a woman who had betrayed him, a woman who was at the root of his endless solitude, he yearned for this dark-haired maid. Yearned for her, as the years passed, as much as he yearned for what had been.

He was drowning in a great, dark sea of alone.

1

It was supposed to be a vacation. It was supposed to be fun, relaxing, enlightening.

It was not supposed to be terrifying.

No, no, terrifying was an exaggeration. Slightly.

A wicked summer storm, a strange road snaking through a dark forest where the trees were like giants cloaked in the armor of mists. Kayleen Brennan of the Boston Brennans wasn't terrified by such things. She was made of sterner stuff. She made a point of reminding herself of that, every ten seconds or so as she fought to keep the rental car on the muddy ditch that had started out as a road.

She was a practical woman, had made the decision to be one quite deliberately and quite clearly when she was twelve. No flights of fancy for Kayleen, no romantic dreams or foolish choices. She had watched—was still watching—such occupations lead her charming, adorable, and baffled mother into trouble.

Financial trouble. Legal trouble. Man trouble.

So Kayleen had become an adult at twelve, and had stayed one.

An adult was not spooked by a bunch of trees and a few streaks of lightning, or by mists that thickened and thinned as if they breathed. A grown woman didn't panic because she'd made a wrong turn. When the road was too narrow, as this one was, to allow her to safely turn around, she simply kept going until she found her way again.

And a sensible person did not start imagining she heard things in the storm.

Like voices.

Should have stayed in Dublin, she told herself grimly as she bumped over a rut. In Dublin with its busy streets and crowded pubs, Ireland had seemed so civilized, so modern, so urbane. But no, she'd just had to see some of the countryside, hadn't she? Just had to rent a car, buy a map, and head out to explore.

But honestly, it had been a perfectly reasonable thing to do. She'd intended to see the country while she was here and perhaps find a few treasures for her family's antique shop back in Boston. She'd intended to wander the roads, to drive to the sea, to visit the pretty little villages, and the great, grand ruins.

Hadn't she booked her stay in a licensed bed-and-breakfast for each night that she'd be traveling?

Confirmed reservations ensured there would be no inconvenience and no surprises at the end of each day's journey.

Hadn't she precisely mapped out her route and each point of interest, how long she intended to stay studying each?

She hadn't anticipated getting lost. No one did. The weather report had indicated some rain, but this was Ireland, after all. It had *not* indicated a wild, windy, wicked thunderstorm that shook her little car like a pair of dice in a cup and turned the long, lovely summer twilight into raging dark.

Still, it was all right. It was perfectly all right. She was just a bit behind schedule, and it was partly her own fault. She'd lingered a bit longer than she intended at Powerscourt Demesne on her way south. And a bit longer again at the churchyard she'd come across when she headed west.

She was certainly still in County Wicklow, certainly somewhere in Avondale Forest, and the guidebook had stated that the population through the forested land was thin, the villages few and far between.

She had expected to find it charming and atmospheric, a delightful drive on her way to her night's stay in Enniscorthy, a destination she'd been scheduled to reach by seven-thirty. She tipped up her arm, risked a quick glance at her watch, and winced when she saw she was already a full hour late.

Doesn't matter. Surely they wouldn't lock the doors on her. The Irish were known for their hospitality. She intended to put that to the test as soon as she came across a town, a village, or even a single cottage. Once she did, she'd get her bearings again.

But for now . . .

She stopped dead in the road, realizing she hadn't even seen another car for over an hour. Her purse, as ruthlessly organized as her life, sat on the seat beside her. She took out the cell phone she'd rented, turned it on.

And swore softly when the readout told her, as it had since she'd driven into the forest far enough to realize she was lost, that she had no signal.

"Why don't I have a signal?" She nearly rapped the phone against the steering wheel in frustration. But that would have been foolish. "What is the point of renting mobile phones to tourists if they're not going to be able to use them?"

She put the phone away, took a deep breath. To calm herself, she closed her eyes, tilted her head back, and allowed herself two minutes of rest.

The rain lashed the windows like whips, the wind continued its feral howl. At jolting intervals the thick darkness was split by yet another lance of blue-edged lightning. But Kayleen sat quietly, her dark hair still tidy in its band, her hands folded in her lap.

Her mouth, full and shapely, gradually relaxed its tight line. When she opened her eyes, blue as the lightning that ripped the sky, they were calm again.

She rolled her shoulders, took one last cleansing breath, then eased the car forward.

As she did, she heard someone—something—whisper her name.

Kayleen.

Instinctively, she glanced to the side, out the rain-spattered window, into the gloom. And there, for an instant, she saw a shadow take shape, the shape of a man. Eyes, green as glass, glittered.

She hit the brakes, jerking forward as the car slid in the mud. Her heart raced, her fingers shook.

Have you dreamed of me? Will you?

Fighting fear, she quickly lowered the window, leaned out into the driving rain. "Please. Can you help me? I seem to be lost."

But there was no one there. No one who would—could—have said, so low and sad, *So am I.*

Of course there was no one. With one icy finger she jabbed the button to send the window back up. Just her imagination, just fatigue playing tricks. There was no man standing in the forest in a storm. No man who knew her name.

It was just the sort of foolishness her mother would have dreamed up. The woman lost in the enchanted forest, in a dramatic storm, and the handsome man, most likely a prince under a spell, who rescued her.

Well, Kayleen Brennan could rescue herself, thank you very much. And there were no spellbound princes, only shadows in the rain.

But her heart rapped like a fist against her ribs. With her breath coming fast, she hit the gas again. She would get off of this damned road, and she would get to where she intended to be.

When she got there, she would drink an entire pot of tea while sitting neck-deep in a hot bath. And all of this . . . inconvenience would be behind her.

She tried to laugh it off, tried to distract herself by mentally composing a letter home to her mother, who would have enjoyed every moment of the experience.

An adventure, she would say. Kayleen! You finally had an adventure!

"Well, I don't want a damn adventure. I want a hot bath. I want a roof over my head and a civilized meal." She was getting worked up again, and this time she couldn't seem to stop. "Won't somebody *please* help me get where I'm supposed to be!"

In answer, lightning shot down, a three-pronged pitch-fork hurled out of the heavens. The blast of it exploded the dark into blinding light.

As she threw up an arm to shield her eyes, she saw, standing like a king in the center of the road, a huge buck. Its hide was violently white in the slash of her headlights, its rack gleaming silver. And its eyes, cool and gold, met her terrified ones through the rain.

She swerved, stomped on the brakes. The little car fish-tailed, seemed to spin in dizzying circles propelled by the swirling fog. She heard a scream— it had to be her own—before the car ran hard into a tree.

And so she dreamed.

Of running through the forest while the rain

slapped down like angry fingers. Eyes, it seemed a thousand of them, watched her through the gloom. She fled, stumbling in the muck stirred up by the storm, her bones jolting as she fell.

Her head was full of sound. The roar of the wind, the booming warning of thunder. And under it a thousand voices chanting.

She wept, and didn't know why. It wasn't the fear, but something else, something that wanted to be wrenched out of her heart as a splinter is wrenched from an aching finger. She remembered nothing, neither name nor place—only that she had to find her way. Had to find it before it was too late.

There was the light, the single ball of it glowing in the dark. She ran toward it, her breath tearing out of her lungs, rain streaming from her hair, down her face.

The ground sucked at her shoes. Another fall tore her sweater. She felt the quick burn on her flesh and, favoring her left arm, scrambled up again. Winded, aching, lost, she continued at a limping run.

The light was her focus. If only she could make it to the light, everything would be all right again. Somehow.

A spear of lightning struck close, so close she felt it sear the air, felt it drench the night with the hot sting of ozone. And in its afterglow she saw that the light was a single beam, from a single window in the tower of a castle.

Of course there would be a castle. It seemed not odd at all that there should be a castle with its tower light glowing in the middle of the woods during a raging storm.

Her weeping became laughter, wild as the night, as she stumbled toward it, tramping through rivers of flowers.

She fell against the massive door and with what strength she had left, slapped a fist against it.

The sound was swallowed by the storm.

"Please," she murmured. "Oh, please, let me in."

BY the fire, he'd fallen into the twilight-sleep he was allowed, had dreamed in the flames he'd set to blaze—of his dark-haired maid, coming to him. But her eyes had been frightened, and her cheeks pale as ice.

He'd slept through the storm, through the memories that often haunted him even in that drifting place. But when she had come into those dreams, when she had turned those eyes on him, he stirred. And spoke her name.

And jolted awake, that name sliding out of his mind again. The fire had burned down nearly to embers now. He could have set it roaring again with a thought, but didn't bother.

In any case, it was nearly time. He saw by the pretty crystal clock on the ancient stone mantel—he was amused by such anachronisms—that it was only seconds shy of midnight.

His week would begin at that stroke. For seven days, and seven nights, he would *be*. Not just a shadow in a world of dreams, but flesh, blood, and bone.

He lifted his arms, threw back his head, and waited to become.

The world trembled, and the clock struck midnight.

There was pain. He welcomed it like a lover. Oh, God, to *feel*. Cold burned his skin. Heat scorched it. His throat opened, and there was the blessed bliss of thirst.

He opened his eyes. Colors sprang out at him, clear and true, without that damning mist that separated him for all the other time.

Lowering his hands, he laid one on the back of his chair, felt the soft brush of velvet. He smelled the smoke from the fire, the rain that pounded outside and snuck in through his partially open window.

His senses were battered, so overwhelmed with the rush of sensations that he nearly swooned. And even that was a towering pleasure.

He laughed, a huge burst of sound that he felt rumble up from his belly. And fisting his hands, he raised them yet again.

"I am."

Even as he claimed himself, as the walls echoed with his voice, he heard the pounding at the door. Jolted, he lowered his arms, turned toward a sound he'd not heard in five hundred years. Then it was joined by another.

"Please." And it was his dream who shouted. "Oh, please, let me in."

A trick, he thought. Why would he be tortured with tricks now? He wouldn't tolerate it. Not now. Not during his week to be.

He threw out a hand, sent lights blazing. Furious, he strode out of the room, down the corridor, down the circling pie-shaped stairs. They would not be allowed to infringe on his week. It was a breach of the sentence. He would not lose a single hour of the little time he had.

Impatient with the distance, he muttered the magic under his breath. And appeared again in the great hall.

He wrenched open the door. Met the fury of the storm with fury of his own.

And saw her.

He stared, transfixed. He lost his breath, his mind. His heart.

She had come.

She looked at him, a smile trembling on her lips and sending the dimple at the corner of her mouth to winking.

"There you are," she said.

And fainted at his feet.

2

SHADOWS and shapes and murmuring voices. They swirled in her head, swelling, fading in a cycle of confusion.

Even when she opened her eyes, they were there. Revolving. What? was her only thought. What is it?

She was cold and wet, and every part of her was a separate ache. An accident. Of course, an accident. But . . .

What is it?

She focused and saw overhead, high overhead, a curved ceiling where plaster faeries danced among ribbons of flowers. Odd, she thought. How odd and lovely. Dazed, she lifted a hand to her brow, felt the damp. Thinking it blood, she let out a gasp, tried to sit up.

Her head spun like a carousel.

"Uh-oh." Trembling now, she looked at her fingers and saw only clear rainwater.

And, turning her head, saw him.

First came the hard jolt of shock, like a vicious strike to the heart. She could feel panic gathering in her throat and fought to swallow it.

He was staring at her. Rudely, she would think later when fear had made room for annoyance. And there was anger in his eyes. Eyes as green as the rain-washed hills of Ireland. He was all in black. Perhaps that was why he looked so dangerous.

His face was violently handsome—"violent" was the word that kept ringing in her ears. Slashing cheekbones, lancing black brows, a fierce frown on a mouth that struck her as brutal. His hair was as dark as his clothing and fell in wild waves nearly to his shoulders.

Her heart pounded, a primal warning. Even as she shrank back, she gathered the courage to speak. "Excuse me. What is it?"

He said nothing. Had been unable to speak since he'd lifted her off the floor. A trick, a new torment? Was she, after all, only a dream within a dream?

But he'd felt her. The cold damp of her flesh, the weight and the shape of her. Her voice came clear to him now, as did the terror in her eyes.

Why should she be afraid? Why should she fear when she had unmanned him? Five hundred years of solitude hadn't done so, but this woman had accomplished it with one quick stroke.

He stepped closer, his eyes never leaving her face. "You are come. Why?"

"I . . . I don't understand. I'm sorry. Do you speak English?"

One of those arching brows rose. He'd spoken in Gaelic, for he most often thought in the language of his life. But five hundred years of alone had given him plenty of time for linguistics. He could certainly speak English, and half a dozen other languages besides.

"I asked why you have come."

"I don't know." She wanted to sit up but was afraid to try it again. "I think there must have been an accident. I can't quite remember."

However much it might hurt to move, she couldn't stay flat on her back looking up at him. It made her feel foolish and helpless. She set her teeth, pushed herself up slowly. Her stomach pitched, her head rang, but she managed to sit.

And sitting, glanced around the room.

An enormous room, she noted, and filled with the oddest conglomeration of furnishings. There was an old and beautiful refectory table that held dozens of candlesticks. Silver, wrought iron, pottery, crystal. Pikes were crossed on the wall, and near them was a dramatic painting of the Cliffs of Moher.

There were display cabinets from various eras. Charles II, James I. Neoclassic bumped up against Venetian, Chippendale against Louis XV. An enormous big-screen television stood near a priceless Victorian davenport.

Placed at random were Waterford bowls, T'ang horses, Dresden vases, and . . . several PEZ dispensers.

Despite discomfort, the eccentricity tickled her humor. "What an interesting room." She glanced up at him again. He'd yet to stop staring. "Can you tell me how I got here?"

"You came."

"Yes, apparently, but how? And . . . I seem to be very wet."

"It's raining."

"Oh." She blew out a breath. The fear had ebbed considerably. After all, the man collected Pez dispensers and Georgian silver. "I'm sorry, Mister . . ."

"I'm Flynn."

"Mister Flynn."

"Flynn," he repeated.

"All right. I'm sorry, Flynn, I can't seem to think very clearly." She was shivering, violently now, and wrapped her arms around her chest. "I was going somewhere, but . . . I don't know where I am."

"Who does?" he murmured. "You're cold." And he'd done nothing to tend to her. He would see to her comfort, he decided, and then . . . He would simply see.

He scooped her off the couch, faintly irritated when she pushed a hand against his shoulder defensively.

"I'm sure I can walk."

"I'm more sure I can. You need dry clothes," he

began as he carried her out of the room. "A warm brew and a hot fire."

Oh, yes, she thought. It all sounded wonderful. Nearly as wonderful as being carried up a wide, sweeping staircase as if she weighed nothing.

But that was a romantic notion of the kind her mother lived on, the kind that had no place here. She kept that cautious hand pressed to a shoulder that felt like a sculpted curve of rock.

"Thank you for . . ." She trailed off. She'd turned her head just a fraction, and now her face was close to his, her eyes only inches from his eyes, her mouth a breath from his mouth. A sharp, unexpected thrill stabbed clean through her heart. The strike was followed by a hard jolt that was something like recognition.

"Do I know you?"

"Wouldn't you have the answer to that?" He leaned in, just a little, breathed. "Your hair smells of rain." Even as her eyes went wide, he skimmed his mouth from her jawline to her temple. "And your skin tastes of it."

He'd learned to savor over the years. To sip even when he wished to gulp. Now he considered her mouth, imagined what flavors her lips would carry. He watched them tremble open.

Ah, yes.

He shifted her, drawing her ever so slightly closer. And she whimpered in pain.

He jerked back, looked down and saw the raw scrape just below her shoulder, and the tear in her sweater. "You're injured. Why the bloody hell didn't you say so before?"

Out of patience—not his strong suit in any case— he strode into the closest bedchamber, set her down on the side of the bed. In one brisk move he tugged the sweater over her head.

Shocked, she crossed her arms over her breasts. "Don't you touch me!"

"How can I tend your wounds if I don't touch you?" His brows had lowered, drawn together. She was wearing a bra. He knew they were called that, as he'd seen them worn on the television and in the thin books that were called magazines.

But it was the first time he had witnessed an actual female form so attired.

He liked it very much.

But such delights would have to wait until he saw what condition the woman was in. He leaned over, unhooked her trousers.

"Stop it!" She shoved, tried to scramble back and was hauled not so gently into place.

"Don't be foolish. I've no patience for female flights. If I was after ravishing you, t'would already be done." Since she continued to struggle, he heaved a breath and looked up.

It was fear he saw—not foolishness but raw fear. A maiden, he thought. For God's sake, Flynn, have a care.

"Kayleen." He spoke quietly now, his voice as soothing as balm on a burn. "I won't harm you. I only want to see where you're hurt."

"Are you a doctor?"

"Certainly not."

He seemed so insulted, she nearly laughed.

"I know of healing. Now be still. I ought to have gotten you out of your wet clothes before." His eyes stayed on hers, seemed to grow brighter. And brighter still, until she could see nothing else. And she sighed. "Lie back now, there's a lass."

Mesmerized, she lay on the heaps of silk pillows and, docile as a child, let him undress her.

"Sweet Mary, you've legs that go to forever." His distraction with them caused the simple spell to waver, and she stirred. "A man's entitled to the view," he muttered, then shook his head. "Look what you've done to yourself. Bruised and scraped one end to the other. Do you like pain, then?"

"No." Her tongue felt thick. "Of course not."

"Some do," he murmured. He leaned over her again. "Look at me," he demanded. "Look here. Stay."

Her eyes drooped, half closed as she floated where he wanted, just above the aches. He wrapped her in the quilt, flicked his mind toward the hearth and set the fire roaring.

Then he left her to go to his workshop and gather his potions.

HE kept her in the light trance as he tended her. He wanted no maidenly fidgets when he touched her.

God, it had been so long since he'd touched a woman, flesh against flesh.

In dreams he'd had her under him, her body eager. He'd laid his lips on her, and his mind had felt her give and arch, her rise, her fall. And so his body had hungered for her.

Now she was here, her lovely skin bruised and chilled.

Now she was here, and didn't know why. Didn't know him.

Despair and desire tangled him in knots.

"Lady, who are you?"

"Kayleen Brennan."

"Where do you come from?"

"Boston."

"That's America?"

"Yes." She smiled. "It is."

"Why are you here?"

"I don't know. Where is here?"

"Nowhere. Nowhere at all."

She reached out, touched his cheek. "Why are you sad?"

"Kayleen." Overcome, he gripped her hand, pressed his lips to her palm. "Do they send you to me so I might know joy again, only to lose it?"

"Who are 'they'?"

He lifted his head, felt the fury burn. So he stepped away and turned to stare into the fire.

He could send her deeper, into the dreaming place. There she would remember what there was, would know what she knew. And would tell him.

But if there was nothing in her, he wouldn't survive it. Not sane.

He drew a breath. "I will have my week," he vowed. "I will have her before it's done. This I will not cast off. This I will not abjure. You cannot break me with this. Not even with her can you break Flynn."

He turned back, steady and resolved again. "The seven days and seven nights are mine, and so is she. What remains here at the last stroke of the last night remains. That is the law. She's mine now."

Thunder blasted like cannon shot. Ignoring it, he walked to the bed. "Wake," he said, and her eyes opened and cleared. As she pushed herself up, he strode to a massive carved armoire, threw the doors open, and selected a long robe of royal blue velvet.

"This will suit you. Dress, then come downstairs." He tossed the robe on the foot of the bed. "You'll want food."

"Thank you, but—"

"We'll talk when you've supped."

"Yes, but I want—" She hissed in frustration as he walked out of the room and shut the door behind him with a nasty little slam.

Manners, she thought, weren't high on the list around here. She dragged a hand through her hair, stunned to find it dry again. Impossible. It had been dripping wet when he'd brought her up here only moments before.

She combed her fingers through it again, frowning. Obviously she was mistaken. It must have been all but dry. The accident had shaken her up, confused her. That was why she wasn't remembering things clearly.

She probably needed to go to a hospital, have X rays taken. Though a hospital seemed silly, really, when she felt fine. In fact, she felt wonderful.

She lifted her arms experimentally. No aches, no twinges. She poked gingerly at the scrape. Hadn't it been longer and deeper along her elbow? It was barely tender now.

Well, she'd been lucky. And now, since she was starving, she'd take the eccentric Flynn up on a meal. After that, her mind was bound to be steadier, and she'd figure out what to do next.

Satisfied, she tossed the covers back. And let out a muffled squeal. She was stark naked.

My God, where were her clothes? She remembered, yes, she remembered the way he'd yanked her sweater off, and then he'd . . . Damn it. She pressed a trembling hand to her temple. *Why* couldn't she remember? She'd been frightened, she'd shoved at him, and then . . . then she'd been wrapped in a blanket, in a room warmed by a blazing fire and he'd told her to get dressed and come down to dinner.

Well, if she was having blackouts, the hospital was definitely first on the agenda.

She snatched up the robe. Then simply rubbed the rich fabric over her cheek and moaned. It felt like something a princess would wear. Or a goddess.

But certainly nothing that Kayleen Brennan of Boston would slip casually into for dinner.

This will suit you, he'd said. The idea of that made her laugh, but she slid her arms into it and let herself enjoy the lustrous warmth against her skin.

She turned, caught her own reflection in a cheval glass. Her hair was a tumble around the shoulders of the deep blue robe that swept down her body and ended in a shimmer of gold lace at the ankles.

I don't look like me, she thought. I look like something out of a fairy tale. Because that made her feel foolish, she turned away.

The bed she'd lain in was covered with velvet as well and lushly canopied with more. On the bureau, and certainly that was a Charles II in perfect condition, sat a lady's brush set of silver with inlays of lapis, antique perfume bottles of opal and of jade. Roses, fresh as morning and white as snow, stood regally in a cobalt vase.

A fairy tale of a room as well, she mused. One fashioned for candlelight and simmering fires. There was a Queen Anne desk in the corner, and tall windows draped in lace and velvet, pretty watercolors of hills and meadows on the walls, lovely faded rugs over the thick planked floors.

If she'd conjured the perfect room, this would have been it.

His manners might be lacking, but his taste was impeccable. Or his wife's, she corrected. For obviously this was a woman's room.

Because the idea should have relieved her, she

ignored the little sinking sensation in her belly and satisfied her curiosity by opening the opal bottle.

Wasn't that strange? she thought after a sniff. The bottle held her favorite perfume.

3

FLYNN had a stiff whiskey before he dealt with the food. It hit him like a hot fist.

Thank God there were still some things a man could count on.

He would feed his woman—for she was unquestionably his—and he would take some care with her. He would see to her comfort, as a man was meant to do, then he would let her know the way things were to be.

But first he would see that she was steadier on her feet.

The dining hall fireplace was lit. He had the table set with bone china, heavy silver, a pool of fragrant roses, the delicacy of slim white candles and the jewel sparkle of crystal.

Then closing his eyes, lifting his hands palms out,

he began to lay the table with the foods that would please her most.

She was so lovely, his Kayleen. He wanted to put the bloom back in her cheeks. He wanted to hear her laugh.

He wanted her.

And so, that was the way things would be.

He stepped back, studied his work with cool satisfaction. Pleased with himself, Flynn went out again to wait at the base of the stairs.

And as she came down toward him, his heart staggered in his chest. "*Speirbhean.*"

Kayleen hesitated. "I'm sorry?"

"You're beautiful. You should learn the Gaelic," he said, taking her hand and leading her out of the hall. "I'll teach you."

"Well, thank you, but I really don't think that'll be necessary. I really want to thank you, too, for taking me in like this, and I wonder if I might use your phone." A little detail, Kayleen thought, that had suddenly come to her.

"I have no telephone. Does the gown please you?"

"No phone? Well, perhaps one of your neighbors might have one I can use."

"I have no neighbors."

"In the closest village," she said, as panic began to tickle her throat again.

"There is no village. Why are you fretting, Kayleen? You're warm and dry and safe."

"That may be, but . . . how do you know my name?"

"You told me."

"I don't remember telling you. I don't remember how I—"

"You've no cause to worry. You'll feel better when you've eaten."

She was beginning to think she had plenty of cause to worry. The well-being she'd felt upstairs in that lovely room was eroding quickly. But when she stepped into the dining room, she felt nothing but shock.

The table was large enough to seat fifty, and spread over it was enough food to feed every one of them.

Bowls and platters and tureens and plates were jammed end to end down the long oak surface. Fruit, fish, meat, soups, a garden of vegetables, an ocean of pastas.

"Where—" Her voice rose, snapped, and had to be fought back under control. "Where did this come from?"

He sighed. He'd expected delight and instead was given shock. Another thing a man could count on, he thought. Women were forever a puzzle.

"Sit, please. Eat."

Though she felt little flickers of panic, her voice was calm and firm. "I want to know where all this food came from. I want to know who else is here. Where's your wife?"

"I have no wife."

"Don't give me that." She spun to face him, steady enough now. And angry enough to stand and demand. "If you don't have a wife, you certainly have a woman."

"Aye. I have you."

"Just . . . stay back." She grabbed a knife from the table, aimed it at him. "Don't come near me. I don't know what's going on here, and I'm not going to care. I'm going to walk out of this place and keep walking."

"No." He stepped forward and neatly plucked what was now a rose from her hand. "You're going to sit down and eat."

"I'm in a coma." She stared at the white rose in his hand, at her own empty one. "I had an accident. I've hit my head. I'm hallucinating all of this."

"All of this is real. No one knows better than I the line between what's real and what isn't. Sit down." He gestured to a chair, swore when she didn't move. "Have I said I wouldn't harm you? Among my sins has never been a lie or the harm of a woman. Here." He held out his hand, and now it held the knife. "Take this, and feel free to use it should I break my word to you."

"You're . . ." The knife was solid in her hand. A trick of the eye, she told herself. Just a trick of the eye. "You're a magician."

"I am." His grin was like lightning, fast and bright. Whereas he had been handsome, now he was devastating. His pleasure shone. "That is what I am, exactly. Sit down, Kayleen, and break fast with me. For I've hungered a long time."

She took one cautious step in retreat. "It's too much."

Thinking she meant the food, he frowned at the table. Considered. "Perhaps you're right. I got a bit carried away with it all." He scanned the selections, nodded, then sketched an arch with his hand.

Half the food vanished.

The knife dropped out of her numb fingers. Her eyes rolled straight back.

"Oh, Christ." It was impatience as much as concern. At least this time he had the wit to catch her before she hit the floor. He sat her in a chair, gave her a little shake, then watched her eyes focus again.

"You didn't understand after all."

"Understand? Understand?"

"It'll need to be explained, then." He picked up a plate and began to fill it for her. "You need to eat or you'll be ill. Your injuries will heal faster if you're strong."

He set the plate in front of her, began to fill one for himself. "What do you know of magic, Kayleen Brennan of Boston?"

"It's fun to watch."

"It can be."

She would eat, she thought, because she did feel ill. "And it's an illusion."

"It can be." He took the first bite—rare roast beef—and moaned in ecstasy at the taste. The first time he'd come to his week, he'd gorged himself so that he was sick a full day. And had counted it worth it. But now he'd learned to take his time, and appreciate.

"Do you remember now how you came here?"

"It was raining."

"Yes, and is still."

"I was going . . ."

"How were you going?"

"How?" She picked up her fork, sampled the fish without thinking. "I was driving . . . I was driving," she repeated, on a rising note of excitement. "Of course. I was driving, and I was lost. The storm. I was coming from—" She stopped, struggling through the mists. "Dublin. I'd been in Dublin. I'm on vacation. Oh, that's right, I'm on vacation and I was going to drive around the countryside. I got lost. Somehow. I was on one of the little roads through the forest, and it was storming. I could barely see. Then I . . ."

The relief in her eyes faded as they met his. "I saw you," she whispered. "I saw you out in the storm."

"Did you now?"

"You were out in the rain. You said my name. How could you have said my name before we met?"

She'd eaten little, but he thought a glass of wine might help her swallow what was to come. He poured it, handed it to her. "I've dreamed of you, Kayleen. Dreamed of you for longer than your lifetime. And dreaming of you I was when you were lost in my forest. And when I awoke, you'd come. Do you never dream of me, Kayleen?"

"I don't know what you're talking about. There was a storm. I was lost. Lightning hit very near, and there was a deer. A white deer in the road. I swerved to avoid it, and I crashed. I think I hit a tree. I probably have a concussion, and I'm imagining things."

"A white hind." The humor had gone from his face again. "You hit a tree with your car? They didn't have to hurt you," he muttered. "They had no *right* to hurt you."

"Who are you talking about?"

"My jailers." He shoved his plate aside. "The bloody Keepers."

"I need to check on my car." She spoke slowly, calmly. Not just eccentric, she decided. The man was unbalanced. "Thank you so much for helping me."

"If you want to check on your car, then we will. In the morning. There's hardly a point in going out in a storm in the middle of the night." He laid his hand firmly on hers before she could rise. "You're thinking, 'This Flynn, he's lost his mind somewhere along the way.' Well, I haven't, though it was a near thing a time or two. Look at me, *leannana*. Do I mean nothing to you?"

"I don't know." And that was what kept her from bolting. He could look at her, as he was now, and she felt tied to him. Not bound by force, but tied. By her own will. "I don't understand what you mean, or what's happening to me."

"Then we'll sit by the fire, and I'll tell you what it all means." He rose, held out his hand. Irritation washed over his face when she refused to take it. "Do you want the knife?"

She glanced down at it, back up at him. "Yes."

"Then bring it along with you."

He plucked up the wine, and the glasses, and led the way.

HE sat by the fire, propped his boots on the hearth, savored his wine and the scent of the woman who sat so warily beside him. "I was born in magic," he began. "Some are. Others apprentice and can learn well enough. But to be born in it is more a matter of controlling the art than of learning it."

"So your father was a magician."

"No, he was a tailor. Magic doesn't have to come down through the blood. It simply has to *be* in the blood." He paused because he didn't want to blunder again. He should know more of her, he decided, before he did. "What is it you are, back in your Boston?"

"I'm an antique dealer. That came through the blood. My uncles, my grandfather, and so on. Brennan's of Boston has been doing business for nearly a century."

"Nearly a century, is it?" he chuckled. "So very long."

"I suppose it doesn't seem so by European standards. But America's a young country. You have some magnificent pieces in your home."

"I collect what appeals to me."

"Apparently a wide range appeals to you. I've never seen such a mix of styles and eras in one place before."

He glanced around the room, considering. It wasn't something he'd thought of, but he'd had only himself to please up until now. "You don't like it?"

Because it seemed to matter to him, she worked up a smile. "No, I like it very much. In my business I see a lot of beautiful and interesting pieces, and I've always felt it was a shame more people don't just toss them together and make their own style rather than sticking so rigidly to a pattern. No one can accuse you of sticking to a pattern."

"No. That's a certainty."

She started to curl up her legs, caught herself. What in the world was wrong with her? She was relaxing into an easy conversation with what was very likely a madman. She cut her gaze toward the knife beside her, then back to him. And found him studying her contemplatively.

"I wonder if you could use it. There are two kinds of people in the world, don't you think? Those who fight and those who flee. Which are you, Kayleen?"

"I've never been in the position where I had to do either."

"That's either fortunate or tedious. I'm not entirely sure which. I like a good fight myself," he added with that quick grin. "Just one of my many flaws. Fact is, I miss going fist to fist with a man. I miss a great many things."

"Why? Why do you have to miss anything?"

"That's the point, isn't it, of this fireside conversation. The why. Are you wondering, *mavourneen*, if I'm off in my head?"

"Yes," she said, then immediately froze.

"I'm not, though perhaps it would've been easier if I'd gone a bit crazy along the way. They knew I had a strong mind—part of the problem, in their thinking, and part of the reason for the sentence weighed on me."

"They?" Her fingers inched toward the handle of the knife. She could use it, she promised herself. She *would* use it if she had to, no matter how horribly sad and lonely he looked.

"The Keepers. The ancient and the revered who guard and who nurture magic. And have done so since the Waiting Time, when life was no more than the heavens taking their first breath."

"Gods?" she said cautiously.

"In some ways of thinking." He was brooding again, frowning into the flames. "I was born of magic, and when I was old enough I left my family to do the work. To heal and to help. Even to entertain. Some of us have more of a knack, you could say, for the fun of it."

"Like, um, sawing a lady in half."

He looked at her with a mixture of amusement and exasperation. "This is illusion, Kayleen."

"Yes."

"I speak of magic, not pretense. Some prophesy, some travel and study, for the sake of it. Others devote their art to healing body or soul. Some choose to make a living performing. Some might serve a worthy master, as Merlin did Arthur. There are as many choices as there are people. And while none may choose to harm or profit for the sake of it, all are real."

He slipped a long chain from under his shirt, held the pendant with its milky stone out for her to see. "A moonstone," he told her. "And the words around are my name, and my title. *Draiodoir*. Magician."

"It's beautiful." Unable to resist, she curved her hand around the pendant. And felt a bolt of heat, like the rush of a comet, spurt from her fingertips to her toes. "God!"

Before she could snatch her hand away, Flynn closed his own over hers. "Power," he murmured. "You feel it. Can all but taste it. A seductive thing. And inside, you can make yourself think there's nothing impossible. Look at me, Kayleen."

She already was, could do nothing else. Wanted nothing else. *There you are*, she thought again. *There you are, at last.*

"I could have you now. You would willingly lie with me now, as you have in dreams. Without fear. Without questions."

"Yes."

And his need was a desperate thing, leaping, snapping at the tether of control. "I want more." His fingers tightened on hers. "What is it in you that makes me crave more, when I don't know what more is? Well, we've time to find the answer. For now, I'll tell you a story. A young magician left his family. He traveled and he studied. He helped and he healed. He had pride in his work, in himself. Some said too much pride."

He paused now, thinking, for there had been times in this last dreaming that he'd wondered if that could be so.

"His skill, this magician's, was great, and he was known in his world. Still, he was a man, with the needs of a man, the desires of a man, the faults of a man. Would you want a man perfect, Kayleen?"

"I want you."

"*Leannana.*" He leaned over, pressed his lips to her knuckles. "This man, this magician, he saw the world. He read its books, listened to its music. He came and went as he pleased, did as he pleased. Perhaps he was careless on occasion, and though he did no harm, neither did he heed the rules and the warnings he was given. The power was so strong in him, what need had he for rules?"

"Everyone needs rules. They keep us civilized."

"Do you think?" It amused him how prim her voice had become. Even held by the spell, she had a strong mind, and a strong will. "We'll discuss that sometime. But for now, to continue the tale. He came to know a woman. Her beauty was blinding, her manner sweet. He believed her to be innocent. Such was his romantic nature."

"Did you love her?"

"Yes, I loved her. I loved the angel-faced, innocent maid I saw when I looked at her. I asked for her hand, for it wasn't just a tumble I wanted from her but a lifetime. And when I asked, she wept, ah, pretty tears down a smooth cheek. She couldn't be mine, she told me, as much as her heart already was. For there was a man, a wealthy man, a cruel man, who had contracted for her. Her father had sold her, and her fate was sealed."

"You couldn't let that happen."

"Ah, you see that, too." It pleased him that she saw it, stood with him on that vital point. "No, how could I let her go loveless to another? To be sold like a horse in the marketplace? I would take her away, I said, and she wept the more. I would give her father twice what had been given, and she sobbed upon my shoulder. It could not be done, for then surely the man would kill her poor father, or see him in prison, or some horrible fate. So long as the man had his wealth and position, her family would suffer. She couldn't bear to be the cause of it, even though her heart was breaking."

Kayleen shook her head, frowned. "I'm sorry, but that doesn't make sense. If the money was paid back and her father was wealthy now, he could certainly protect himself, and he would have the law to—"

"The heart doesn't follow such reason," he interrupted, impatiently because if he'd had the wit in his head at the time, instead of fire in his blood, he'd have come to those same conclusions. "It was saving her that was my first thought—and my last. Protecting her, and yes, perhaps, by doing so having her love me the more. I would take this cruel man's wealth and his position from him. I vowed this, and oh, how her eyes shone, diamonds of tears. I would take what he had and lay it at her feet. She would live like a queen, and I would care for her all my life."

"But stealing—"

"Will you just listen?" Exasperation hissed through his voice.

"Of course." Her chin lifted, a little tilt of resentment. "I beg your pardon."

"So this I did, whistling the wind, drawing down the moon, kindling the cold fire. This I did, and did freely for her. And the man woke freezing in a crofter's cot instead of his fine manor house. He woke in rags instead of his warm nightclothes. I took his life from him, without spilling a drop of blood. And when it was done, I stood in the smoldering dark of that last dawn, triumphant."

He fell into silence a moment, and when he continued, his voice was raw. "The Keepers encased me in a shield of crystal, holding me there as I cursed them, as I shouted my protests, as I used the heart and innocence of my young maid as my defense for my crime. And they showed me how she laughed as she gathered the wealth I'd sent to her, as she leapt into a carriage laden with it and fell into the arms of the lover with whom she'd plotted the ruin of the man she hated. And my ruin as well."

"But you loved her."

"I did, but the Keepers don't count love as an excuse, as a reason. I was given a choice. They would strip me of my power, take away what was in my blood and make me merely human. Or I would keep it, and live alone, in a half world, without companionship, without human contact, without the pleasures of the world that I, in their estimation, had betrayed."

"That's cruel. Heartless."

"So I claimed, but it didn't sway them. I took the second choice, for they would not empty me. I would not abjure my birthright. Here I have existed, since that night of betrayal, a hundred years times five, with only one week each century to feel as a man does again.

"I am a man, Kayleen." With his hand still gripping hers, he got to his feet. Drew her up. "I am," he murmured, sliding his free hand into her hair, fisting it there.

He lowered his head, his lips nearly meeting hers, then hesitated. The sound of her breath catching, releasing, shivered through him. She trembled under his hand, and he felt, inside himself, the stumble of her heart.

"Quietly this time," he murmured. "Quietly." And brushed his lips, a whisper, once . . . twice over hers. The flavor bloomed inside him like a first sip of fine wine.

He drank slowly. Even when her lips parted, invited, he drank slowly. Savoring the texture of her mouth, the easy slide of tongues, the faint, faint scrape of teeth.

Her body fit against his, so lovely, so perfect. The heat from the moonstone held between their hands spread like sunlight and began to pulse.

So even drinking slowly he was drunk on her.

When he drew back, her sigh all but shattered him.

"A ghra." Weak, wanting, he lowered his brow to hers. With a sigh of his own he tugged the pendant free. Her eyes, soft, loving, clouded, began to clear. Before the change was complete, he pressed his mouth to hers one last time.

"Dream," he said.

4

SHE woke to watery sunlight and the heady scent of roses. There was a low fire simmering in the grate and a silk pillow under her head.

Kayleen stirred and rolled over to snuggle in.

Then shot up in bed like an arrow from a plucked bow.

My God, it had really happened. All of it.

And for lord's sake, for *lord's* sake, she was naked again.

Had he given her drugs, hypnotized her, gotten her drunk? What other reason could there be for her to have slept like a baby—and naked as one—in a bed in the house of a crazy man?

Instinctively, she snatched at the sheets to cover herself, and then she saw the single white rose.

An incredibly sweet, charmingly romantic crazy

man, she thought and picked up the rose before she could resist.

That story he'd told her—magic and betrayal and five hundred years of punishment. He'd actually believed it. Slowly she let out a breath. So had she. She'd sat there, listening and believing every word— then. Hadn't seen a single thing odd about it, but had felt sorrow and anger on his behalf. Then . . .

He'd kissed her, she remembered. She pressed her fingertips to her lips, stunned at her own behavior. The man had kissed her, had made her feel like rich cream being gently lapped out of a bowl. More she'd *wanted* him to kiss her. Had wanted a great deal more than that.

And perhaps, she thought, dragging the sheets higher, there had been a great deal more than that.

She started to leap out of bed, then changed her mind and crept out instead. She had to get away, quickly and quietly. And to do so, she needed clothes.

She tiptoed to the wardrobe, wincing at the creak as she eased the door open. It was one more shock to look inside and see silks and velvets, satins and lace, all in rich, bold colors. Such beautiful things. The kind of clothes she would covet but never buy. So impractical, so frivolous, really.

So gorgeous.

Shaking her head at her foolishness, she snatched out her own practical trousers, her torn sweater . . . but it wasn't torn. Baffled, she turned it over, inside out, searching for the jagged rip in the arm. It wasn't there.

She hadn't imagined that tear. She couldn't have imagined it. Because she was beginning to shake, she dragged it over her head, yanked the trousers on. Trousers that were pristine, though they had been stained and muddy.

She dove into the wardrobe, pushing through evening slippers, kid boots, and found her simple black flats. Flats that should have been well worn, caked with dirt, scarred just a little on the inside left where she had knocked against a chest the month before in her shop.

But the shoes were unmarked and perfect, as if they'd just come out of the box.

She would think about it later. She'd think about it all later. Now she had to get away from here, away from him. Away from whatever was happening to her.

Her knees knocked together as she crept to the door, eased it open, and peeked out into the hallway. She saw beautiful rugs on a beautiful floor, paintings and tapestries on the walls, more doors, all closed. And no sign of Flynn.

She slipped out, hurrying as quickly as she dared. Wild with relief, she bolted down the stairs, raced to the door, yanked it open with both hands.

And barreling through, ran straight into Flynn.

"Good morning." He grasped her shoulders, steadying her even as he thought what a lovely thing it would be if she'd been running toward him instead of away from him. "It seems we've done with the rain for now."

"I was—I just—" Oh, God. "I want to go check on my car."

"Of course. You may want to wait till the mists burn off. Would you like your breakfast?"

"No, no." She made her lips curve. "I'd really like to see how badly I damaged the car. So, I'll just go see and . . . let you know."

"Then I'll take you to it."

"No, really."

But he turned away, whistled. He took her hand, ignoring her frantic tugs for release, and led her down the steps.

Out of the mists came a white horse at the gallop, the charger of folklore with his mane flying, his silver bridle ringing. Kayleen managed one short shriek as he arrowed toward them, powerful legs shredding the mists, magnificent head tossing.

He stopped inches from Flynn's feet, blew softly, then nuzzled Flynn's chest.

With a laugh, Flynn threw his arms around the horse's neck. With the same joy, she thought, that a boy might embrace a beloved dog. He spoke to the horse in low tones, crooning ones, in what she now recognized as Gaelic.

Still grinning, Flynn eased back. He lifted a hand, flicked the wrist, and the palm that had been empty now held a glossy red apple. "No, I would never forget. There's for my beauty," he said, and the horse dipped his head and nipped the apple neatly out of Flynn's palm.

"His name is Dilis. It means faithful, and he is." With economical and athletic grace, Flynn vaulted into the saddle, held down a hand for Kayleen.

"Thank you all the same, and he's very beautiful, but I don't know how to ride. I'll just—" The words slid back down her throat as Flynn leaned down, gripped her arm, and pulled her up in front of him as though she weighed less than a baby.

"I know how to ride," he assured her and tapped Dilis lightly with his heels.

The horse reared, and Kayleen's scream mixed with Flynn's laughter as the fabulous beast pawed the air. Then they were leaping forward and flying into the forest.

There was nothing to do but hold on. She banded her arms around Flynn, buried her face in his chest. It was insane, absolutely insane. She was an ordinary woman who led an ordinary life. How could she be galloping through some Irish forest on a great white horse, plastered against a man who claimed to be a fifteenth-century magician?

It had to stop, and it had to stop now.

She lifted her head, intending to tell him firmly to rein his horse in, to let her off and let her go. And all she did was stare. The sun was slipping in fingers through the arching branches of the trees. The air glowed like polished pearls.

Beneath her the horse ran fast and smooth at a breathless, surely a reckless, pace. And the man who rode him was the most magnificent man she'd ever seen.

His dark hair flew, his eyes glittered. And that sadness he carried, which was somehow its own strange appeal, had lifted. What she saw on his face was joy, excitement, delight, challenge. A dozen things, and all of them strong.

And seeing them, her heart beat as fast as the horse's hooves. "Oh, my God!"

It wasn't possible to fall in love with a stranger. It didn't happen in the real world.

Weakly, she let her head fall back to his chest. But maybe it was time to admit, or at least consider, that she'd left the real world the evening before when she'd taken that wrong turn into the forest.

Dilis slowed to a canter, stopped. Once again, Kayleen lifted her head. This time her eyes met Flynn's. This time he read what was in them. As the pleasure of it rose in him, he leaned toward her.

"No. Don't." She lifted her hand, pressed it to his lips. "Please."

His nod was curt. "As you wish." He leapt off the horse, plucked her down. "It appears your mode of transportation is less reliable than mine," he said, and turned her around.

The car had smashed nearly headlong into an oak. The oak, quite naturally, had won the bout. The hood was buckled back like an accordion, the safety glass a surrealistic pattern of cracks. The air bag had deployed, undoubtedly saving her from serious injury. She'd been driving too fast for the conditions, she remembered. Entirely too fast.

But how had she been driving at all?

That was the question that struck her now. There was no road. The car sat broken on what was no more than a footpath through the forest. Trees crowded in everywhere, along with brambles and wild vines that bloomed with unearthly flowers. And when she slowly turned in a circle, she saw no route she could have maneuvered through them in the rain, in the dark.

She saw no tracks from her tires in the damp ground. There was no trace of her journey; there was only the end of it.

Cold, she hugged her arms. Her sweater, she thought, wasn't ripped. Cautiously, she pushed up the sleeve, and there, where she'd been badly scraped and bruised, her skin was smooth and unmarred.

She looked back at Flynn. He stood silently as his horse idly cropped at the ground. Temper was in his eyes, and she could all but see the sparks of impatience shooting off him.

Well, she had a temper of her own if she was pushed far enough. And her own patience was at an end. "What is this place?" she demanded, striding up to him. "Who the hell are you, and what have you done? How have you done it? How the devil can I be here when I can't possibly be here? That car—" She flung her hand out. "I couldn't have driven it here. I couldn't have." Her arm dropped limply to her side. "How could I?"

"You know what I told you last night was the truth."

She did know. With her anger burned away, she did know it. "I need to sit down."

"The ground's damp." He caught her arm before she could just sink to the floor of the forest. "Here, then." And he lowered her gently into a high-backed chair with a plump cushion of velvet.

"Thank you." She began to laugh, and burying her face in her hands, shook with it. "Thank you very much. I've lost my mind. Completely lost my mind."

"You haven't. But it would help us both considerably if you'd open it a bit."

She lowered her hands. She was not a hysterical woman, and would not become one. She no longer feared him. However savagely handsome his looks, he'd done her no harm. The fact was, he'd tended to her.

But facts were the problem, weren't they? The fact that she couldn't be here, but was. That he couldn't exist, yet did. The fact that she felt what she felt, without reason.

Once upon a time, she thought, then drew a long breath.

"I don't believe in fairy tales."

"Now, then, that's very sad. Why wouldn't you? Do you think any world can exist without magic?

Where does the color come from, and the beauty? Where are the miracles?"

"I don't know. I don't have any answers. Either I'm having a very complex dream or I'm sitting in the woods in a"—she got to her feet to turn and examine the chair—"a marquetry side chair. Dutch, I believe, early eighteenth century. Very nice. Yes, well." She sat again. "I'm sitting here in this beautiful chair in a forest wrapped in mists, having ridden here on that magnificent horse, after having spent the night in a castle—"

" 'Tisn't a castle, really. More a manor."

"Whatever, with a man who claims to be more than five hundred years old."

"Five hundred and twenty-eight, if we're counting."

"Really? You wear it quite well. A five-hundred-and-twenty-eight-year-old magician who collects PEZ dispensers."

"Canny little things."

"And I don't know how any of it can be true, but I believe it. I believe all of it. Because continuing to deny what I see with my own eyes makes less sense than believing it."

"There." He beamed at her. "I knew you were a sensible woman."

"Oh, yes, I'm very sensible, very steady. So I have to believe what I see, even if it's irrational."

"If that which is rational exists, that which is irrational must as well. There is ever a balance to things, Kayleen."

"Well." She sat calmly, glancing around. "I believe in balance." The air sparkled. She could feel it on her face. She could smell the deep, dark richness of the woods. She could hear the trill of birdsong. She was where she was, and so was he.

"So, I'm sitting in this lovely chair in an enchanted forest having a conversation with a five-hundred-and-twenty-eight-year-old magician. And, if all that isn't crazy enough, there's one more thing that tops it all off. I'm in love with him."

The easy smile on his face faded. What ran through him was so hot and tangled, so full of layers and routes he couldn't breathe through it all. "I've waited for you, through time, through dreams, through those small windows of life that are as much torture as treasure. Will you come to me now, Kayleen? Freely?"

She got to her feet, walked across the soft cushion of forest floor to him. "I don't know how I can feel like this. I only know I do."

He pulled her into his arms, and this time the kiss was hungry. Possessive. When she pressed her body to his, wound her arms around his neck, he deepened the kiss, took more. Filled himself with her.

Her head spun, and she reveled in the giddiness. No one had ever wanted her—not like this. Had ever touched her like this. Needed her. Desire was a hot spurt that fired the blood and made logic, reason, sanity laughable things.

She had magic. What did she need of reason?

"Mine." He murmured it against her mouth. Said it

again and again as his lips raced over her face, her throat. Then, throwing his head back, he shouted it.

"She's mine now and ever. I claim her, as is my right."

When he lifted her off her feet, lightning slashed across the sky. The world trembled.

THEY rode through the forest. He showed her a stream where golden fish swam over silver rocks. Where a waterfall tumbled down into a pool clear as blue glass.

He stopped to pick her wildflowers and thread them through her hair. And when he kissed her, it was soft and sweet.

His moods, she thought, were as magical as the rest of him, and just as inexplicable. He courted her, making her laugh as he plucked baubles out of thin air and painted rainbows in the sky.

She could feel the breeze on her cheeks, smell the flowers and the damp. What was in her heart was like music. Fairy tales *were* real, she thought. All the years she'd turned her back on them, dismissed the happily-ever-after that her mother sighed over, her own magic had been waiting for her.

Nothing would ever, could ever, be the same again.

Had she known it somehow? Deep inside, had she known it had only been waiting, that he had only been waiting for her to awake?

They walked or rode while birds chorused around them and mists faded away into brilliant afternoon.

There beside the pool he laid a picnic, pouring wine out of his open hand to amuse her. Touching her hair, her cheek, her shoulders dozens of times, as if the contact was as much reassurance as flirtation.

She'd never had a romance. Never taken the time for one. Now it seemed a lifetime of love and anticipation could be fit into one perfect day.

He knew something about everything. History, culture, art, literature, science. It was a new thrill to realize that the man who held her heart, who attracted her so completely, appealed to her mind as well. He could make her laugh, make her wonder, make her yearn. And he brought her a contentment she hadn't known she'd lived without.

If this was a dream, she thought, as twilight fell and they mounted the horse once more, she hoped never to wake.

5

A perfect day deserved a perfect night. She had thought, hoped, that when they returned from their outing, he would take her inside. Take her to bed.

But he had only kissed her in that stirring way that made her weak and jittery and asked if she might like to change for the evening.

So she had gone up to her room to worry and wonder how a woman prepared, after the most magical of days, for the most momentous night of her life. Of one thing she was certain. It wouldn't do to think. If she let her thoughts take shape, the doubts would creep in. Doubts about everything that had happened—and about what would happen yet.

For once, she would simply act. She would simply be.

The bath that adjoined her room was a testament to modern luxury. Stepping from the bedchamber

with its antiques and plush velvets into this sea of
tile and glass was like stepping from one world into
another.

Which was, she supposed, something she'd done
already. She filled the huge tub with water and scent
and oil, let the low hum of the motor and quiet jets
relax her as she sank in up to her chin.

Silver-topped pots sat on the long white counter.
From them she scooped out cream to smooth over
her skin. And watched herself in the steam-hazed
window. This was the way women had prepared for
a lover for centuries. Scenting and softening themselves for a man's hands. For a man's mouth.

A woman's magic.

She wouldn't be afraid, she wouldn't let anxiety
crowd out the pleasure.

In the wardrobe she found a long gown of silk in
the color of ripe plums. It slid over her body like
sin and scooped low over her breasts. She slipped
her feet into silver slippers, started to turn to the
glass.

No, she thought, she didn't want to see herself
reflected in a mirror. She wanted to see herself reflected in Flynn's eyes.

HE felt like a green youth, all eager nerves and
awkward moves. In his day, he'd had quite a way
with the ladies. Though five hundred years could
certainly make a man rusty in certain areas, he'd had
dreams.

But even in dreams, he hadn't wanted so much.

How could he? he thought as Kayleen started down the staircase toward him. Dreams paled next to the power of her.

He reached out, almost afraid that his hand would pass through her and leave him nothing but this yearning. "You're the most beautiful woman I've ever known."

"Tonight"—she linked her fingers with his—"everything's beautiful." She stepped toward him and was confused when he stepped back.

"I thought . . . Will you dance with me, Kayleen?"

As he spoke, the air filled with music. Candles, hundreds of them, spurted into flame. The light was pale gold now, and flowers blossomed down the walls, turning the hall into a garden.

"I'd love to," she said, and moved into his arms.

They waltzed in the Great Hall, through the swaying candlelight and the perfume of roses that bloomed everywhere. Doors and windows sprang open, welcoming the glow of moon and stars and the fragrance of the night.

Thrilled, Kayleen threw back her head and let him sweep her in stirring circles. "It's wonderful! Everything's wonderful. How can you know how to waltz like this when there was no waltz in your time?"

"Watching through dreams. I see the world go by in them, and I take what pleases me most. I've

danced with you in dreams, Kayleen. You don't remember?"

"No," she whispered. "I don't dream. And if I do,
I never remember. But I'll remember this." She
smiled at him. "Forever."

"You're happy."

"I've never in my life been so happy." Her hand
slid from his shoulder, along his neck, to rest on his
cheek. The blue of her eyes deepened. Went dreamy.
"Flynn."

"Wine," he said, when fresh nerves kicked in his
belly. "You'll want wine."

"No." The music continued to swell as they
stood. "I don't want wine."

"Supper, then."

"No." Her hand trailed over, cupped the back of
his neck. "Not supper either," she murmured and
drew his mouth to hers. "You." She breathed it.
"Only you."

"Kayleen." He'd intended to romance her, charm
her. Seduce her. Now she had done all of that to
him. "I don't want to rush you."

"I've waited so long, without even knowing.
There's never been anyone else. Now I think there
couldn't have been, because there was you. Show
me what it's like to belong."

"There's no woman I've touched who mattered.
They're shadows beside you, Kayleen. This," he
said and lifted her into his arms, "is real."

He carried her through the music and candlelight,
up the grand stairs. And though she felt his arms,

the beat of his heart, it was like floating.

"Here is where I dreamed of you in the night."
He took her into his bedchamber, where the bed was
covered with red silk and the petals of white roses,
where candles stood flaming and the fire shimmered.
"And here is where I'll love you, this first time.
Flesh to flesh."

He set her on her feet. "I won't hurt you, that I
can promise. I'll give you only pleasure."

"I'm not afraid."

"Then be with me." He cupped her face in his
hands, laid his lips on hers.

In dreams there had been longing, and echoes of
sensations. Here and now, with those mists parted,
there was so much more.

Gently, so gently, his mouth took from hers.
Warmth and wanting. With tenderness and patience,
his hands moved over her. Soft and seductive. When
she trembled, he soothed, murmuring her name, and
promises. He slid the gown off her shoulders, trailed
kisses over that curve of flesh. And thrilled to the
flavor and the fragrance.

"Let me see you now, lovely Kayleen." He
skimmed his lips along her throat as he eased the
gown down her body. When it pooled at her feet,
he stepped back and looked his fill.

There was no shyness in her. The heat that rose
up to bloom on her skin was anticipation. The tremble that danced through her was delight when his
gaze finished its journey and his eyes locked on hers.

He reached out, caressed the curve of her breast,

let them both absorb the sensation. When his fingertips trailed down, he felt her quiver under his touch.

She reached for him, her hands not quite steady as she unbuttoned his shirt. And when she touched him, it was like freedom.

"A ghra." He pulled her against him, crushed her mouth with his, lost himself in the needs that stormed through him. His hands raced over her, took, sought more, until she gasped out his name.

Too fast, too much. God help him. He fought back through the pounding in his blood, gentled his movements, chained the raw need. When he lifted her again, laid her on the bed, his kiss was long and slow and gentle.

This, she thought, was what the poets wrote of. This was why a man or a woman would reject reason for even the chance of love.

This warmth, this pleasure of another's body against your own. This gift of heart, and all the sighs and secrets it offered.

He gave her pleasure, as he had promised, drowning floods of it that washed through her in slow waves. She could have lain steeped in it forever.

She gave to him a taste, a touch, so that sensation pillowed the aches. He savored, and lingered, and held fast to the beauty she offered.

When flames licked at the edges of warmth, she welcomed them. The pretty clouds that had cushioned her began to thin. Falling through them, she cried out. A sound of triumph as her heart burst inside her.

And heard him moan, heard the quick whispers, a kind of incantation as he rose over her. Through the candlelight and the shimmer of her own vision she saw his face, his eyes. So green now they were like dark jewels. Swamped with love, she laid a hand on his cheek, murmured his name.

"Look at me. Aye, at me." His breath wanted to tear out of his lungs. His body begged to plunge. "Only pleasure."

He took her innocence, filled her, and gave her the joy. She opened for him, rose with him, her eyes swimming with shocked delight. And with the love he craved like breath.

And this time, when she fell, he gathered himself and plunged after her.

Her body shimmered. She was certain that if she looked in the mirror she would see it was golden. And his, she thought, trailing a hand lazily up and down his back. His was so beautiful. Strong and hard and smooth.

His heart was thundering against hers still. What a fantastic sensation that was, to be under the weight of the man you loved and feel his heart race for you.

Perhaps that was why her mother kept searching, kept risking. For this one moment of bliss. Love, Kayleen thought, changes everything.

And she loved.

Was loved. She repeated that over and over in her head. She was loved. It didn't matter that he hadn't said it, in those precise words. He couldn't look at her as he did, couldn't touch her as he did and not love her.

A woman didn't change her life, believe in spells and fairy tales after years of denial, and not be given the happy ending.

Flynn loved her. That was all she needed to know.

"Why do you worry?"

She blinked herself back. "What?"

"I feel it. Inside you." He lifted his head and studied her face. "The worry."

"No. It's only that everything's different now. So much is happening to me in so little time." She brushed her fingers through his hair and smiled. "But it's not worry."

"I want your happiness, Kayleen."

"I know." And wasn't that love, after all? "I know." And laughing, she threw her arms around him. "And you have it. You make me ridiculously happy."

"There's often not enough ridiculous in a life." He pulled her up with him so they were sitting tangled together on silk roses. "So let's have a bit."

The stone in his pendant glowed brighter as he grinned. He fisted his hands, shot them open.

In a wink the bed around them was covered with platters of food and bottles of wine. It made her jolt. She wondered if such things always would. Angling her head, she lifted a glass.

"I'd rather champagne, if you please."

"Well, then."

She watched the glass fill, bottom to top, with the frothy wine. And laughing, she toasted him and drank it down.

6

ALL of her life Kayleen had done the sensible thing. As a child, she'd tidied her room without being reminded, studied hard in school and turned in all assignments in a timely fashion. She had grown into a woman who was never late for an appointment, spent her money wisely, and ran the family business with a cool, clear head.

Looking back through the veil of what had been, Kayleen decided she had certainly been one of the most tedious people on the face of the planet.

How could she have known there was such freedom in doing the ridiculous or the impulsive or the foolish?

She said as much to Flynn as she lay sprawled over him on the bed of velvety flowers.

"You couldn't be tedious."

"Oh, but I could." She lifted her head from his

chest. She wore nothing but her smile, with its dimple, and flowers in her hair. "I was the queen of tedium. I set my alarm for six o'clock every morning, even when I didn't have to get up for work. I even set alarms when I was on vacation."

"Because you didn't want to miss anything."

"No. Because one must maintain discipline. I walked to work every day, rain or shine, along the exact same route. This was after making my bed and eating a balanced breakfast, of course."

She slithered down so that she could punctuate her words with little kisses over his shoulders and chest. "I arrived at the shop precisely thirty minutes before opening, in order to see to the morning paperwork and check any displays that might require updating. Thirty minutes for a proper lunch, fifteen minutes, exactly, at four for a cup of tea, then close shop and walk home by that same route."

She worked her way up his throat. "Mmmm. Watched the news during dinner—must keep up with current affairs. Read a chapter of a good book before bed. Except for Wednesdays. Wednesdays I went wild and took in an interesting film. And on my half day, I would go over to my mother's to lecture her."

Though her pretty mouth was quite a distraction, he paid attention to her words, and the tone of them. "You lectured your mother?"

"Oh, yes." She nibbled at his ear. "My beautiful, frivolous, delightful mother. How I must have irritated her. She's been married three times, engaged double that, at least. It never works out, and she's heartbroken about it for, oh, about an hour and a half."

With a laugh, Kayleen lifted her head again. "That's not fair, of course, but she manages to shake it all off and never lose her optimism about love. She forgets to pay her bills, misses appointments, never knows the correct time, and has never been known to be able to find her keys. She's wonderful."

"You love her very much."

"Yes, very much." Sighing now, Kayleen pillowed her head on Flynn's shoulder. "I decided when I was very young that it was my job to take care of her. That was after her husband number two."

He combed his fingers through her flower-bedecked hair. "Did you lose your father?"

"No, but you could say he lost us. He left us when I was six. I suppose you could call him frivolous, too, which was yet another motivation for me to be anything but. He never settled into the family business well. Or into marriage, or into fatherhood. I hardly remember him."

He stroked her hair, said nothing. But he was beginning to worry. "Were you happy, in that life?"

"I wasn't unhappy. Brennan's was important to me, maybe all the more so because it wasn't important to my father. He shrugged off the tradition of it, the responsibility of it, as carelessly as he shrugged off his wife and his daughter."

"And hurt you."

"At first. Then I stopped letting it hurt me."

Did you? Flynn wondered. Or is that just one more pretense?

"I thought everything had to be done a certain way to be done right. If you do things right, people don't leave," she said softly. "And you'll know exactly what's going to happen next. My uncle and grandfather gradually let me take over the business because I had a knack for it, and they were proud of that. My mother let me handle things at home because, well, she's just too good-natured not to."

She sighed again, snuggled into him. "She's going to get married again next month, and she's thrilled. One of the reasons I took this trip now is because I wanted to get away from it, from those endless plans for yet another of her happy endings. I suppose I hurt her feelings, leaving the way I did. But I'd have hurt them more if I'd stayed and spoke my mind."

"You don't like the man she'll marry?"

"No, he's perfectly nice. My mother's fiancés are always perfectly nice. Funny, since I've been here I haven't worried about her at all. And I imagine, somehow, she's managing just fine without me picking at her. The shop's undoubtedly running like clockwork, and the world continues to spin. Odd to realize I wasn't indispensable after all."

"To me you are." He wrapped his arms around her, rolled over so he could look down at her. "You're vital to me."

"That's the most wonderful thing anyone's ever

said to me." It was better, wasn't it? she asked herself. Even better than "I love you." "I don't know what time it is, or even what day. I don't need to know. I've never eaten supper in bed unless I was ill. Never danced in a forest in the moonlight, never made love in a bed of flowers. I've never known what it was like to be so free."

"Happy, Kayleen." He took her mouth, a little desperately. "You're happy."

"I love you, Flynn. How could I be happier?"

He wanted to keep her loving him. Keep her happy. He wanted to keep her beautifully naked and steeped in pleasures.

More than anything, he wanted to keep her.

The hours were whizzing by so quickly, tumbling into days so that he was losing track of time himself. What did time matter now, to either of them?

He could give her anything she wanted here. Anything and everything. What would she miss of the life she had outside? It was ordinary and tedious. Hadn't she said so herself? He would see that she never missed what had been. Before long she wouldn't even think of it. The life before would be the dream.

HE taught her to ride, and she was fearless. When he thought of how she'd clung to him in terror when he'd pulled her up onto Dilis the first time, he rationalized the change by saying she was simply quick to learn. He hadn't changed her basic nature, or forced her will.

That was beyond his powers and the most essential rule of magic.

When she galloped off into the forest, her laughter streaming behind her, he told himself he let his mind follow her only to keep her from harm.

Yet he knew, deep inside himself, that if she traveled near the edge of his world, he would pull her back.

He had that right, Flynn thought, as his hands fisted at his sides. He had claimed her. What he claimed during his imprisonment was his to keep.

"That is the law." He threw his head back, scowling up at the heavens. "It is *your* law. She came to me. By rights of magic, by the law of this place, she is mine. No power can take her from me."

When the sky darkened, when lightning darted at the black edges of clouds, Flynn stood in the whistling wind, feet planted in challenge. His hair blew wild around his face, his eyes went emerald-bright. And the power that was his, that could not be taken from him, shimmered around him like silver.

In his mind he saw Kayleen astride the white horse. She glanced uneasily at the gathering storm, shivered in the fresh chill of the wind. And turned her mount to ride back to him.

She was laughing again as she raced out of the trees. "That was wonderful!" She threw her arms recklessly in the air so that Flynn gripped the halter to keep Dilis steady. "I want to ride every day. I can't believe the *feeling*."

Feeling, he thought with a vicious tug of guilt, was the one thing he wouldn't be able to offer her much longer.

"Come, darling." He lifted his arms up to her. "We'll put Dilis down for the night. A storm's coming."

SHE welcomed it too. The wind, the rain, the thunder. It stirred something in her, some whippy thrill that made her feel reckless and bold. When Flynn set the fire to blaze with a twist of his hand, her eyes danced.

"I don't suppose you could teach me to do that?"

He glanced back at her, the faintest of smiles, the slightest lift of brow. "I can't, no. But you've your own magic, Kayleen."

"Have I?"

"It binds me to you, as I've been bound to no other. I will give you a boon. Any that you ask that is in my power to give."

"Any?" A smile played around her mouth now as she looked up at him from under her lashes. The blatantly flirtatious move came to her much more naturally than she'd anticipated. "Well, that's quite an offer. I'll have to consider very carefully before making any decision."

She wandered the room, trailing a fingertip over the back of the sofa, over the polished gleam of a table. "Would that offer include, say, the sun and the moon?"

Look at her. He thought. She grows more beautiful by the hour. "Such as these?" He held out his hands. From them dripped a string of luminous white pearls with a clasp of diamonds.

She laughed, even as her breath caught. "Those aren't bad, as an example. They're magnificent, Flynn. But I didn't ask for diamonds or pearls."

"Then I give them freely." He crossed to her, laid the necklace over her head. "For the pleasure of seeing you wear them."

"I've never worn pearls." Surprised by the delight they brought her, she lifted them, let them run like moonbeams through her fingers. "They make me feel regal."

Holding them out, she turned a circle while the diamond clasp exploded with light. "Where do they come from? Do you just picture them in your mind and ... poof?"

"Poof?" He decided she hadn't meant that as an insult. "More or less, I suppose. They exist, and I move them from one place to another. From there, to here. Whatever is, that has no will, I can bring here, and keep. Nothing with heart or soul can be taken. But the rest ... It's sapphires, I'm thinking, that suit you best."

As Kayleen blinked, a string of rich black pearls clasped with brilliant sapphires appeared around her neck. "Oh! I'll never get used to ... Move them?" She looked back at him. "You mean take them?"

"Mmm." He turned to pour glasses of wine.

"But . . ." Catching her bottom lip between her teeth, she looked around the room. The gorgeous antiques, the modern electronics—which she'd noticed ran without electricity, the glamour of Ming vases, the foolishness of pop art.

Almost nothing in the room would have existed when he'd been banished here.

"Flynn, where do all these things come from? Your television set, your piano, the furniture and rugs and art. The food and wine?"

"All manner of places."

"How does it work?" She took the wine from him. "I mean, is it like replicating? Do you copy a thing?"

"Perhaps, if I've a mind to. It takes a bit more time and trouble for that process. You have to know the innards, so to speak, and the composition and all matter of scientific business to make it come right. Easier by far just to transport it."

"But if you just transport it, if you just take it from one place and bring it here, that's stealing."

"I'm not a thief." The idea! "I'm a magician. The laws aren't the same for us."

Patience was one of her most fundamental virtues. "Weren't you punished initially because you took something from someone?"

"That was entirely different. I changed a life for another's gain. And I was perhaps a bit . . . rash. Not that it deserved such a harsh sentence."

"How do you know what lives you've changed

by bringing these here?" She held up the pearls. "Or any of the other things? If you take someone's property, it causes change, doesn't it? And at the core of it, it's just stealing." Not without regret, she lifted the jewels over her head. "Now, you have to put these back where you got them."

"I won't." Fully insulted now, he slammed his glass down. "You would reject a gift from me?"

"Yes. If it belongs to someone else. Flynn, I'm a merchant myself. How would I feel to open my shop one morning and find my property gone? It would be devastating. A violation. And beyond that, which is difficult enough, the inconvenience. I'd have to file a police report, an insurance claim. There'd be an investigation, and—"

"Those are problems that don't exist here," he interrupted. "You can't apply your ordinary logic to magic. Magic is."

"Right is, Flynn, and even magic can't negate what's right. These may be heirlooms. They may mean a great deal to someone even beyond their monetary value. I can't accept them."

She laid the pearls, the glow and the sparkle, on the table.

"You have no knowledge of what governs me." The air began to tremble with his anger. "No right to question what's inside me. Your world hides from mine, century by century, building its pale layers of reason and denial. You come here, and in days you stand in judgment of what you can't begin to comprehend?"

"I don't judge you, Flynn, but your actions." The wind had come into the room. It blew over her face, through her hair. And it was cold. Though her belly quaked, she lifted her chin. "Power shouldn't take away human responsibility. It should add to it. I'm surprised you haven't learned that in all the time you've had to think."

His eyes blazed. He threw out his arms, and the room exploded with sound and light. She stumbled back, but managed to regain her balance, managed to swallow a cry. When the air cleared again, the room was empty but for the two of them.

"This is what I might have if I lived by your rules. Nothing. No comfort, no humanity. Only empty rooms, where even the echoes are lifeless. Five hundred years of alone, and I should worry that another whose life comes and goes in a blink might do without a lamp or a painting?"

"Yes."

Temper snapped off him, little flames of gold. Then he vanished before her eyes.

What had she done? Panicked, she nearly called out for him, then realized he would hear only what he chose to hear.

She'd driven him away, she thought, sinking down in misery to sit on the bare floor. Driven him away with her rigid stance on right and wrong, her own unbending rules of conduct, just as she had kept so many others at a distance most of her life.

She'd preached at him, she admitted with a sigh. This incredible man with such a magnificent gift.

She had wagged her finger at him, just the way she
wagged it at her mother. Taken on, as she habitually
did, the role of adult to the child.

It seemed that not even magic could burn that
irritating trait out of her. Not even love could overcome it.

Now she was alone in an empty room. Alone, as
she had been for so long. Flynn thought he had a
lock on loneliness, she thought with a half laugh.
She'd made a career out of alone.

She drew up her knees, rested her forehead on
them. The worst of it, she realized, was that even
now—sad, angry, aching—she believed she was
right.

It wasn't a hell of a lot of comfort.

7

IT took him hours to work off his temper. He walked, he paced, he raged, he brooded. When temper had burned off he sulked, though if anyone had put this term on his condition, he'd have swung hard back into temper again.

She'd hurt him. When anger cleared away enough for that realization to surface, it came as a shock. The woman had cut him to the bone. She'd rejected his gift, questioned his morality, and criticized his powers. All in one lump.

In his day such a swipe from a mere woman would have . . .

He cursed and paced some more. It wasn't his day, and if there was one thing he'd learned to adjust to, it was the changes in attitudes and sensibilities. Women stood toe-to-toe with men in this age, and in his readings and viewings over the years, he'd come to believe they had the right of it.

He was hardly steeped in the old ways. Hadn't he embraced technology with each new development? Hadn't he amused himself with the quirks of society and fashion and mores as they shifted and changed and became? And he'd taken from each of those shifts what appealed most, what sat best with him.

He was a well-read man, had been well read and well traveled even in his own time. And since that time, he'd studied. Science, history, electronics, engineering, art, music, literature, politics. He had hardly stopped using his mind over the last five hundred years.

The fact was, he rarely had the chance to use anything else.

So, he used it now and went over the argument in his head.

She didn't understand, he decided. Magic wasn't bound by the rules of her world, but by itself. It was, and that was all. No conscientious magician brought harm to another deliberately, that was certain. All he'd done was take a few examples of technology, of art and comfort, from various points in time. He could hardly be expected to live in a bloody cave, could he?

Stealing? Why, the very idea of it!

He sat on a chair in his workshop and indulged in more brooding.

It wasn't meant to be stealing, he thought now. Magicians had moved matter from place to place since the beginning of things. And what were jewels but pretty bits of matter?

Then he sighed. He supposed they were considerably more, from her point of view. And he'd wanted her to see them as more. He'd wanted her to be dazzled and delighted, and dote on him for the gift of them.

Much as he had, he admitted, wanted to dazzle and delight the woman who'd betrayed him. Or, to be honest, the woman who'd tempted him to betray himself and his art. That woman had greedily gathered what he'd given, what he'd taken, and left him to hang.

What had Kayleen done? Had she been overpowered by the glitter and the richness? Seduced by them?

Not in the least. She'd tossed them back in his face.

Stood up for what she believed was right and just. Stood up to him. His lips began to curve with the image of that. He hadn't expected her to, he could admit that. She'd looked him in the eye, said her piece, and stuck to it.

God, what a woman! His Kayleen was strong and true. Not a bauble to ride on a man's arm but a partner to stand tall with him. That was a grand thing. For while a man might indulge himself in a pretty piece of fluff for a time, it was a woman he wanted for a lifetime.

He got to his feet, studied his workroom. Well, a

woman was what he had. He'd best figure out how to make peace with her.

KAYLEEN considered having a good cry, but it just wasn't like her. She settled instead for hunting up the kitchen which was no easy task. On the search she discovered Flynn had chosen to make his point with only that one empty room. The rest of the house was filled to brimming, and in his fascinatingly eclectic style.

She softened by the time she brewed tea in a kitchen equipped with a restaurant-style refrigerator, a microwave oven, and a stone fireplace in lieu of stove. It took her considerable time to get the fire going and to heat water in the copper pot. But it made her smile.

How could she blame him, really, for wanting things around him? Pretty things, interesting things. He was a man who needed to use his mind, amuse himself, challenge himself. Wasn't that the man she'd fallen in love with?

She carried the tea into the library with its thousands of books, its scrolls, its manuscripts. And its deep-cushioned leather chairs and snappy personal computer.

She would light the fire, and enough candles to read by, then enjoy her tea and the quiet.

Kneeling at the hearth, she tried to light the kindling and managed to scorch the wood. She rearranged the logs, lodged a splinter painfully in her thumb, and tried again.

She created a hesitant little flame, and a great deal of smoke, which the wind cheerfully blew back in her face. She hissed at it, sucked on her throbbing thumb, then sat on her heels to think it through.

And the flames burst into light and heat.

She set her teeth, fought the urge to turn around. "I can do it myself, thank you."

"As you wish, lady."

The fire vanished but for the smoke. She coughed, waved it away from her face, then got to her feet. "It's warm enough without one."

"I'd say it's unnaturally chilly at the moment." He walked up behind her, took her hand in his. "You've hurt yourself."

"It's only a splinter. Don't," she said when he lifted it to his lips.

"Being strong-minded and being contrary are two different matters." He touched his lips to her thumb, and the throbbing eased. "But not contrary enough, I notice, to ignore the comforts of a cup of tea, a book, and a pleasant chair."

"I wasn't going to stand in an empty room wringing my hands while you worked out your tantrum."

He lifted his eyebrows. "Disconcerting, isn't it? Emptiness."

She tugged her hand free of his. "All right, yes. And I have no true conception of what you've dealt with, nor any right to criticize how you compensate. But—"

"Right is right," he finished. "This place and what I possessed was all I had when first I came here. I could fill it with things, the things that appealed to me. That's what I did. I won't apologize for it."

"I don't want an apology."

"No, you want something else entirely." He opened his hands, and the rich loops of pearls gleamed in them.

"Flynn, don't ask me to take them."

"I am asking. I give you this gift, Kayleen. They're replicas, and belong to no one but me. Until they belong to you."

Her throat closed as he placed them around her neck. "You made them for me?"

"Perhaps I'd grown a bit lazy over the years. It took me a little longer to conjure them than it might have, but it made me remember the pleasure of making."

"They're more beautiful than the others. And much more precious."

"And here's a tear," he murmured, and caught it on his fingertip as it spilled onto her cheek. "If it falls from happiness, it will shine. If it's from sorrow, it will turn to ashes. See."

The drop glimmered on his finger, shimmered, then solidified into a diamond in the shape of a tear. "And this is your gift to me." He drew the pendant from beneath his shirt, passed his hand over it. The diamond drop sparkled now beneath the moonstone. "I'll wear it near my heart. Ever."

She leapt into his arms, clung to his neck. "I missed you!"

"I let temper steal hours from us."

"So did I." She leaned back. "We've had our first fight. I'm glad. Now we never have to have a first one again."

"But others?"

"We'll have to." She kissed his cheek. "There's so much we don't understand about each other. And even when we do, we won't always agree."

"Ah, my sensible Kayleen. No, don't frown," he said, tipping up her chin. "I like your mind. It stimulates my own."

"It annoyed you."

"At the first of it." He circled her around, lighting the fire, the candles as he did. "And I spent a bit of time pondering on how much more comfortable life would be if you'd just be biddable and agree with everything I said and did. 'Yes, Flynn, my darling,' you would say. 'No indeed, my handsome Flynn.' "

"Oh, really?"

"But then I'd miss that battle light in your eyes, wouldn't I, and the way your lovely mouth goes firm. Makes me want to . . ." He nipped her bottom lip. "But that's another kind of stimulation altogether. I'm willing to fight with you, Kayleen, as long as you're willing to make up again with me."

"And I'm willing to have you stomp off in a temper—"

"I didn't stomp."

"Metaphorically speaking. As long as you come

back." She laid her head on his shoulder, closed her eyes. "The storm's passed," she murmured. "Moonlight's shining through the windows."

"So it is." He scooped her up. "I have the perfect way to celebrate our first fight." He closed her hand over his pendant. "Would you like to fly, Kayleen?"

"Fly? But—"

And she was soaring through the air, through the night. Air swirled around her, then seemed to go fluid so it was like cutting clean through a dark sea. The stone pulsed against her palm. She cried out in surprise, and then in delight, reaching out as if she could snatch one of the stars that shone around her.

Fearless, Flynn thought, even now. Or perhaps it was more a thirst for all the times she'd denied herself a drink. When she turned her face to his, her eyes brighter than the jewels, brighter than the stars, he spun her in dizzying circles.

They landed in a laughing tumble to roll over the soft cushion of grass by the side of his blue waterfall.

"Oh! That was amazing. Can we do it again?"

"Soon enough. Here." He lifted a hand, and a plump peach balanced on the tips of his fingers. "You haven't eaten your supper."

"I wasn't hungry before." Charmed, she took the peach, bit into the sweetness. "So many stars," she murmured, lying back again to watch them. "Were we really flying up there?"

"It's a kind of manipulation of time and space and matter. It's magic. That's enough, isn't it?"

"It's everything. The world's magic now."

"But you're cold," he said when she shivered.

"Mmm. Only a little." Even as she spoke, the air warmed, almost seemed to bloom.

"I confess it." He leaned over to kiss her. "I stole a bit of warmth from here and there. But I don't think anyone will miss it. I don't want you chilled."

"Can it always be like this?"

There was a hitch in his chest. "It can be what we make it. Do you miss what was before?"

"No." But she lowered her lashes, so he was unable to read her eyes. "Do you? I mean, the people you knew? Your family?"

"They've been gone a long time."

"Was it hard?" She sat up, handed him the peach. "Knowing you'd never be able to see them again, or talk to them, or even tell them where you were?"

"I don't remember." But he did. This was the first lie he'd told her. He remembered that the pain of it had been like death.

"I'm sorry." She touched his shoulder. "It hurts you."

"It fades." He pushed away, got to his feet. "All of that is beyond, and it fades. It's the illusion, and this is all that's real. All that matters. All that matters is here."

"Flynn." She rose, hoping to comfort, but when he spun back, his eyes were hot, bright. And the desire in them robbed her of breath.

"I want you. A hundred lifetimes from now I'll want you. It's enough for me. Is it enough for you?"

"I'm here." She held out her hands. "And I love you. It's more than I ever dreamed of having."

"I can give you more. You still have a boon."

"Then I'll keep it. Until I need more." Because he'd yet to take her offered hands, she cupped his face in them. "I've never touched a man like this. With love and desire. Do you think, Flynn, that because I've never felt them before I don't understand the wonder of knowing them now? Of feeling them now for one man? I've watched my mother search all of her life, be willing to risk heartbreak for the chance—just the chance—of feeling what I do right at this moment. She's the most important person to me outside this world you've made. And I know she'd be thrilled to know what I've found with you."

"Then when you ask me for your heart's desire, I'll move heaven and earth to give it to you. That's my vow."

"I have my heart's desire." She smiled, stepped back. "Tell me yours."

"Not tonight. Tonight I have plans for you that don't involve conversation."

"Oh? And what might they be?"

"Well, to begin . . ."

He lifted a hand and traced one finger down through the air between them. Her clothes vanished.

8

"Oh!" this time she instinctively covered herself. "You might have warned me."

"I'll have you bathed in moonlight, and dressed in starshine."

She felt a tug, gentle but insistent, on her hands. Her arms lowered, spread out as if drawn by silken rope. "Flynn."

"Let me touch you." He kept his eyes on hers as he stepped forward, as he traced his fingertips down her throat, over the swell of her breasts. "Excite you." He took her mouth in quick, little bites. "Possess you."

Something slid through her mind, her body, at the same time. A coiled snake of heat that bound both together. The rise of it, so fast, so sharp, slashed through her. She hadn't the breath to cry out, she could only moan.

He had barely touched her.

"How can you . . . how could I—"

"I want to show you more this time." Now his hands were on her, rough and insistent. Her skin was so soft, so fragrant. In the moonlight it gleamed so that wherever he touched, the warmth bloomed on it. Roses on silk. "I want to take more this time."

For a second time he took her flying. Though her feet never left the ground, she spun through the air. A fast, reckless journey. His mouth was on her, devouring flesh. She had no choice but to let him feed. And his greed erased her past reason so that her one desire was to be consumed.

Abandoning herself to it, she let her head fall back, murmuring his name like a chant as he ravished her.

He mated his mind with hers, thrilling to every soft cry, every throaty whimper. She stood open to him in the moonlight, soaked with pleasure and shuddering from its heat.

And such was his passion for her that his fingers left trails of gold over her damp flesh, trails that pulsed, binding her in tangled ribbons of pleasure.

When his mouth found hers again, the flavor exploded, sharp and sweet. Drunk on her, he lifted them both off the ground.

Now freed, her arms came tight around him, her nails scraping as she sought to hold, sought to find. She was hot against him, wet against him, her hips arching in rising demand.

He drove himself into her, one desperate thrust,

then another. Another. With her answering beat for urgent beat, he let the animal inside him spring free.

His mind emptied but for her and that primal hunger they shared. The forest echoed with a call of triumph as that hunger swallowed them both.

SHE lay limp, useless. Used. A thousand wild horses could have stampeded toward her, and she wouldn't have moved a muscle.

The way Flynn had collapsed on her, and now lay like the dead, she imagined he felt the same.

"I'm so sorry," she said on a long, long sigh.

"Sorry?" He slid his hand through the grass until it covered hers.

"Umm. So sorry for the women who don't have you for a lover."

He made a sound that might have been a chuckle. "Generous of you, *mavourneen.* I prefer being smug that I'm the only man who's had the delights of you."

"I saw stars. And not the ones up there."

"So did I. You're the only one who's given me the stars." He stirred, pressing his lips to the side of her breast before lifting his head. "And you give me an appetite as well—for all manner of succulent things."

"I suppose that means you want *your* supper and we have to go back."

"We have to do nothing but what pleases us. What would you like?"

"At the moment? I'd settle for some water. I've never been so thirsty."

"Water, is it?" He angled his head, grinned. "That I can give you, and plenty." He gathered her up and rolled. She managed a scream, and he a wild laugh, as they tumbled off the bank and hit the water of the pool with a splash.

IT seemed miraculous to Kayleen how much she and Flynn had in common. Considering the circumstance and all that differed between them, it was an amazing thing that they found any topic to discuss or explore.

But then, Flynn hadn't sat idle for five hundred years. His love of something well made, even if its purpose was only for beauty, struck home with her. All of her life she'd been exposed to craftsmanship and aesthetics—the history of a table, the societal purpose of an enameled snuffbox, or the heritage of a serving platter. The few pieces she'd allowed herself to collect were special to her, not only because of their beauty but also because of their continuity.

She and Flynn had enjoyed many of the same books and films, though he had read and viewed far more for the simple enjoyment of it than she.

He listened to her, posing questions about various phases of her life, until she was picking them apart for him and remembering events and things she'd seen or done or experienced that she'd long ago forgotten.

No one had ever been so interested in her before, in who she was and what she thought. What she felt. If he didn't agree, he would lure her into a debate or tease her into exploring a lighter side of herself rarely given expression.

It seemed she did the same for him, nudging him out of his brooding silences, or leaving him be until the mood had passed on its own.

But whenever she made a comment or asked a question about the future, those silences lasted long.

So she wouldn't ask, she told herself. She didn't need to know. What had planning and preciseness gotten her, really, but a life of sameness? Whatever happened when the week was up—God, why couldn't she remember what day it was—she would be content.

For now, every moment was precious.

He'd given her so much. Smiling, she wandered the house, running her fingers along the exquisite pearls, which she hadn't taken off since he'd put them around her neck. Not the gifts, she thought, though she treasured them, but romance, possibilities, and above all, a vision.

She had never seen so clearly before.

Love answered all questions.

What could she give him? Gifts? She had nothing. What little she still possessed was in the car she'd left abandoned in the wood. There was so little there, really, of the woman she'd become, and was still becoming.

She wanted to do something for him. Something that would make him smile.

Food. Delighted with the idea, she hurried back toward the kitchen. She'd never known anyone to appreciate a single bite of apple as much as Flynn.

Of course, since there wasn't any stove, she hadn't a clue what she could prepare, but . . . She swung into the kitchen, stopped short in astonishment.

There certainly was one beauty of a stove now. White and gleaming. All she'd done was mutter about having to boil water for tea over a fire and—poof!—he'd made a stove.

Well, she thought, and pushed up her sleeves, she would see just what she could do with it.

IN his workroom, Flynn gazed through one of his windows on the world. He'd intended to focus on Kayleen's home so that he could replicate some of her things for her. He knew what it was to be without what you had, what had mattered to you.

For a time he lost himself there, moving his mind through the rooms where she had once lived, studying the way she'd placed her furniture, what books were on her shelves, what colors she'd favored.

How tidy it all was, he thought with a great surge in his heart. Everything so neatly in place, and so tastefully done. Did it upset her sense of order to be in the midst of his hodgepodge?

He would ask her. They could make some adjustments. But why the hell hadn't the woman had more color around her? And look at the clothes in the closet. All of them more suited to a spinster— no, that wasn't the word used well these days. Plain attire without the richness of fabric and the brilliance of color that so suited his Kayleen.

She would damn well leave them behind if he had any say in it.

But she would want her photographs, and that lovely pier glass there, and that lamp. He began to set them in his mind, the shape and dimensions, the tone and texture. So deep was his concentration that he didn't realize the image had changed until the woman crossed his vision.

She walked through the rooms, her hands clasped tightly together. A lovely woman, he noted. Smaller than Kayleen, fuller at the breasts and hips, but with the same coloring. She wore her dark hair short, and it swung at her cheeks as she moved.

Compelled, he opened the window wider and heard her speak.

"Oh, baby, where are you? Why haven't you called? It's almost a week. Why can't we find you? Oh, Kayleen." She picked up a photograph from a table, pressed it to her. "Please be all right. Please be okay."

With the picture hugged to her heart, she dropped into a chair and began to weep.

Flynn slammed the window shut and turned away.

He would not be moved. He would not.

Time was almost up. In little more than twenty-four hours, the choice would be behind him. Behind them all.

He closed his mind to a mother's grief. But he wasn't fully able to close his heart.

His mood was edgy when he left the workroom. He meant to go outside, to walk it off. Perhaps to whistle up Dilis and ride it off. But he heard her singing.

He'd never heard her sing before. A pretty voice, he thought, but it was the happiness in it that drew him back to the kitchen.

She was stirring something on the stove, something in the big copper kettle that smelled beyond belief.

It had been a very long time since he'd come into a kitchen where cooking was being done. But he was nearly certain that was what had just happened. Since it was almost too marvelous to believe, he decided to make sure of it.

"Kayleen, what are you about there?"

"Oh!" Her spoon clattered, fell out of her hand and plopped into the pot. "Damn it, Flynn! You startled me. Now look at that, I've drowned the spoon in the sauce."

"Sauce?"

"I thought I'd make spaghetti. You have a very unusual collection of ingredients in your kitchen. Peanut butter, pickled herring, enough chocolate to make an entire elementary school hyper for a month. However, I managed to find plenty of herbs, and some lovely ripe tomatoes, so this seemed the safest bet. Plus you have ten pounds of spaghetti pasta."

"Kayleen, are you cooking for me?"

"I know it must seem silly, as you can snap up a five-star meal for yourself without breaking a sweat. But there's something to be said for home cooking. I'm a very good cook. I took lessons. Though I've never attempted to make sauce in quite such a pot, it should be fine."

"The pot's wrong?"

"Oh, well, I'd do better with my own cookware, but I think I've made do. You had plenty of fresh vegetables in your garden, so I—"

"Just give me a few moments, won't you? I'll need a bit of time."

And before she could answer, he was gone.

"Well." She shook her head and went back to trying to save the spoon.

She had everything under control again, had adjusted the heat to keep the sauce at low simmer, when a clatter behind her made her jolt. The spoon plopped back into the sauce.

"Oh, for heaven's sake!" She turned around, then stumbled back. There was a pile of pots and pans on the counter beside her.

"I replicated them," Flynn said with a grin. "Which took me a little longer, but I didn't want to argue with you about it. Then you might not feed me."

"My pots!" She fell on them with the enthusiasm of a mother for lost children.

More enthusiasm, Flynn realized as she chattered and held up each pan and lid to examine, than she'd shown for the jewels he'd given her.

Because they were hers. Something that belonged to her. Something from her world.

And his heart grew heavy.

"This is going to be good." She stacked the cookware neatly, selected the proper pot. "I know it must seem a waste of time and effort to you," she said as she transferred the sauce. "But cooking's a kind of art. It's certainly an occupation. I'm used to being busy. A few days of leisure is wonderful, but I'd go crazy after a while with nothing to do. Now I can cook."

While the sauce simmered in the twenty-first-century pot, she carried the ancient kettle to the sink to wash it. "And dazzle you with my brilliance," she added with a quick, laughing glance over her shoulder.

"You already dazzle me."

"Well, just wait. I was thinking, as I was putting all this together, that I could spend weeks, months, really, organizing around here. Not having a pattern is one thing, but having no order at all is another. You could use a catalogue system for your books. And some of the rooms are just piled with things. I don't imagine you even know what there is. You could use a listing of your art, and the antiques, your music. You have the most extensive collection of antique toys I've ever seen. When we have children . . ."

She trailed off, her hands fumbling in the soapy water. Children. Could they have children? What were the rules? Might she even now be pregnant? They'd done nothing to prevent conception. Or she hadn't, she thought, pressing her lips together.

How could she know what he might have done?

"Listen to me." She shook her hair back, briskly rinsed the pot. "Old habits. Lists and plans and procedures. The only plan we need right now is what sort of dressing I should make for the salad."

"Kayleen."

"No, no, this is my performance here. You'll just have to find something to do until curtain time." She heard the sorrow in his voice, the regret. And had her answers. "Everything should be ready in an hour. So, out."

She turned, smiling, shooing at him. But her voice was too thick.

"I'll go and tend to Dilis, then."

"Good, that's fine."

He left the room, waited. When the tear fell from her eye he brought it from her cheek into his palm. And watched it turn to ashes.

9

He brought her flowers for the table, and they ate her meal with the candles glowing.

He touched her often, just a brush of fingers on the back of her hand. A dozen sensory memories stored for an endless time of longing.

He made her laugh, to hear the sound of it and store that as well. He asked her questions only to hear her voice, the rise and fall of it.

When the meal was done, he walked with her, to see how the moonlight shone in her hair.

Late into the night, he made love with her, as tenderly as he knew how. And knew it was for the last time.

When she slept, when he sent her deep into easy dreams, he was resolved, and he was content with what needed to be done.

* * *

SHE dreamed, but the dreams weren't easy ones. She was lost in the forest, swallowed by the mists that veiled the trees and smothered the path. Light shimmered through it, so drops of moisture glittered like jewels. Jewels that melted away at the touch of her hand, and left her nothing.

She could hear sounds—footsteps, voices, even music—but they seemed to come from underwater. Drowning sounds that never took substance. No matter how hard she tried to find the source, she could come no closer.

The shapes of trees were blurred, the color of the flowers deadened. When she tried to call out, her voice seemed to carry no farther than her own ears.

She began to run, afraid of being lost and being alone. She only had to find the way out. There was always a way out. And her way back to him. As panic gushed inside her, she tried to tear the mists away, ripping at them with her fingers, beating at them with her fists.

But her hands only passed through, and the curtain stayed whole.

Finally, through it, she saw the faint shadow of the house. The spear of its turrets, the sweep of its battlements were softened like wax in the thick air. She ran toward it, sobbing with relief. Then with joy as she saw him standing by the massive doors.

She ran to him now, her arms flung out to embrace, her lips curved for that welcoming kiss.

When her arms passed through him, she understood he was the mist.

And so was she.

She woke weeping and reaching out for him, but the bed beside her was cold and empty. She shivered, though the fire danced cheerfully to warm the room. A dream, just a dream. That was all. But she was cold, and she got out of bed to wrap herself in the thick blue robe.

Where was Flynn? she wondered. They always woke together, almost as if they were tied to each other's rhythms. She glanced out the windows as she walked toward the fire to warm her chilled hands. The sun was beaming and bright, which explained why Flynn hadn't been wrapped around her when she woke.

She'd slept away the morning.

Imagine that, she thought with a laugh. Slept away the morning, dreamed away the night. It was so unlike her.

So unlike her, she thought again as her hands stilled. Dreaming. She never remembered her dreams, not even in jumbled pieces. Yet this one she remembered exactly, in every detail, almost as though she'd lived it.

Because she was relaxed, she assured herself. Because her mind was relaxed and open. People were always saying how real dreams could be, weren't they? She'd never believed that until now.

If hers were going to be that frightening, that heartbreaking, she'd just as soon skip them.

But it was over, and it was a beautiful day. There were no mists blanketing the trees. The flowers were basking in the sunlight, their colors vibrant and true. The clouds that so often stacked themselves in layers over the Irish sky had cleared, leaving a deep and brilliant blue.

She would pick flowers and braid them into Dilis's mane. Flynn would give her another riding lesson. Later, perhaps she'd begin on the library. It would be fun to prowl through all the books. To explore them and arrange them.

She would *not* be obsessive about it. She wouldn't fall into that trap again. The chore would be one of pleasure rather than responsibility.

Throwing open the windows, she leaned out, breathed in the sweet air. "I've changed so much already," she murmured. "I like the person I'm becoming. I can be friends with her."

She shut her eyes tight. "Mom, I wish I could tell you. I'm so much in love. He makes me so happy. I wish I could let you know, and tell you that I understand now. I wish I could share this with you."

With a sigh, she stepped back, leaving the windows open.

HE kept himself busy. It was the only way he could get through the day. In his mind, in his heart, he'd said goodbye to her the night before. He'd already let her go.

There was no choice but to let her go.

He could have kept her with him, drawing her into the long days, the endless nights of the next dreaming. His solitude would be broken, the loneliness diminished. And at the end of it, she would be there for that brief week. To touch. To be.

The need for her, the desire to have her close, was the strongest force he'd ever known. But for one.

Love.

Not just with the silken beauty of the dreams he'd shared with her. But with the pains and joys that came from a beating heart.

He would not deny her life, steal from her what she had known, what she would be. How had he ever believed he could? Had he really thought that his own needs, the most selfish and self-serving of them, outweighed the most basic of hers?

To live. To feel heat and cold, hunger, thirst, pleasure and pain.

To watch herself change with the years. To shake the hand of a stranger, embrace a loved one. To make children and watch them grow.

For all his power, all his knowledge, he could give her none of those things. All he had left for her was the gift of freedom.

To comfort himself, he pressed his face to Dilis's neck, drew in the scents of horse and straw, of oat and leather. How was it he could forget, each time forget the wrenching misery of these last hours? The sheer physical pain of knowing it was all ending again.

He was ending again.

"You've always been free. You know I have no claim to keep you here, should you choose to go." He lifted his head, stroking the stallion's head as he looked into his eyes. "Carry her away safe for me. And if you go beyond, I'll not count it against you."

He stepped back, drew his breath. There was work yet, and the morning was passing fast.

When it was done, the last spell, the thin blanket of forget spread at the edges of his prison, he saw Kayleen in his mind's eye.

She wandered through the gardens toward the verge of the forest. Looking for him, calling his name. The pain was like an arrow in the heart, almost driving him to his knees.

So, he was not prepared after all. He fisted his hands, struggled for composure. Resolved but not prepared. How would he ever live without her?

"She will live without me," he said aloud. "That I want more. We'll end it now, quick and clean."

He could not will her away, will her back into her world and into life. But he could drive her from him, so that the choice to go was her own.

Taking Dilis's reins, only for the comfort of contact, he walked for the last time as a man, for yet a century to come, through the woods toward home.

SHE heard the jingle of harness and the soft hoofbeats. Relieved, she turned toward the sound, walking quickly as Flynn came out of the trees.

"I wondered where you were." She threw her arms around his neck, and he let her. Her mouth pressed cheerfully to his, and he absorbed the taste of it.

"Oh, I had a bit of work." The words cut at his throat like shards of glass. "It's a fine day for it, and for your travels."

"For my travels."

"Indeed." He gave her a little pat, then moved away to adjust the stirrups of Dilis's saddle. "I've cleared the path, so you'll have no trouble. You'll find your way easily enough. You're a resourceful woman."

"My way? Where?"

He glanced back, gave her an absent smile. "Out, of course. It's time for you to go."

"Go?"

"There, that should do." He turned to her fully. Every ounce of power he owned went into the effort. "Dilis will take you as far as you need. I'd go with you myself, but I've so much to see to yet. I saw you have one of those little pocket phones in your car. Fascinating things. I have to remember to get one myself for the study of it. You should be able to use it once you're over the border."

"I don't understand what you're saying." How could she when her mind had gone numb, when her heart had stopped beating. "I'm not going."

"Kayleen, darling, of course you are." He patted her cheek. "Not that it hasn't been a delight having you here. I don't know when I've been so diverted."

"Di . . . *diverted*?"

"Mmm. God, you're a tasty bit," he murmured, then leaned down to nip at her bottom lip. "Perhaps we could take just enough time to . . ." His hands roamed down her, giving her breasts a teasing squeeze.

"Stop!" She stumbled back, came up hard against Dilis, who shifted, restless. "A diversion? That's all this was to you? A way to pass the time?"

"Passed it well, didn't we? Ah, sweetheart, I gave as much pleasure as I got. You can't deny it. But we've both got things to get back to, don't we?"

"I love you."

She was killing him. "God bless the female heart." And he said it with a chuckle. "It's so generous." Then he lifted his brows, rolled his eyes under them. "Ah, don't be making a scene and spoil this parting moment. We've enjoyed each other, and that's the end. Where did you think this was going? It's time out of time, Kayleen. Now don't be stubborn."

"You don't love me. You don't want me."

"I loved you well enough." He winked at her. "And wanted you plenty." When the tears swam into her eyes, he threw up his hands as if exasperated. "For pity's sake, woman, I brought some magic and romance into a life you yourself said was tedious. I gave you some sparkle." He lifted her pearls with a fingertip.

"I never asked for jewels. I never wanted anything but you."

"Took them, though, didn't you? Just as another took the sparkles from me once. Do you think, after having a woman damn me to this place, I'd want another around for longer than it takes to amuse myself?"

"I'm not like her. You can't believe—"

"A woman's a woman," he said carelessly. "And I've given you a pretty holiday, with souvenirs besides. The least you can do is be grateful and go along when I bid you. I've no more time for you, and none of the patience to dry your tears and cuddle. Up you go."

He lifted her, all but tossed her into the saddle.

"You said you wouldn't hurt me." She dragged the pearls over her head, hurled them into the dirt at his feet. She stared at him, and in his face she saw the savageness again, the brutality, and none of the tenderness. "You lied."

"You hurt yourself, by believing what wasn't there. Go back to your tame world. You've no place in mine."

He slapped a hand violently on Dilis's flank. The horse reared, then lunged forward.

When she was gone, swallowed up by the forest, Flynn dropped to his knees on the ground—and grieved.

10

SHE wanted to find anger. Bitterness. Anything that would overpower this hideous pain. It had dried up even her tears, had smothered any rage or sorrow before it could fully form.

It had all been a lie. Magic was nothing but deceit.

In the end, love hadn't been the answer. Love had done nothing but make her a fool.

Didn't it prove she'd been right all along? Her disdain of the happy ending her mother had regaled her with had been sense, not stubbornness. There were no fairy tales, no loves that conquered all, no grand sweep of romance to ride on forever.

Letting herself believe, even for a little while, had shattered her.

Yet how could she not have believed? Wasn't she even now riding on a white horse through the forest?

That couldn't be denied. If she'd misplaced her heart, she couldn't deny all that she'd seen and done and experienced. How did she, logical Kayleen, resolve the unhappy one with the magnificent other?

How could he have given her so much, shown her so much, and thought of her as only a kind of temporary entertainment? No, no, something was wrong. Why couldn't she think?

Dilis walked patiently through the trees as she pondered. It had all happened so quickly. This change in him had come like a fingersnap, and left her reeling and helpless. Now, she willed her mind to clear, to analyze. But after only moments, her thoughts became scattered and jumbled once again.

Her car was unmarked, shining in the sunlight that dappled through the trees. It sat tidily on a narrow path that ran straight as a ruler through the forest.

He'd cleared the path, he'd said. Well, he certainly was a man of his word. She slid off the horse, slowly circled the car. Not a scratch, she noted. Considerate of him. She wouldn't have to face the hassle that a wrecked car would have caused with the rental company.

Yes, he'd cleared that path as well. But why had he bothered with such a mundane practicality?

Curious, she opened the car door and sliding behind the wheel, turned the key. The engine sprang to life, purred.

Runs better than it did when I picked it up, she

thought. And look at that, to top things off, we have a full tank.

"Did you want me out of your life so badly, Flynn, that you covered all contingencies? Why were you so cruel at the end? Why did you work so hard to make me hate you?"

He'd given her no reason to stay, and every rational reason to go.

With a sigh, she got out of the car to say goodbye to Dilis. She indulged herself, running her hands over his smooth hide, nuzzling at his throat. Then she patted his flank. "Go back to him now," she murmured, and turned away to spare her heart as the horse pranced off.

Because she wanted some tangible reminder of her time there, she picked a small nosegay of wildflowers, twined the stems together, and regardless of the foolishness of the gesture, tucked them into her hair.

She got into the car again and began to drive.

The sun slanted in thin beams through the trees, angled over the little lane. As she glanced in her mirror, she saw the path shimmer, then vanish behind her in a tumble of moss and stones and brambles. Soon there would be nothing but the silent wood, and no trace that she had ever walked there with a lover.

But she would remember, always, the way he'd looked at her, the way he would press his lips to the heart of her hand. The way he'd bring her flowers and scatter them over her hair.

The way his eyes would warm with laughter, or heat with passion when . . . His eyes. What color were his eyes? Slightly dizzy, she stopped the car, pressed her fingers to her temples.

She couldn't bring his face into her mind, not clearly. How could she not know the color of his eyes? Why couldn't she quite remember the sound of his voice?

She shoved out of the car, stumbled a few steps. What was happening to her? She'd been driving from Dublin on the way to her bed-and-breakfast. A wrong turn. A storm. But what . . .

Without thinking, she took another step back down the now overgrown path. And her mind snapped clear as crystal.

Her breath was coming short. She turned, stared at the car, the clear path in front of it, the impassable ground behind.

"Flynn's eyes are green," she said. His face came clearly into her mind now. And when she took a cautious step forward, her memory of him went hazy.

This time she stepped back quickly, well back. "You wanted me to forget you. Why? Why if none of it mattered did you care if I remembered you or not? Why would it matter if I broke my heart over you?"

A little shaky, she sat down on the ground. And she began to do what she'd always done best. Be logical.

* * *

FLYNN sat as he had on the night it had begun. In the chair in front of the fire in the tower. He'd watched in the flames until Kayleen had gotten into her car. After that, he hadn't been able to bear it, so he had hazed the vision with smoke.

He'd lost track of the time that he'd sat there now, chained by his own grief. He knew the day was passing. The slant of sunlight through the window had shortened and was dimming.

She would be beyond now, and would have forgotten him. That was for the best. There would be some confusion, of course. A loss of time never fully explained. But she would put that behind her as well.

In a year or two, or twenty, he might look into the fire again, and see how she was. But he would never open his mind to her in dreams, for that would be more torment than he could ever possibly bear.

She would be changed a little by what had passed between them. More open to possibilities, to the magic of life. He lifted the strings of pearls, watched them glow in the light of the dying fire. At least that was a gift she hadn't been able to hurl at his feet.

With the pearls wrapped around his fingers, he lowered his face into his hands. He willed the time to come when pain could strike only his mind, when every sense wasn't tuned so sharply that he could smell her even now. That soft scent that whispered in the air.

"Bring on the bloody night," he muttered and threw his head back.

Then he was stumbling to his feet, staring. She stood not three feet away. Her hair was tangled, her clothes torn. Scratches scored her hands and face.

"What trick is this?"

"I want my boon. I want what you promised me."

"What have you done?" His knees unlocked and he lunged toward her, grabbing her hard by the arms. "How are you hurt? Look at you. Your hands are all torn and bleeding."

"You put briars in my way." She gave him a shove, and such was his shock that she knocked him back two full steps. "You bastard. It took hours to get through them."

"Get through." His head snapped back, as if she'd slapped him. "You have to go. Go! Now! What's the time?" He was pushing her out of the room, and when that wasn't quick enough he began to drag her.

"I'm not going. Not until you grant my boon."

"You damn well are." Terrified, he tossed her over his shoulder and began to run. As she struggled and cursed him, he began to fly.

The night was closing in. Time that had dripped began to flood. He went as deep into the forest as he dared. The edges of his prison seemed to hiss around him.

"There." Fear for her slicked his skin. "Your car's just up ahead. Get in it and go."

"Why? So I can drive a little farther and forget

all this? Forget you? You'd have stolen that from me."

"I've no time to argue with you." He grabbed her shoulders and shook. "There is no time. If you stay past the last stroke of twelve, you're trapped here. A hundred years will pass before you can walk away again."

"Why do you care? It's a big house. A big forest. I won't get in your way."

"You don't understand. Go. This place is mine, and I don't want you here."

"You're trembling. Flynn. What frightens you?"

"I'm not frightened, I'm angry. You've abused my hospitality. You're trespassing."

"Call the cops," she suggested. "Call your Keepers. Or . . . why don't you just flick me out, the way you flick things in? But you can't, can you?"

"If I could, you'd be gone already." He yanked her a few steps toward the car, then swore when the ground in front of his boots began to spark and smoke. That was the edge of his prison.

"Big, powerful magician, but you can't get rid of me that way. You couldn't bring me here, and you can't send me away. Not with magic, because I have heart and soul. I have will. So you tried to drive me away with careless words. Cruel, careless words. You didn't think I'd see through them, did you? Didn't think I'd figure it all out. You forgot who you were dealing with."

"Kayleen." He took her hands now, squeezing desperately. "Do this thing I ask now, won't you?"

"A diversion," she said. "That's a crock. You love me."

"Of course I love you." He shook her harder, shouted so his voice boomed through the forest. "That's the bloody point. And if you care for me, you'll do what I tell you, and do it now."

"You love me." Her breath came out on a sob as she flung herself against him. "I knew it. Oh, I'm so angry with you. I'm so in love with you."

His arms ached to grip, to hold. He made himself push her away, hold her at arm's length. "Listen to me, Kayleen. Clear the stars out of your eyes and be sensible. I've no right to love you. Be quiet!" he snapped when she started to speak. "You remember what I told you about this place, about me. Do you feel my hands on you, Kayleen?"

"Yes. They're trembling."

"After midnight, one breath after, you won't feel them, or anything else. No touch, no contact. You'll pick a flower, but you won't feel the stem or the petals. Its perfume will be lost to you. Can you feel your own heart beat? Beating inside you? You won't. It's worse than death to be and yet not be. Day by day into the decades with nothing of substance. Nothing but what's in your mind. And, *a ghra*, you haven't even the magic to amuse yourself into some sanity. You'll be lost, little more than a ghost."

"I know." Like the dream, she thought. A mist within the mist.

"There's more. There can be no children. During

the dreaming nothing can grow in you. Nothing can change in or of you. You will have no family, no comfort. No choice. This is my banishment. It will not be yours."

Though her nerves began to dance, her gaze stayed steady. "I'll have my boon."

He swore, threw up his hands. "Woman, you try me to the bone. All right, then. What will you?"

"To stay."

"No."

"You took a vow."

"And so I break it. What more can be done to me?"

"I'll stay anyway. You can't stop me."

But he could. There was one way to save her in the time left him. One final way. "You defeat me." He drew her close, rocked her against him. "You've a head like a rock. I love you, Kayleen. I loved you in dreams, when dreams were all there was for me. I love you now. It killed me to hurt you."

"I want to be with you, no matter how short the time or how long. We'll dream together until we can live together again."

He took her mouth. A deep kiss, a drugging one that spun in her head, blurred her vision. Joy settled sweetly in her heart.

When she sighed, he stepped back from her. "Five hundred years," he said quietly. "And only once have I loved. Only you."

"Flynn." She started to move toward him, but the air between them had hardened into a shield. "What is this?" She lifted her fisted hands to it, pushed. "What have you done?"

"There's a choice, and it's mine to make. I will not damn you to my prison, Kayleen. No power can sway me."

"I won't go." She pounded a fist on the shield.

"I know it, and understand it as well. I should have before. I would never leave you, either. *Manim astheee hu.*" My soul, he said in the language of his birth, is within you. "You brought me a gift, Kayleen. Love freely given."

The wind began to kick. From somewhere a sound boomed, slow and dull, like a clock striking the hour.

"I give you a gift in return. Life to be lived. I have a choice, one offered me long ago. A hundred years times five."

"What are you . . . No!" She flung herself at the shield, beat against it. "No, you can't. You'll die. You're five hundred years old. You can't live without your powers."

"It's my right. My choice."

"Don't do this." How many strikes of the clock had there been? "I'll go. I swear it."

"There's no time now. My powers," he said, lifting his arms. "My blood, my life. For hers." Lightning spewed from the sky, struck like a comet between them. "For foolishness, for pride, for arrogance I abjure my gifts, my skills, my birthright. And for love I cast them away."

His eyes met Kayleen's through the wind and

light as the clock struck. "For love, I offer them freely. Let her forget, for there is no need for her to suffer."

He fisted his hands, crossed his arms over his chest. Braced as the world went mad around him. "Now."

And the clock struck twelve.

The world went still. Overhead the skies broke clear so the stars poured free. The trees stood as if carved out of the dark. The only sound was of Kayleen's weeping.

"Do I dream?" Flynn whispered. Cautious, he held out a hand, opened and closed his fist. Felt the movement of his own fingers.

The air began to stir, a soft, sweet breeze. An owl called.

"I am." Flynn dropped to his knees beside Kayleen, with wonder in his eyes. "I am."

"Flynn!" She threw her arms around him, dragging him close, breathing him in. "You're real. You're alive."

"I am restored." He dropped his head on her shoulder. "I am freed. The Keepers."

He was breathless, fighting to clear his mind. Drawing her back, he framed her face in his hands. Solid, warm. His.

"You're free." She pressed her hands against his. The tears that fell from her eyes shimmered into diamonds on the ground between them. "You're alive! You're here."

"The Keepers said I have atoned. I was given

love, and I put the one I loved before myself. Love."
He pressed his lips to her brow. "They told me it is
the simplest, and most potent of magic. I took a very
long time to learn it."

"So have I. We saved each other, didn't we?"

"We loved each other. *Manim astheee hu*," he
said again. "These are the words I give you." He
opened his hand and held out the pearls. "Will you
take them, and this gift, as a symbol of betrothal?
Will you take them, and me?"

"I will."

He drew her to her feet. "Soon, then, for I've a
great respect for time, and the wasting of it. Now,
look what you've done." He trailed his fingers gently over the scratch on her cheek. "There's a mess
you've made of yourself."

"That's not very romantic."

"I'll fill you with romance, but first I'll tend those
hurts." He scooped her off her feet.

"My mother's going to be crazy about you."

"I'm counting on it." Because he wanted to savor,
he walked for a bit. "Will I like Boston, do you
think?"

"Yes, I think you will." She twirled a lock of his
hair around her fingers. "I could use someone who
knows something about antiques in my family business."

"Is that so? Ha. A job. Imagine that. I might consider that, if there was thought of opening a branch
here in Ireland, where a certain wildly-in-love married couple could split their time, so to speak."

"I wouldn't have it any other way."

She laughed as he spun her around, pressed her lips to his, and held on tight as they leaped into space and flew toward home.

And happily-ever-afters.

#1 *New York Times* bestselling author

NORA ROBERTS

Northern Lights

"You can't bottle wish fulfillment, but Nora Roberts
certainly knows how to put it on the page."
—*New York Times*

**The colorful, compelling novel about
two lonely souls who find love—and
redemption—in Lunacy, Alaska.**

The official
Nora Roberts
seal guarantees
that these are
new books.

*Premium Edition—Specially designed
for comfortable reading.*

0-515-13974-2

Available wherever books are sold or at
penguin.com

J990